UNDER A COPPER MOON

THE ADVENTURES OF A MAIL-ORDER BRIDE
IN
JEROME, ARIZONA TERRITORY
1894

ALSO BY GREG LILLY:

FINGERING THE FAMILY JEWELS — *A Derek Mason Mystery*

DEVIL'S BRIDGE

UNDER A
COPPER MOON

THE ADVENTURES OF A MAIL-ORDER BRIDE
IN
JEROME, ARIZONA TERRITORY
1894

2/2008
Amos –
Thanks for all
your support.
Greg Lilly

Greg Lilly

Cherokee McGhee

Sedona, Arizona

ISBN 978-0-9799694-0-9
0-9799694-0-9

First Printing 2008

Cover illustration by Jonathan G. Spenser
Author photograph by Mike Blevins

Published by:
Cherokee McGhee, L.L.C.
Sedona, Arizona 86336

Find us on the World Wide Web at:
WWW.CHEROKEEMCGHEE.COM

Printed in the United States of America

Acknowledgements

Thanks to...

My editors Viki Cupaiuolo and Michelle Moore for their gentle diligence and wholehearted encouragement

Archivist Ronne Roope of the Jerome Historical Society who read the early manuscript to help keep me grounded in reality

My first readers Brad Dorris, Angela McCoy, and Joyice Gere when they didn't growl when I dropped the manuscript at their doorsteps, and then they actually returned it in one piece

Jerome, Arizona, called the "Wickedest Town in America" by the *New York Post* in 1903 – thanks for the inspiration

To my grandmother Athna McGhee
and mother Jean Lilly
—two pure-hearted and strong women

CHAPTER ONE

She knew one thing as a solid truth: no one would love her as her mother had. Inez closed the door of the small home to the clop, clop, clop of horses on hard red clay and the rattle of wagons wallowing down the rutted road. She avoided the few mourners who still lingered in the parlor of her mother's house and crept into her bedroom. The quiet murmurs of "Ain't it pitiful" and "She got to learn things early" and "Inez is so young" combined with the sad and sorry stares of neighbors and church members clouded her mind from the events of the day, but a chilly stream of understanding woke her from the haze. Now, at sixteen, she was alone in the world.

A timid knock at her bedroom door, followed by the gray walnut-head of Mrs. Hammonds peeking through startled Inez. The slight gap Mrs. Hammonds had pushed open allowed for privacy and confidential talk without a full commitment of entering the room. "Dear," she began, "you holding up?"

Supporting herself with the help of the old cedar wardrobe, Inez considered the question; no, she was raw; no, things would never be the same; no, her mother was dead. "I'm fine." Her own voice troubled her by its steady and strong resolution.

The door creaked open a little more, but Mrs. Hammonds still did not allow her body to step into the bedroom. "When your pappy passed on all those years ago, I never thought Sara would last this long—all alone... Well, if there is anything me or Thomas can do for you, you just yell." With that, she pulled the door closed as her little head retreated back.

Inez wanted to scream, to stretch her mouth as wide as the river and shriek like a bobcat. And cry; cry like she had when she was a baby in her mother's arms—strong arms that would never hold her again.

✕ ✕ ✕

William Grayson, the town bachelor, stopped by her house a few days later. He held his hat in his hand, twisting it as she opened the door. "Miss Inez," he stepped back from the threshold and off the stoop, crushing a two-foot high milkweed, "would you come out to talk to me for a while?"

The sight of 28-year-old William, nervous as a rabbit because of her, intrigued Inez. He had never married and still lived with his mother, which she thought displayed a fine quality for a man. To sacrifice starting a family of his own to help his mama with her seamstress work, well that just showed fine character, at least that's what her own mother had always said when the other women whispered about William.

"William, it's awful hot out. You can come inside." She pulled the door open wide for him as the summer heat spilled into the house.

"No, no, Miss Inez. It ain't right for an unmarried man and woman to be alone inside. You can come out here in the yard. Sit over here in the shade of the woodshed with me."

Propriety didn't mean scratch to her; who cared what people thought? Maybe seeing her and William going into the house together would give the old ladies something to talk about. But, she could see sweat rolling down the side of William's flushed face either from standing there in the sun waiting for her or from his nervousness, so she stepped down to the split-log step and out across the barren yard to the shed, shooing away a couple of chickens. William followed a few tentative feet behind her.

"Yes, William? What'd you want to talk about?"

He settled a respectable distance from her on the bench. "I

wanted to tell you I was sorry about your mama's passing. She was a fine woman."

The familiar hurt rumbled in her soul as his words brought the reality to her mind again. "Thank you."

"I brung you this newspaper from Charlotte," he handed her a creased paper. "It has your mama's listing in it. Thought you might like to save it."

From the fold, she saw the simple notice that her mother had left the world. She imagined her mama reading it and being proud that she had made the city paper. Now, Inez, just a shadow of her mother's size, but with the same cornhusk-colored hair and weary blue eyes, carried on the family name. She wondered if she would be the end of the Watkins line.

William sat still, sweat lingering on his forehead.

"Thank you," she said and placed the newspaper in her apron pocket. "That's the end of us."

"And that's... I... Well, it's..." The words refused to come to him, and Inez feared she knew where those forced beginnings would lead.

"William, you don't have to—"

"Yes," he awkwardly slipped from the bench with a crack of his knee hitting the packed red-clay dirt. "Miss Inez, I know you're all alone. One day I will be too. Mama ain't as spry as she used to be. I been thinking. Well, me and you..." He inhaled deep, then let the words wash out, "You should come live with us, as my wife."

She had hoped a proposal of marriage would come from love, or want, or even barnyard desire, but she knew that at sixteen with no family and no dowry but the slumping house in front of her, she couldn't expect much. Although, she did expect something more than pity, and that was what he and Mrs. Grayson had for her. She wanted a husband; someone to take care of her and she could take care of him. They could be as happy as her parents had been. William searched her eyes, so she glanced at the few logs left in the wood stack. "Thank you for asking, but I can't say yes. It's too soon after Mama died."

His body had stopped shivering in the heat; she felt he must be relieved. "But," he sat back up on the bench, "how will you live alone?"

"I have my garden out back, these few chickens, and that old cow for milk. Besides, my aunt and cousins aren't that far. Maybe just a couple of days travel. I'm fine," she said. Then added, "Thank you for asking. There probably ain't another man in town who would take in an orphan like me."

✕ ✕ ✕

Her letters to a cousin in Greenville, an aunt in Charleston, and another cousin in Kershaw didn't receive replies. She considered loading up her trunk of clothes and a few of her mother's books and quilts, packing the wagon, and arriving uninvited on her aunt's doorstep, but the thought of traveling that far, alone, and with an uncertain reception, frightened her more than staying in the house and surviving on what she could find in the garden. Her few hens had stopped laying eggs on a regular basis; she had fried the rooster, maybe the hens protested that decision. The cow's milk had dried up, and she had exchanged that old cow for the overdue bills at the mercantile. Using her father's rifle, she tracked through the woods and fields searching for rabbits, but once she had one in her sights, she dropped her aim when she saw it had a mate nearby. She couldn't bring herself to widow a rabbit.

The legend of Annie the Witch came to mind as she wandered back to her empty house and yard. Annie had lost her husband and sons to Yankee cannon fire, then living by herself, she ran out of food and roamed into the woods to scavenge. Town people later said they caught sight of Annie with tangled hair, torn clothes, and no shoes dancing in a forest clearing to the full moon's light. They said the devil had married her to keep her from dying alone.

The summer sun warmed Inez's back as she hummed a childhood song about Annie the Witch and scratched in the dusty rows of wilting potatoes. By her side, a skinny white chicken called Sally kept her company. "Sally," Inez said stopping to rest under a shady sycamore, "we don't have much left. As a matter of fact, we didn't have much to begin with." Sally cocked her head then picked at a feather on her wing.

Her tears had dried up with the summer drought, but Inez remembered her mother every time she walked into the old house; the air still held her smell: warm cornbread and butter. Milk thistle, polk, and dandelions had grown up in the front yard, but she didn't have the energy to keep it cut back, and besides, she substituted polk and dandelion leaves for lettuce in her meals. None of the neighbors checked on her anymore, not that she expected them to continue; she wasn't their responsibility. Pecking the chalky dirt, Sally fished for a June bug. Inez watched, then pulled the tattered newspaper out of her apron pocket and re-read the advertisement.

Two other chickens, each a bit plumper than Sally, roamed the yard. With the advertisement safely tucked back in her pocket, Inez grabbed a startled rust-colored hen and held it down by the neck on a hickory stump, then with one swift hatchet chop, severed its head from its body. Inez turned away until she guessed the bird had stopped flopping on the stump. One last scrawny chicken and stewed weeds supper in South Carolina, she reasoned, then a new life rises with the sun.

✕ ✕ ✕

Rattling over rough tracks, the train pitched back and forth into a steady rhythm that Inez let her body sway along with. She sat near an open window that allowed in some fresh air, but coal smoke drifted in with it every time the train twisted to the right. The women surrounding her seemed to be just the same country folk as her, except Inez knew she had to be the youngest. The other women in the passenger car had the appearance of years of working a farm in the sun, raising babies, scrubbing clothes, and gathering firewood. Maybe these women are here because their husbands died, she thought, because surely they had had husbands to look so haggard. Her hands held tight to her canvas bag containing her money, change of unmentionables, her mother's Bible, and her father's traveling pistol.

The woman sitting across from her forced a smile and asked "Are you as scared as I am?"

"Yes, I think so," Inez smiled back at the woman with crow-black hair and a barrel of a bosom. The woman's face held a grin, or a grimace, that Inez hoped meant she was friendly and not going to take her bag away from her with those big bear-claw hands. Face powder had settled into the creases of the woman's jowls giving her the lines of a catfish.

"This is as far from home as I ever been," the woman said and shifted her weight in a quick waddle on the pine bench. "What 'bout you?"

"Yes ma'am, this is as far as I been too." Calm settled on her as she talked to the big woman. She leaned forward, over her canvas bag, "I drove my wagon up to Charlotte this morning to meet with Mr. Dula; he took it as my payment for this ticket."

The big woman tipped toward her, and Inez sat back to stay a safe distance away. The woman whispered, "Honey, you didn't need to pay for this ticket. The man out west is paying expenses."

Anger burned her cheeks as she realized Mr. Dula had talked her out of her horse and wagon, but she didn't have anywhere to put them... But, dang it, she could have sold a horse and wagon in the streets of Charlotte for some good money. A deep breath to settle her nerves helped, but Inez bet the woman thought she was a foolish little girl for letting Dula take her horse and wagon.

"By the way," the woman smiled crooked teeth at her, "my name is Gertrude. Just call me Gert. What they call you, Honey?"

She thought about making up a name, to become a whole new person with a new past, a different past, a more exciting past, but her imagination failed her. "Inez," she finally said.

Gert held out one of her big bear hands, but Inez pulled her bag closer to her. "Pleased to make your acquaintance," Gert pretended to shake hands with Inez. "I find this quite exciting, going to a new place, but I hear stories about the West, you know about Indians snatching white women." Something funny must have occurred to Gert because she laughed a little covering her mouth with her large hand. "I'm probably too much woman for some Indian to throw over his saddle and ride off with."

The image of Gert being thrown over anything brought a giggle out of Inez too. "I don't worry none about Indians. The few around home are just as nice and polite as the preacher's wife."

"Well, that may be," Gert said, "but I still heard a lot of stories." She glanced out at the thick trees sweeping by the window. "Any idea where we might be? That looks like the Smoky Mountains coming up. Once we get over them, it's pretty much down hill from then on."

The question Inez yearned to ask surfaced, but she dismissed it as being too personal. But, weren't they all going for the same reason? Why not ask? Why not talk about it? She sat her bag at her feet and leaned toward Gert. A faint scent of roses lingered around the woman. "Do you know him?"

Gert sat back, "The man I'm going to marry?"

"Yes, ma'am."

"No, Honey. Do you know yours?"

She guessed she could admit it, since Gert didn't know either. "No, but I was told he's a fine gentleman with wealth from mining."

"Mr. Dula told you that?" Gert asked.

"Yes, ma'am."

"Honey, he told me the same thing. You think we're marrying the same man?" Gert laughed a hearty laugh and slapped Inez on the knee.

Afraid she might be going after the bag, Inez kicked it under her seat. "You don't think so, do you? I mean I heard of Mormons out there having a whole herd of wives. You don't think we're heading for Mormons, do you?"

Gert sat back and crossed her arms over her vast chest. "Better not or I'll grab me an Indian and throw him over my shoulder to be my husband. I ain't putting up with no other wives."

Inez ventured another of her list of questions, "Do you know exactly where you're going? Which town?"

"All I know is I ride this train and," she looked at her papers, "switch in Chattanooga, then Memphis, then up to Kansas City, then

I jump on the Kansas Pacific line going to Denver. Whew, that's a lot of train hopping. What about you?"

Inez pulled her bag from under the bench and dug out her own piece of paper wrapped around her tickets. "Me too, but in Kansas City, I go on the Santa Fe line to the Arizona Territory, switch in Flagstaff to a local train, then" she caught her breath, "to Ash Fork then to Jerome Junction." She looked up and smiled. "A copper mining town," she revealed to Gert as if she might be impressed.

"Honey, sounds like we're not marrying the same man." Gert rummaged through a straw bag next to her and pulled out a fried chicken leg. "Here, Honey, eat something, it's way past supper time and I don't think this train is going to stop until we hit Chattanooga in the morning."

Inez thanked her and sank her teeth into the cold chicken that tasted a hundred times better than her old, tough, skinny hens back at her mother's house in South Carolina.

✕ ✕ ✕

After helping each other learn the ways of the different train stations and eating a lot of greasy food in the railroad establishments, Inez and Gert parted ways in Kansas City, but Gert promised to write as soon as she got settled in Denver. Back on another rattling train, Inez daydreamed about the life of luxury and romance that the gentleman in Jerome would give her. Her budgeted money allowed her one good meal a day at a whistle stop around noon, then she would snack on bread or crackers until the next day. She tracked the amount of money she spent against how much she had expected, then adjusted accordingly; her mother had always stressed the importance of money and how to keep track of it. The Santa Fe line didn't have as many single women as the Eastern trains. Families and men now out-numbered the lone women; Inez kept to herself, but always sat near a family instead of a group of men. If some man said howdy to her, she would respectfully smile and then look down at her open Bible, not that she was actually reading the Good Book, but she held it in her hands as a lucky charm.

She watched the women. Did she know how to act like a lady? Had her mother taught her right? These women sat quietly with their babies and young children; even a five-year-old girl had the teaching to stay calm while her brother pointed out the window with excitement at buzzards coasting circles above a field. Ladies learned the proper way to behave: no bloomers, petticoats; no slang, speak correctly; no face paint, no flouncy clothes, no exposed limbs, no imbibing alcohol. She knew what to do; she could be a good wife, as good a wife as any. With that settled in her mind, Inez pushed up the window allowing the wind to blow past her face.

The flat lands of the prairie seemed to stretch for a thousand miles as she watched bigheaded, woolly cattle, which someone called buffalo and bison, graze near the tracks the train sped over. She missed the lush green trees and grass of the Mississippi Valley; all she saw now was dirt-colored. The land, the animals, the people, the buildings, everything had settled in hues of brown. As if her prayers had been answered, the train chugged up hills, higher and greener. Shrubs of juniper and pinyon and sporadic stands of pines spotted the sharp, rugged ridges and valleys, so unlike the rolling, gentle slopes of the East. The Western landscape intrigued Inez with its raw beauty, a little dangerous looking, but definitely a refreshing change from the dusty bland plains.

Before the train stopped in Gallup, of the New Mexico Territory, the conductor walked through the car taking lunch orders for the restaurant. "Eat one of the best meals in your life," he announced. "See the world famous Harvey Girls and be served in luxury. This is a treat for the weary traveler. Gentlemen need to wear their coats in this establishment." He walked down the aisle, jotting things in his notebook, and when he came to Inez, he asked, "Lunch counter or dining room?"

"How much?" She worried that such a fancy place wouldn't fit her budget.

The conductor grinned, "35 cents for lunch counter, but for 50 cents in the dining room, you'll get your choice of steak, chicken, duck, turkey, a lot of vegetables, and plenty of dessert. All you can eat. Plus," he glanced down at her budget scrawled with numbers, "it'll fill you up until tomorrow morning."

She ordered the dining room meal, and as they pulled into the Gallup restaurant. Young girls, not much older than her, in starched aprons and simple black dresses, their hair tied in back by a single white ribbon, escorted the passengers to their tables and immediately began serving food. Inez drank iced tea and ate roast sirloin, English peas au gratin, sweet potatoes, some sugar cured ham, beets, French slaw, and for dessert, she tried cantaloupe, peaches, and custard. The Harvey Girls kept bringing food, until Inez could eat no more.

"Do you like the West?" Inez asked a Harvey Girl who looked about her age as the girl refilled her iced tea.

"Yes, ma'am. We meet a lot of interesting traveling people. And," the girl looked around as if getting ready to share a trade secret, "most of the girls find husbands. It's rare to find a Harvey Girl that has worked for more than a year."

"Good men?" Inez asked.

"Bankers, lawyers, company men," she boasted and collected empty plates from Inez's small table, "and a few cowboys and miners, but mostly impressive successful men."

"I'm on my way to Jerome, a copper mining town," Inez said. "I have a man waiting for me there. It's been a long trip. I'm a bit scared."

"Don't worry," the girl said. "The men here are so much better than the Eastern men. They have respect for women because there's just so few of us." She glanced around, "Do you want me to wrap up some ham biscuits for your traveling?"

"That would be right kind of you," Inez said.

"I know how the trains can get," the Harvey Girl said. "Take something with you. How many more days do you have?"

"I should be there by morning. The biscuits will make a nice supper." She wondered if things didn't work out if she could be a Harvey Girl. "Does Mr. Harvey hire girls with no experience serving?"

"If you can stand on your feet all day and be sociable then you can work here. Like I said, we're always looking to replace newly wed girls."

Back on the train, she napped a few hours then snacked on her ham biscuits and slept again until the sun rose and the conductor walked through announcing Flagstaff of the Arizona Territory. Her new life was budding.

CHAPTER TWO

She stood on the wooden platform with her trunk and bag at her feet; cool wind whipped at her skirt and blew her hair into her eyes. Tall pines swayed in the breeze as fat clouds tumbled across a pure blue sky. The swaying sensation of the train still clung to her body, so she walked back and forth as she had learned from past stops to get her "land limbs" back. Just a few hours and she'd meet her future husband. One more leg of the trip lay in front of her: a local train to take her to Ash Fork, then down the Santa Fe, Prescott, and Phoenix line to Jerome Junction. She paced the platform in Flagstaff wondering how she had come so far on her own.

A woman in a yellow silk dress and painted lips walked by Inez and smiled. She went into the station in a rustle of petticoats. My, Inez thought, this place has some fancy women. Touching her hair, she realized how tangled it had gotten from the wind of the train. She tried to smooth it down, but finally pulled it back and tied it with a ribbon as she had seen the Harvey Girls do.

When her train arrived, the fancy woman boarded it too. She sat a few rows behind Inez. Worry crept into Inez's mind that the woman might be a miner's bride too and that her future husband might see them both and feel he'd been slighted. She knew her travels hadn't allowed her to look her best, but hopefully, she could clean up before she met him.

The train whipped around mountain curves as it headed south toward Prescott causing Inez to have to hold on to the bench to keep from sliding. Smoke from the engine poured in the open window as they hooked around a knoll, and Inez actually saw the engine pass her window as it headed back down a switchback pulling its cars like a snake descending a rock wall.

Finally, the conductor announced Jerome Junction. Inez looked out the window to see a small cluster of buildings around the station. After collecting her trunk and bag, she stretched and walked around on the platform to shake the rickety train sensation from her body, except this time she knew she wouldn't be boarding a train again, this time, she was done with riding noisy, hot, smoky trains.

Several wagons waited near the station with steady horses or mules harnessed to guide travelers on to their final destinations. Inez hooked her bag over one shoulder and pulled her heavy trunk behind her, across the platform, to the ticket window.

A white-haired, stoop-shouldered man looked up and smiled at her, "Help you?"

"I was wondering if a ride for Inez Watkins was waiting for me."

"You Inez Watkins?" he asked, checking a list held down from the breeze with railroad spikes laid at the top and bottom of the paper.

"Yes, sir." Inez peeked through the window to scan the list, but his finger had traced to the bottom before she could make out any names. "You must be here early." He reached for a book packed with loose sheets and strummed through them shaking his head. "No, I don't see no one coming for no Inez Watkins."

Disappointment shook her tired body. Had she traveled for so long and for so far to be abandoned, left at the station like unclaimed luggage? Her mind raced with alternatives: did she have money to find a place to stay for the night, should she try to go back to South Carolina, could she get to Denver to stay with Gert?

"Hold on," the man laughed and tapped a paper with his finger. "You aren't early; you're late. A man looking for you came in yesterday. That train of yours was a day late."

"Did he leave? Is he coming back?" she asked leaning forward, nose against the wooden bars of the window.

"I need to send my boy to fetch him from the hotel. You just take a seat in the waiting area, and he'll be here directly." The man turned to an open door behind him and hollered, "Charlie, go get that Mr. Caldwell from the hotel. Tell him his bride is here."

Inez's cheeks burned from the old man knowing why she had come to his town. She grabbed her bag and trunk, pushing them toward the door of the station, and she almost forgot her manners in her embarrassment, but said over her shoulder, "Thank you kindly."

Settled inside on a long bench, she wondered what this Mr. Caldwell was like and what he would think of her. A long mirror hung by a door to the street, so she walked over to see what Mr. Caldwell would find when he came to get her. Dust and dirt smudged her face; her cream-colored hair was loose in places and hanging free like a wild woman. Licking her sleeve, she rubbed her face clean, then re-tied the ribbon in her hair. Pinching her cheeks for color, she then tried to straighten her wrinkled dress.

She caught the reflection of the fancy woman watching her preen. This woman, in her beautiful corn-yellow silk dress, smiled at her and walked toward Inez. "Dear, you look good enough for whatever farmer or miner is coming to get you."

Did everyone in town know she was waiting for an unseen husband? Did this Mr. Caldwell tell all of the Arizona Territory he was collecting his new wife from the train? The woman was so close that Inez could see the paint on her face and smell the flowery perfume hovering around her. That pretty yellow dress wasn't as respectable as her own pale blue calico, in fact, Inez could see the top of the woman's breasts, all squeezed together and popping out of the low neckline. She knew this was what the women back home called a "fallen woman." The fine clothes and hair the color of sunsets might look glamorous, but Satan himself dwelled in that woman. Inez excused herself, then a gentle touch to Inez's arm, stopped her.

"Dear," the woman said, "I have some sweet smelling cologne to help hide the traveler's grime that won't rub off without a bath. You do want to smell good for him, don't you?" she produced a small violet bottle out of her silk purse.

Inez considered the length of time since she had bathed and the man on his way to meet her. "Thank you. I appreciate it." She took the bottle and unstopped it; a quick sniff of the lavender scent brought back thoughts of the romance she hoped for. Dabbing the stopper on her wrists and behind her ears transformed her image of herself. Maybe Mr. Caldwell would like her, even if she wasn't as pretty as the woman in yellow. But, a thought struck her, she couldn't be seen standing next to this woman because people might think... Well, forget what other people would think, her original concern surfaced: she couldn't be compared to this fancy woman when Mr. Caldwell came in. She would look scrawny and plain next to this pretty lady—fallen or not. "Thank you," she handed the bottle back to the woman.

"Linda," the woman said.

"Thank you, Miss Linda." Inez smiled. "I'm Inez. I need to get back. My ride is coming to fetch me."

"Good luck, Inez," Linda said as she sashayed out the side door of the station.

Watching the oak-panel door swing shut behind her, Inez wondered exactly what a fallen woman did to be called that. She knew from the whispers of the women back home that they did favors for men without expecting anything but payment, but was that so different than what a wife was expected to do? Was that any different than what she had traveled so far for? The difference, she was sure from her church lessons, was that those women took pleasure in the act. Pleasure for pleasure's sake—that's no way to go about life.

The boy, Charlie, came into the lobby with a lanky man about the age of William Grayson, but she could tell this man didn't work with his seamstress mother. His hand, as big as Gert's, smoothed his black, unruly hair, while his other hand held a bouquet of daisies. The smile spread across his thin face showed pearly straight teeth; his green eyes sparkled in the sunlight streaming through the dusty windows of the station. Broad, straight shoulders bent a little as he nodded his head toward Charlie to thank him. He walked in wide strides across the plank floor to Inez.

"You must be Miss Inez Watkins," he bowed a little and held out the daisies.

She liked his look; she liked his manners. "Yes, sir. That would be me. Are you Mr. Caldwell?"

"Yes, ma'am." He smiled, then motioned for her to take a seat on the bench. He sat next to her, still grinning.

"You are the one I'm supposed to go to Jerome with? Are you the man who asked for me to come out here?" She wanted to make sure that this handsome man wasn't just driving her to meet some old grouchy man.

"Yes, ma'am." He said again. Then, he laughed and shook his head, "You sure are prettier than I thought you'd be."

"So are you," she confessed. "What should I call you?"

"Oh, pardon me," then added with a slow drawl like he was trying on her name, "Inezzzz." He straightened up on the bench and said, "I'm Josiah Benjamin Caldwell."

"Pleased to meet you, Josiah," Inez smiled and tipped her head toward him. So, this was her man. His manner was sociable, and she didn't smell spirits, a prize, that's what she thought of him.

"Can I get you anything before we start our trip to Jerome?" he asked, then apologized. "I would say we could stay here for a little bit, let you rest up from the trip, but I got to be at work tomorrow."

"That's alright," she said. "I ain't done nothing but stare out the train window for days. I'm ready to get this traveling over with."

"Okay," Josiah slapped his knees and stood. "Let's get your trunk in the wagon and head down the mountain. It's a pretty ride," then he added, "and will be all the prettier with you sitting beside me."

She smiled at the compliment and took his extended hand to help her up from the bench. The touch of his strong, rough hand comforted her; she knew she had made the right decision.

✗ ✗ ✗

Inez sneaked another peek at Josiah and clinched her fists tight with excitement, yes, she had made a good choice, yes, she would have a happy life in these green hills, yes, Josiah handled the wagon with a steady grip and strong command to the horse, he would be a good husband.

Maneuvering the wagon and horse around a deep rut, but sliding into it anyway, Josiah glanced at Inez, "Sorry 'bout that. We had some gully-washers yesterday that left the roads a bit rough."

A tall pine forest surrounded the trail, layering it with soft yellow needles. "Is your house in the woods?" Inez asked.

"My house?" He almost laughed, leaving Inez taut with worry that she had asked something she shouldn't have. Josiah corrected her question, "Our house."

Relief spread through her like dropped reins on a mule. "Our house," she repeated. "Is our house in the woods?"

"No ma'am. In fact, we don't have a house—not yet." He raised his eyebrows and took a slow look at her.

Trying to disguise her confusion and not reveal her disappointment, she managed a smile. "Where are we heading?"

"Miss Inez," he said, "we ain't married yet, so you are going to stay with my friend, Samuel, and his wife, Lottie, in a family community down the mountain and I go back up to Jerome to work. Besides, you got some planning to do."

"Like what?" Inez asked. The wagon rolled over smoother, winding roads, sloping down the mountain. A mother deer and two fawns leaped through the underbrush. "You mean wedding planning?"

A smile spread across his face, "Well, some, 'course no wedding is too fancy around here; I was thinking about the house. I have some land staked out just down the mountain, near the river. The land I got has room for a garden and a few cottonwood trees to build a house under."

"But," Inez started, then stopped, wondering just how to phrase it without making herself look bad compared to all the other frontier women. "I don't know how to build a house."

"Ha," he laughed and slapped his knee, startling the horse that picked up her pace to a gallop. "Inez, you don't have to build the house, just make sure it's what you want. Some of the miners will help me build it."

"Well, thank the Lord," she dug through her canvas bag and pulled out her bonnet. "I was scared you wanted me to build the thing." The forest canopy thinned, allowing sunlight to streak through and the temperature to rise a few degrees. Inez tied the bonnet under her chin and adjusted the wooden slats in the bill to shade her eyes.

"Nothing too fancy," she said watching the horse's black tail swing back and forth, losing rhythm momentarily to swat a fly from its rump. "Just a small house to raise a few young'uns and some livestock." She studied Josiah's thick, muscled forearms as he guided the horse down a steep part of the road. What would it be like to couple with this man? As schoolgirls, she and her friends had talked about such things, wondering about what went on behind bedroom doors. The physical acts she knew from growing up on their small farm, but the leading-up-to, the courtship, the wooing, she wasn't sure about. Then, she wondered, what do you say to each other after it's done? Her mother had never given her the rules of courting; no one had ever come to suit Inez except William Grayson and his clumsy attempt. She had read a book once that a girl in school had hidden in her lunch pail and passed to Inez in the school yard behind a tree. According to the woman in the story, she should expect to be pursued, while rebuffing all advances, but then reluctantly give in to the man. The scandalous part of the story was how the woman took pleasure in the amorous dalliance. Would Josiah give her tenderness and attention? Would he talk her through things she didn't know? Her cheeks burned from her thoughts, so she fanned her face under her bonnet.

"You doing alright?" he asked. "Look up ahead," he pointed to where the road seemed to drop off the end of the earth. Clear blue sky hovered above the disappearing road, but even as the wagon approached, Inez couldn't see past the crest. They wobbled over rocks and pulled up to the ridge where her astonishment caused her to stand up in the wagon to get a better look. Spread before her like a feast at a banquet, the Arizona landscape reached for miles in the valley before them with streaks of amber, rust, crimson, pale white, speckled with a scattering of evergreen shrubs. The steep, rock walls of the valley appeared to have been carved into faces, church spires, and lavish columns of scarlet limestone. In the distance as if standing guard, two mountain peaks towered in the north. To the east, she saw more of the rusty red rocks that hemmed in the valley and a glittering river running from the west toward the foot of the ridge they were perched on.

Pulling off her bonnet for a better look, she laughed. "It's beautiful. Is this Jerome?" The wind whipped up the canyon walls whirling her skirt around her ankles. She tucked her bonnet in her bag and tugged the ribbon out of her hair, shaking her head to let the breeze flow through her almond locks.

The wagon shook, and she found Josiah standing with her; he draped one arm casually around her shoulders. "There," he pointed to down the ridge, "that is Cleopatra Hill. Half-way up is Jerome; there at the bottom, those few houses, that's where Sam and Lottie live."

"It's not what I expected," she smiled and leaned into him.

"What did you expect?"

She sighed, "I guess to look more like home: lots of trees, rolling green hills..." her words left her as he held her shoulders in a firm grasp turning her to face him.

"This is home." He bowed in and brushed her lips with his.

The sensation of his mouth touching hers, the scratch of his beard stubble against her lip, she wanted more. She pressed harder back against him, but he pulled away slightly, and she moved in closer to regain what he had taken back. Without realizing it, her arms had wrapped around his shoulders and tugged him toward her; she knew this didn't qualify as lady-like behavior, but she was to be his wife, still the appearance of being too free with yourself could cast the wrong impression. She relinquished her hold on him, and flashed a coy smile before turning away to breathe in the view from the ridge again. "I think this will be a heavenly home."

The wide grin on Josiah's face seemed to attest to the shared expectation they had of their life together, a life of first kisses, of first embraces, of a home, and of children.

✕ ✕ ✕

Lottie, with her squat face and rolled body, informed Inez every time she made a misstep; her righteousness, when compared to the whispering, judging women of Inez's childhood, made them seem like hurdy-gurdy girls. And another downfall pointed out to Inez was her slang, "Where did you hear, I hate to say it out loud," Lottie paced the kitchen, tapping the table in front of Inez with her palm each time she passed, "the term 'hurdy-gurdy'?"

Avoiding her accusing eyes, Inez decided not to tell her the truth that it came from Lottie's husband, Sam. "I don't know, probably from someone on the train."

"Well, young lady, to be treated with respect, you must show respect in the way you," her staccato tone bounced off her list, "talk, walk, dress, eat, clean, stand, sit, laugh, smile," her voice rose with the excitement of teaching, "think, and obey." She stopped her pacing and sat in the chair opposite Inez. "Your slangy speech will reflect badly on Josiah."

"But, I learned good back home. I'm not free with my speech. Hearing new words out here, I'm just not sure when to use them and when not to." Inez sat up straighter to imitate Lottie's posture.

"I know what words to use," Lottie assured. "You ask me if you don't know. There is a social order I read about called The Cult of True Womanhood. All the ladies of the day follow the guide. A 'True Woman' should be pure, pious, domestic, and submissive. Your man will take care of you."

"That sounds fine for a city woman," Inez said. "But, what about here? I just thought man and wife would have to work side-by-side to get things accomplished."

"That's the domestic part. You will need to manage the household and children. Now, that would include cutting firewood, tending the garden, drawing water. In fact Missy, you need to put on some weight. Josiah will have plenty of work for you, and you need to be strong." She held up a beefy arm and made a fist.

Lottie appeared to be the model frontier woman with her stout, strong, no-nonsense body. Inez often thought of her as a horse turd come-to-life: something you see everyday, but don't mess with unless you have to. Sam, by contrast, laughed and teased everyone without one smidgen of seriousness, a cheerful butterfly, gravity not corralling him long to one subject or person. How those two got hitched together, the horse turd and the butterfly, Inez couldn't figure, but she confessed their marriage did work. Lottie called Sam 'husband' and he called her 'wife' as if those roles defined their existence. Inez called Josiah by his name, like she was his friend and an equal; every once in a while, Josiah would call her 'Honey' or 'Sweetheart' which made her insides melt like butter left in the desert sun. Lottie had to have been Sam's 'Honey' at some point, maybe in private she still was. Inez chewed those thoughts as Lottie reiterated, "As to your language, you just ask me if you don't know a word."

Lottie stood and smoothed her apron, "Now, let's start the laundry so we can get it on the line before noon."

"I wanted to take the horse up to Jerome and meet Josiah for lunch." A thought hit Inez to help soothe Lottie's opinion of her, "Why don't you come too? Sam would be glad to have lunch with you."

"No, respectable women don't roam the streets of Jerome. Families stay down here. Jerome is for the single men with all its saloons and such. Best not for a young lady to go by herself."

"That's why I wanted you to go with me."

"You can wait for Josiah to come back after his shift." Lottie clanged a bucket out the back door, "Inez, bring the laundry basket out."

By mid-morning, the chill in the air had lifted along with Lottie's temperament, and Inez knew both had to do with the whiskey Lottie sipped from a coffee cup. She conceded that Inez could take the horse up the mountain to deliver lunch to Josiah and Sam, but she needed to stay home to nurse a headache caused by her monthly condition. "Inez," she yelled from the front porch, "you ride side-saddle and keep your hair pinned under your bonnet."

The winding trail allowed Inez to study the valley she had first seen a month before. Beautiful, she thought, with the scattering of red buttes and mesas in the distance and the wide open valley below her where herds of white-faced cattle grazed on clumps of rough grasses. She shifted her focus on the town clinging to the hills above her. The road wrapped up the mountain like a slithering rattlesnake; crooked, wood-framed buildings, partly on sloped dirt, partly on stilts, burred to the side of the mountain and fed off the town's mine like ticks. In that copper mine, Josiah worked in the dark, damp, heat to chip the coppery veins from the limestone bones of Cleopatra Hill and haul it out to the smelting pots. Over and over, in and out of the mine, he breathed harsh vapors until the shift ended at five o'clock.

Then, he would come down the same road each evening to have supper with Inez and discuss plans for the wedding and house, never complaining about her cooking, although she watched Lottie watch him to catch his reaction which always consisted of his wide grin and a pat to his belly and "Fine cooking, Inez, mighty fine."

She spotted a clump of buttercups along the road and wondered if he saw them as he passed the same way. At that moment, she wanted to climb into the flowers like a bee and wait for him to pass, so she could ride with him, spend more time with him than the few hours each evening they had, seldom any alone time, always with Lottie and Sam, at the very least, in the next room.

She didn't think she would love so quickly, in all honesty to herself, if love would come at all, but it had. She loved Josiah. She marveled at his chin, the cleft where his razor missed the whiskers; she wanted his calloused hands holding hers while he smiled his wide smile at the words she spoke; she longed for his strong arms embracing her shoulders and how that simple gesture settled such a sense of comfort around her. She wanted to set him down on the porch to trim his thick, dark hair and let her fingers smooth it against his sturdy neck.

Plans for the simple wedding would conclude that coming Sunday in the Methodist church in Cottonwood. Sam would give her away; Lottie would stand in for her as matron-of-honor. Few others would be there except for the preacher and his wife. Then, they would live in a tent on Josiah's land until the emerging house was rainproof. These thoughts so engaged her mind, she didn't notice the nervous prance of the horse or the low rumble building in the ground until the mountain swayed with the force of the explosion.

CHAPTER THREE

Inez slid off the horse and steadied herself by holding onto the reins—the involuntary impulse anchored the prancing mare to her. A thin wisp of smoke curled into the serene blue sky.

The crows had grounded themselves.

The bees burrowed into the grass.

A distant rabbit flashed its white tail as it shot into a rock crevice.

Her mind savaged with too many thoughts issued a flight response. Over her shoulder, the homes looked orderly as always, but ahead of her, Jerome came alive with the disturbing, panicked yells of men and a distorted siren shriek. Small figures in the distance rushed from the town's buildings toward the mines. Only one other thought squeezed through her terror: Josiah. With her skirt flying, Inez hooked one leg over the horse, straddling the animal, riding like a boy, kicking the mare with her heels to charge it up the trail toward the mine shafts.

Dreamlike images flooded by her blurred eyes as she blasted into town: people moved as if suspended in thick buttermilk, their progression hampered as each ticking second dragged them back a step; the saloons, hardware store, boarding houses felt as if they tilted in on her as she hammered the horse up the street. Wiping the tears and sweat from her eyes, she pulled the horse to a halt behind a crowd gathered in front of one of the shafts. Dangling timber supports almost blocked the entrance, but ragged, bleeding men struggled out of the mouth of the black, smoke-belching hole; crying miners helped their brothers from the darkness and laid them out in the noon sun—some moved, others didn't.

Her single arrow-point focus was Josiah. She stood in the stirrups for a good look over the crowd, then swung off the horse, bonnet hanging down her back, her hair loose and tangled, with dread pushing her forward through the pack. She searched each man's face, but none of the worried, worn, craggy faces favored her young buck who, she knew, wasn't in that mine, probably not down any of the shafts at that moment; perhaps, he and Sam had been outside the mine. Her thoughts didn't calm her as she had hoped.

The foul odor of the smoke, like a nervous polecat, surrounded the crowd, but the deafening siren screech assaulted her senses as much as the tainted air. Her eyes, still blurred, couldn't focus on faces anymore; the smoke coated her tongue so that she tasted the polecat as well as smelled it. A touch to her shoulder ignited hope, but she swung around to find the hazy figure of a woman, an Indian woman, guiding her out of the swarm of panic to a twisted alligator juniper with patulous branches protecting them from the chaos. The Indian woman wore a long white smock and thick black hair hung in two braids behind her ears. She set Inez on a boulder next to the bent tree trunk and handed her a tin cup of water.

Inez drank, then wiped her eyes with her apron and attempted to get her breathing back to normal. "Thank you," she began to the Indian woman, "my future husband is..." The words choked emerging from her mouth. "He's somewhere in... there." She pointed back toward the mine.

"Pearl," a deep baritone came from the Indian woman motioning to a girl with raven-black hair.

The girl ran over and plopped down next to Inez with a flash of red and gold stockings beneath the hem of her simple straw-colored dress. "Is she okay? She looks right blanched. Was she near the explosion?"

"Pearl, settle down," the Indian woman said. "Her betrothed might be in the mine."

"Oh, damn," Pearl said, then she grabbed Inez's hand. "Don't you worry. Onalee will get the girls together to find him."

The shrieking siren from the mine caught her attention again, but the warmth of Pearl's little hands helped calm Inez. The strangeness of the woman called Onalee brought Lottie's instructions to mind: if you don't know, ask. She studied Pearl's hands and her own, then Onalee's; she was in the league of Gert, but different. Gert's big round hands had a softness to them, Onalee's reminded her of Josiah, strong, wide, masculine. "Are you," she raised her voice to be heard over the commotion, "Onalee, a..." she searched for the right way to ask.

Onalee smiled and nodded her head. "Yes, I am from the Diné tribe." Her voice hid a truth when she said it.

The Navajo called themselves Diné, this Inez had learned from Sam. Although, Onalee had the dark brow and straight nose of the Navajo, something didn't fit.

Her face was smooth and features delicate, but her eyes held knowledge that no woman, Indian or white, could know. Those eyes, deep and dark as coffee, seemed to read Inez down to her very soul, the mellow voice vibrated through her bones when Onalee said, "I am a nádleehí, or a two-moon man, different names for my kind. A shaman of sorts for the tribe, before the Navajo reservation, when we were still a tribe."

Berdaches, that's the term Inez had heard before, about this kind of person. Her mama had said they were between men and women, a combination of the best from each. "I'm sorry," Inez said, "I thought you was a woman."

"Nothing to be sorry for; the tribal women were the strong ones. It is the white people taking strength and pride from women."

"Speaking of being strong, I need to find Josiah." Inez stood with the help of Pearl and tucked her hair under her bonnet.

"Wait," Onalee said. "I will gather up some of my girls to help find him. Pearl, go get Molly, Toy, Frenchy, and Lois."

Although unsophisticated in the ways of a mining town, Inez knew what these girls were, and she knew Lottie would throw her out of the house if word got back that she had fraternized with jezebels. "Thank you kindly, Mr. Onalee, but I need to look on my own." She nodded to Pearl, then hurried back into the crowd and pushed her way to the front, remembering Onalee's words that the women of the tribe were the strong ones.

Springing forward, she almost stumbled over miners laid out on the dirt in a line as a doctor picked through them indicating with a flick of his wrist which ones might be helped and which ones should be left there.

The pale faces, the mask of death she remembered from her mother, and the open, motionless eyes staring to the heavens, along with the silent yawning mouths of these men should have, she reasoned, scared her, but an odd acceptance saddled her: if Josiah lay among these men, he was in a better place and their life together wasn't meant to be.

Slow, measured steps took her down the line of men passed over by the doctor. A white-haired, big-mustached Irishman cradled his dead son's head in his lap and cried; two Chinamen bent over their friend reciting a solemn chant; a young light-skinned Negro paced away and then back to the body of an older thin-bearded Mexican. Mournful wails and sobbing burdened her ears so that even tightening the ribbons of her bonnet didn't block them.

Inez stopped to stare at a face she knew. The familiar spark in his eyes was dulled by death, although a joyful smile still graced his now ashen face; she could almost hear his buoyant laugh and his light, barmy jokes.

Josiah's tear-streaked face looked up at Inez standing before him, Sam's lifeless body in his arms.

She and Josiah held each other in a tight embrace standing behind Sam's corpse; they swayed to a primal soundless tune in their grief and relief to be back in the other's arms. The mass of Josiah's body didn't burden her; she knew she held him on his rickety legs, giving him the physical and emotional support he needed. His body started to convulse in tears coming from deep down in the mines where he had lost his friend. Inez lowered Josiah back to the ground, still holding him like a baby, cuddling and consoling.

"I tried to get to him," he strained to say.

"I know, I know."

"The blast knocked him against me, shoving me down in the dirt—"

"It's alright."

"Then, he hit the wall, hard."

"Oh, Honey."

"I heard the crack."

Inez just rocked him.

"I heard his soul leave." His wide wet eyes bored into Inez, "In a breath, he was gone."

✕ ✕ ✕

She stared across the emerald Verde Valley in a daze as Josiah guided Sam's wagon down the mountain, the mare tied to the back, following them in procession. Inez, thankful to have Josiah by her side, turned to him from time to time and kissed his shoulder while he held both reins to drive the horse along the road. His sleeve still had the dirt from the mine floor where Sam had pushed him out of the way of the blast. Sam had saved his life, directly or indirectly she wasn't sure, but she knew she owed him for Josiah sitting there beside her. Lottie concerned her now, how to tell Lottie?

They had left Sam's body with the mine officials who had gathered up the dead and wounded and transported them to the new hospital perched on the road above O'Keefe's general store. Lottie would have to decide where Sam would be buried. Fate and Sam kept Inez from having to make that decision for Josiah.

The Red Rock country to the northeast, at the mouth of Oak Creek Canyon attracted her attention; she had heard that it was a sacred place for the local Indians. A few white settlers farmed there along the creek; maybe, she thought, that would be a nice place to raise children, a safe place, away from the copper mines of Cleopatra Hill.

Rolling into the small community of family homes, Inez felt the mid-afternoon hung askew. The usual business of the day had ceased, no wet laundry hung on the lines, no simmering beef stew scented the breeze, no children played in the lane. Women lined the street, asking each returning man about the accident, had he seen her beloved, was her husband coming down the road behind him? A few of the women cried in each other's arms. Some mounted horses or took their carriages or wagons and charged up the hill to find their men themselves, apparently not believing the miners returning from Jerome. Tears clouded Inez's eyes as she witnessed the reality she almost lived.

She spotted Lottie sitting on the front porch in a rocking chair watching them approach. Lottie stringed and broke green beans in a bowl on her lap; her movements, slow and deliberate, signaled to Inez that she had heard, but probably didn't believe the horrifying news. She didn't leave her chair as Inez and Josiah climbed off the wagon.

"Lottie," Josiah began, then tears stopped his next words.

Inez hurried up the steps of the porch before Josiah and knelt next to Lottie; when she tried to remove the bowl of beans, Lottie pulled them back. "Dear," Inez started in a soft voice near Lottie's ear, "Sam was a brave man." Inez felt the grip of Lottie's cold hand on her arm as the bowl slid from Lottie's lap and tumbled off the porch spreading beans across the yard.

✕ ✕ ✕

A total of thirteen men died from the accident. Within two days, all funerals and burials were held. Sam's burial was on the edge of town where several of the other men were laid to rest. Lottie didn't say much until they returned home from the gravesite.

"All I have left is this house and my wits, what's left of them," she paced the back porch where Inez sat folding laundry. "Some of the other widows are going to Prescott, but I'm staying. I figure that with the money Josiah pays for you staying here and by taking in laundry of some of the single men, I can get by."

"I'll be glad to help you with the wash," Inez said.

"Yes ma'am, I will need you to. Josiah pays only enough to cover your food; your boarding can come from you helping as laundress." She turned her back to Inez; clothes flapped on a rope stretched between a cottonwood and the corner of the house.

Inez considered the hurt Lottie must feel and ignored the sharp tone she had adopted, especially when addressing Inez.

"I bet we can bring in a lot of wash," Inez offered. "Why, between the two of us we could do six, maybe seven loads a day."

"Yes, but once you and Josiah marry, I will need to take in another boarder. That woman might want the job as assistant laundress."

"That's okay," Inez said. "I don't think I'll have much time for wash work once we're married. We have a house to build, a family to get commenced…" She noticed that Lottie had turned away from her again, and she realized how she had carried on about her future with Josiah when Lottie had just buried her husband. "Dear," she stood and gently touched Lottie's shoulder, "I'm sorry. I owe you so much. If you need me to help as a washer woman after I get married, I'd be proud to."

"Thank you," Lottie patted her hand and turned to face her, tears welled in her eyes. "You are a kind girl."

✂ ✂ ✂

Crickets chorused as a coyote yapped and howled on the near ridge of the black mountain. Josiah mashed tobacco into his pipe, then struck a match and pulled the flame into the pipe bowl with three puffs; each breath flared the match to illuminate his face in a soft bronze-hue that reminded Inez of copper—the blood of Jerome.

"I think we could live in our little house for a couple of years while I set aside some money," he explained, holding Inez's hand in the darkness of Lottie's porch. "Then, maybe buy a few acres near Prescott and do some farming, raise a few cattle, and" he took the pipe out of his mouth and smiled at Inez, eyes sparkling, "raise a few children."

His words delivered happiness tinged with euphoria and eased the worries Inez had held since the mine disaster and the postponement of their wedding. Bride-white had been replaced by widow-black on their day, but she felt no bad luck hovered over them because of it. With Josiah talking about their future and eventually leaving the occupation of miner, she believed fate had better times planned for them. "And children," Inez repeated his words.

"Yes, ma'am," he patted her hand. "A passel of young'ens to help their father and mother with the chores."

"I always fancied that stretch of land over near Oak Creek," she ventured her opinion of where their dream ranch would grow.

"Honey, your fancy is my fancy." Josiah puffed on his pipe. "I'll go wherever you want. I just thought you might like to be closer to a big town like Prescott where you and the children would have more people around."

"You are all the people I need," she leaned over and kissed his cheek; his beard stubble tickled her nose.

He turned to face her, setting his pipe down on the window ledge, then cupping her face in his hands, brought her lips to his. The gust of passion she experienced from his touch flamed her enchantment, her desire, her love for him. She reluctantly broke from his embrace. A decision had been made after the mine disaster, not from her urges or anything he had said or done, but from the reasoning of sleepless nights with him not by her side. She hadn't revealed her intention to Josiah, and she prayed he wouldn't think less of her. This moment fit her plan, in fact for her, the timing made it seem less a scheme on her part than a natural reaction. Inez stood, then pulled him to his feet. She didn't speak, but led him off the porch and down the road to his little canvas tent on the site of their future home.

CHAPTER
FOUR

In the dark quiet of the tent, Inez listened to Josiah's steady breathing and planned their future. Their house would be built on this same site; children would come from more nights like this one; their marriage would be forever passionate, gentle, satisfying, and content as this first night had been for them. As she began to pull on her drawers and petticoats, Josiah propped himself up on one elbow.

"What're you looking at?" Inez smiled, but a bit unsure of his reaction to their passion. She had hoped to slip out before he woke.

"The woman I love," he answered, leaning over to kiss her lightly on the lips.

Relief settled over her, snug like his embrace. She was home. Not the tent, not a cabin, house, ranch, mansion, or palace would be more of a home to her than Josiah's love. She cuddled back into his arms and fell asleep.

With the glow of daybreak fading out the stars and bleaching the dark blue sky, Inez crept through Lottie's back door and into her room. Within the hour, she heard Lottie up and fixing breakfast in the kitchen. She slept a little longer, dreaming of Josiah's touch.

The clang of pots roused her from sleep as if Lottie meant to wake her up. Her room beamed bright from the sun, and she jerked her head to check the clock on the dresser. Almost nine o'clock, half the day is gone, she thought, Lottie will have my hide. She hurried to get dressed and brush her hair, then emerged to find Lottie in the kitchen wearing a Sunday dress and hat.

"Sorry, I didn't feel well this morning," Inez made up the excuse as she said it. "I felt worn out before I even got out of bed. You look awful nice; where are you off to?"

Lottie seemed to ignore her explanation of sleeping late. "I didn't wait breakfast for you. I'm going into town to spread the word that I'll take in laundry. I need to get some extra money in here."

"What can I do?" Inez asked.

"You just thank the Good Lord that you still got Josiah," Lottie said. "Being out here with no family and no husband is not easy. I can already see that."

Inez placed her hand gently on Lottie's arm. "Think of me and Josiah as your family. We'll help you."

Lottie smiled and nodded her head, then retied her bonnet. "Thank you for saying so, but I know I need to survive on my own, and I will. I have this house. I can sew, mend, and clean clothes. But just now, I need to make sure everybody knows it and that I'm hanging out my shingle as a laundress."

"You'll do fine," Inez encouraged. "I'll ask Josiah to spread the word among the miners." She stood at the door and watched Lottie walk down the dusty road toward the general store. An idea occurred to her: Lottie needed a sign for her house. The blacksmith back home in South Carolina would make a sign for businesses by burning the letters into a piece of pine with a glowing poker. What a nice surprise that would be for Lottie when she returned home, she thought as she headed out the door.

The blacksmith worked in a barn about a mile away, on the road to Cottonwood. Inez planned the sign as she walked; it would be a nice square of oak with letters as high as her hand that spelled out laundress. She considered putting Lottie's name below or coming up with something clever like Laundress Lottie or Lottie's Laundry, but didn't believe Lottie would find it as witty as she had, so a simple sign that notified all who passed that a laundress worked in the house would be sufficient.

The bright sun warmed her shoulders as she walked. Different houses attracted her attention, and she began to take the features she liked from each and construct her dream home in her mind. A wide front porch, a parlor with stairs that go to a couple of rooms tucked under the eaves for children, a big kitchen with a covered back porch, then one side of the house for her and Josiah's bedroom. She imagined a large iron bed with a feather and down mattress and layered with quilts; a fireplace in the bedroom—they would need that. Another fireplace in the parlor would heat it and the upstairs rooms, and the kitchen would have the stove for heat. She would place the windows to catch the mountain breeze for cooling in the summer. With the house building itself in her mind, she lost track of time until she realized she'd walked past the blacksmith's barn.

She returned to the road that led to the blacksmith's; cottonwoods and sycamores spread their branches across the dirt road. She heard the clank, clank, clang of the ironsmith banging the metal into a useful form. As a child, she would watch the blacksmith shape out horseshoes, hinges, and gate locks in the heat of his fire and anvil. The smell of sweat and molten metal greeted Inez as she pushed through the small entry cut into the sliding barn door. To her surprise, the blacksmith wasn't an old, fat, hairy man like the one in South Carolina, this one was a young, solid man, not much older than Inez. His auburn hair hung in his red face as he hammered a rod of burning iron. He wore no shirt under his leather apron, and his muscles strained in the effort of shaping the metal. A thought came to Inez that she attributed to the past night of passion with Josiah, surely her thoughts were of Josiah, not this young man she didn't know.

"Help you?" he asked, looking up from his work, laying the hammer and iron rod on the anvil.

"Uh, yes," Inez looked away from the young man sweating before her. "I wanted to get a sign made for my friend. She's a laundress, and I want an oak board, a nice oak board, with 'laundress' burned into it. We're going to hang it on the porch to let people know we're in business."

He wiped his forehead with a handkerchief, "Just write what you want on that piece of paper." He motioned to a stack of paper on a table by the door. "And pick out a board over there."

Inez went to the stack of boards in the corner of the barn and found a nice square of oak that she knew she could polish into a work of art. "This one will do."

He smiled at her with slightly crooked teeth and walked over to take the selection from her. She could smell his brute scent before he reached out to take the oak board; her head began to swim as her emotions stirred. Could this man treat her the way Josiah had? Did he know how to make her knees buckle from his touch, could he make her forget to be a lady, to act on animal instincts like she had with Josiah? The questions plagued her as he walked away with the board. What was wrong with her? She loved Josiah. Why did another man raise the same feelings and desires in her? Was she no better than the floozies in the cribs in Jerome, standing by the door, asking passing men to come in for a quick release for 25 cents?

She turned and patted herself in the face briskly to drive her mind back to where it should be.

"Hey!" the blacksmith said. "You gonna write down the letters you want on this sign?"

"Yes sir," she took a deep breath, grabbed a piece of paper from the pile, and wrote LAUNDRESS in large letters so he wouldn't mess it up. She held the paper out to him.

He took it and stared at the letters, then said "That'll be one dollar."

Pulling out her purse, she counted out her coins and handed them to him. "Do a real good job, and I'll throw in another ten cents." She had learned this tactic from her mother.

"Yes, ma'am," the blacksmith nodded his clump of red hair at her.

He set his iron back in the fire, then took three clamps and secured the square of oak to a granite topped table. Wisps of light fragrant smoke rose from the crackling wood as he seared the first letter. His quick glances to the paper she had written on caused Inez to wonder if this man could read or if he just copied the lines from the paper; she wanted to get closer to make sure he didn't do it wrong, but the proper distance needed to be maintained.

She inspected his workshop, examining common objects and the uncommon. A pile of wagon hitches leaned on a stack of iron lace sections reminding her of the metalwork of her aunt's garden wall in Charleston. A shelf held ornate silver candlestick holders and pewter pitchers and mugs. She glanced back to make sure the sign progressed correctly and found that he had just about finished. The lettering stood thick and bold against the golden oak square.

"Since this here's a sign for your business, I'll add two loop screws and a chain at no charge." He took a rag from a bucket of water and wiped the lettering. "Want me to hang it for you, Miss?"

"No, no thank you," she answered quick. "My intended can do that. He's mighty handy with such things." She smiled.

"Fine. What's this fella's name? I might know him."

"Josiah Caldwell, he's a miner in Jerome."

He shook his head as he attached the loops and chain. "No, can't say that I know him." He held up the sign by the chain, "How's that look?"

"Wonderful," Inez grinned knowing that Lottie would love the simplicity of it. She held out an extra ten cents. "Thank you."

He opened his grimy hand and she placed the coins in his warm palm.

"Thank you, ma'am," he nodded to her, then swiped a lock of auburn hair out of his eyes. "You come back any time," he winked at her.

A rush of blood heated her face, she smiled, then tucked the sign under her arm and headed for home.

Lottie hadn't returned when Inez walked into the house. She set the sign on the kitchen table for Lottie to see, then busied herself with building a fire in the backyard to heat water for a load of wash.

As the water began to boil, Inez added soap and stirred before dumping in the clothes. One advantage of the new roads between Jerome and Cottonwood was that dirt and mud were always clinging to pant legs and skirt hems and regular washing kept it from setting in the fabric, which meant, Inez figured, that she and Lottie could become rich washing other people's clothes. A movement on the back porch caught her eye—Lottie held the Laundress sign in front of her, smiling through tears.

"Bless your heart," Lottie said. "This is the most thoughtful thing anyone has done for me in a long time."

"You're more than welcome," Inez stepped up on the porch and hugged her. "I hoped you'd like it. I can get Josiah to hang it tonight after supper."

Lottie leaned the sign against the doorjamb, then stood back to admire it. "Where'd you get it?"

"I went down to the blacksmith's barn and asked him to make it." Inez smiled knowing that Lottie would be impressed with her initiative.

"Is Caleb's son still working there?" Lottie asked.

"I don't know Caleb or his son," she explained, "but the man who did this was red-headed and about my age."

"Oh, that must have been Red Dale. He's from a good family back East," Lottie thought for a moment, "Boston, I reckon. Anyway," she pulled Inez's arm to sit with her on the porch steps, then leaned in and whispered as if the laundry would soak up the gossip she was about to spill, "I heard he got in trouble back there and had to come here to escape the law."

"No?"

"Yes."

"He didn't seem the type."

"They never do."

"Go on," Inez urged, "What did he do?"

"Well, the way I heard it, and you must realize this is all just hearsay, but I heard it was..." Lottie glanced around to make sure no one had sneaked up to listen to them, "fornication." Her eyebrow arched and she nodded her chin as if she had known all along that red-headed people were likely to be fornicators.

"But," Inez tried to understand how that drove him West, "why would the law be after him for that?"

"I don't know the specifics," Lottie admitted, "but I know he has lust in his heart. Caleb's a good man to give Red Dale a job, but I never would put a boy like that next to a fire all day long; Lord, he's liable to get all heated up and attack some unsuspecting woman."

So that's what I felt, Inez thought, his lust radiating from him, causing me to think such things. "Oh my, I was alone with him while he made that sign."

"You mean Caleb wasn't there?"

"No, just me and Red Dale," Inez said.

Lottie shook her head in disbelief, "I don't know how you made it out of that barn without being molested, but thank the heavens you did."

"He didn't seem that bad," Inez said. "I mean he's polite and worked hard to get your sign made."

With slow movements, Lottie's fingers traced the burned letters while her eyes stared at the boiling pot of laundry. After a moment, she roused herself from her thoughts, "Inez, we shouldn't be talking of such things. I wanted to tell you I have more washing lined up for tomorrow and the next day. I think we're in business."

✕ ✕ ✕

Josiah spooned more bean pie into his plate. "Inez," he grinned, "this is my favorite dish. It's got all the stuff I like."

"Well, I like it too," Inez said. "It's easy to fix and it makes you happy."

"Dear," Lottie spoke up, "this might be good for family, but I wouldn't serve it for company."

Josiah's eyes darted from Inez to Lottie, then back again. She knew he thought they were getting ready to scrap over the meal, but Inez breathed deep and forced a smile. "You're probably right, Lottie. I wouldn't serve this to the mine boss."

Between bites, Josiah said, "Just the same, it's mighty good for me."

A pile of green peppers had been sorted out of Lottie's portion, and she picked at the red beans, ground beef, and remaining onions.

All she seemed to eat was the cornbread crust. Inez didn't want to comment on it, but she wished Lottie would eat more. Maybe it was her cooking, she thought, or maybe it was Sam. How could she keep going without him?

After they cleaned up the supper plates, Josiah nailed up the Laundress sign that Inez had polished to a golden glow. Lottie commented again on how much she appreciated it. After a while, she retired to her room, and Inez and Josiah sat on the front porch listening to the crickets and a distant coyote on his nightly prowl.

Josiah whistled a bouncy tune in rhythm with the chorus of crickets and the coyote solo. "I been happy all day."

"Have anything to do with last night?" she asked.

He took her hand in his rough, strong fingers, lifted it to his lips, and kissed each knuckle.

"Stop," she giggled, "my hands are coarse from the lye soap and they smell like bleach."

"You have beautiful hands." He kept kissing, then still holding her hand, slipped down on his knee. "Miss Inez, marry me."

"Well, I don't know," she kidded him, "I have my eye on this boy with a tent and a plot of land. He's handsome and loves my bean pie, no matter what some fussy, bossy woman says."

"Sounds like a smart man," he pulled himself back up on the chair. "We should re-set our date. I don't know if I can wait for you to become my wife, not after last night." He winked at her.

"I'm not busy this Sunday, are you?" she asked.

"Sunday it is." Josiah kicked his boots up on the porch railing and began whistling his playful tune again. His notes slowed and drifted into the night. "I'm working on clearing the North mine."

Shock grabbed her. "The one that Sam died in?"

"Yeah, I didn't want to mention it in front of Lottie, but we're going back in to shore up the walls and inspect the supports. It needs to be operational by next week."

She didn't want him back there. The memory of that day still haunted her as a nightmare specter who visited her bed each evening, staying with her throughout the night. "Doesn't it bother you going back?"

"Gotta be done," he said.

Just like a man, she thought, push the emotion out of the way, get on with the job at hand. The strange Indian came into her thoughts. "The women are the strong ones."

"What?" he asked.

"I heard that in the Navajo tribe, the women are considered the strong ones. They build the houses, care for the fields, hunt and prepare the food. The men protect the tribe, but leave most else to the women. If women owned that mine, it would stay closed."

Josiah smiled and lit his pipe, "How's keeping that mine closed mean women are stronger?"

"Cause, we don't think the money is worth more than lives."

He puffed out a bellow of creamy smoke, "Don't you worry. I'm careful and I won't let that mine bite me twice. Losing Sam was enough of a lesson to me on how dangerous those copper veins can be."

She studied his profile as the last rays of the sunset sank behind Cleopatra Hill. "You remember that you belong to me, not to that mining company."

"Yes, ma'am," he saluted her as if she had just given him an order.

She didn't want to turn into Lottie. "Sorry, I just worry."

"I know. That's part of loving someone. I love you too, Inez."

She leaned over and hugged him, "Oh, I love you, Mr. Caldwell."

The next morning brought clouds and a cold drizzle, so the drying laundry hung in the kitchen and the back porch. Tromping back and forth to the kettle and the wash board, Inez noticed Lottie talking to someone at the front door. "More wash?" Inez muttered stirring the kettle in the rain. "You'd think a person would wait for the mud to dry."

Lottie's continued absence caused her to sneak another look at the visitor in the house. A man in a dark suit coat stood in the parlor talking with Lottie. With her hand over her mouth, Lottie shook her head slowly. Inez guessed it was one of the mine officials delivering more reports on Sam's accident and what the company would pay or not pay his widow.

Fishing out clothes with a broom handle and dropping them into a tub of cold water for rinsing, Inez wondered how long Lottie would be; I'll have this load done before she gets back to work. Just as the thought entered her mind, a sorrow-burdened Lottie braced the threshold of the back door. She appeared weaker, smaller than before the man arrived. What had he said to her? What more could the mine do to poor Lottie?

"Inez," her voice cracked, "please come here for a minute."

Inez searched Lottie's steady eyes for the meaning of the man, his visit, why she was summoned. The broom handle fell to the muddy ground pulling a petticoat with it.

The wind blew a loose strand of her damp hair across her face, and she looked in the direction of the gust to see if, perhaps, it wanted her to follow it—away from Lottie, away from the man, away from the future. She jerked from the touch of Lottie guiding her up the steps. "It's not?" she pleaded.

Lottie just kept her eyes down and led her to the man in the parlor.

"Miss Inez Watkins?" he asked with a deep downy voice.

She didn't look at his face, but concentrated on her apron hem. "Yes sir."

"I regret to inform you that Mr. Josiah Caldwell was killed this morning while working in a mine. His body has been recovered..."

White fluttered across her eyes, then a black veil dropped.

CHAPTER FIVE

The world should have stopped. The sun should not have risen the next morning. No finches should fly or sing; only the scavenging ravens should haunt the skies. The creak of wagon wheels rolling past Inez's bedroom seemed foreign and strange—why did the world continue without Josiah?

Nothing could be the same, yet Cleopatra Hill and the valley below trudged along as if he had never existed. Inez refused to leave her bed, finding solitude more comforting than witnessing life without him. She closed her eyes and imagined him there with her; tears soaked the pillow that she hugged. She wanted to die to ease her pain, for surely, she thought, death would be easier than life. Yet, with all these thoughts, she didn't have the strength to retrieve a knife from the kitchen. Each time she drifted into the numbing arms of sleep, she prayed not to wake.

Lottie convinced her to attend the funeral that Sunday, but her deadened mind didn't register the activity, partly from grief and partly from the morphine the doctor had given to calm her nerves. Only later did she realize she had buried Josiah on what would have been their wedding day.

The days continued, to her amazement since she knew the world would stop, and she re-joined the living. The ache burned in her, but she knew she had to survive on her own. She couldn't depend on anyone else to take care of her.

✗ ✗ ✗

Unlike Lottie, Inez had no claim to any death benefits from the mine. She and Josiah were not legally married, although in her mind, Inez considered herself a widow. She wore black for a month and mourned as was appropriate. She and Lottie, two copper mine widows surviving on their own. Lottie possessed her house and had a small pension from Sam's death. Inez had nothing but, as she would say to Lottie, "the smarts to stay alive and the gumption to keep living."

Doubts crawled into her thoughts even with the brave exterior constructed for Lottie. Am I being punished for lying with him before God said it was alright? The question twisted in her mind as she wrung out a mustard-colored dress over the rinse tub. Why? Why Josiah? He was a good man. I couldn't have asked for any man better. If I was wrong to couple with him, then why didn't I die? I'm the harlot. The woman is supposed to say no. She had hoped for a child to be born from their night together, to keep some part of Josiah alive, to still be part of her, but as the weeks passed, she faced the fact no child was to come.

"Inez," Lottie called from the back porch. "You about finished with that rinse? You need to get that load on the line to dry. I promised Anna May it would be ready this afternoon."

"Yes, ma'am," she answered and slung the wet dress into a grapevine basket. "Yes, Miss Bossy," she muttered as she hoisted the basket to her hip and heaved it to the line. "Well, 'course the line is full. Would it have killed Miss Business Woman to take this load off?" Inez pulled up her apron and clipped clothespins at each corner. She snapped off the pins from the line with one hand, letting them fall into her apron pouch, and tossed the dry clothes on her shoulder as she worked her way down the line to the cottonwood tree, then back up to the house on a second line. Inez dropped the dry load into an empty basket, then made the trip down the line again, pinning up the wet clothes.

"Yes," she nodded to herself, "I'm being punished. Daddy died, Jackson died, then Mama, and now Josiah. It's damn dangerous to know Inez Watkins. Even poor ole Sam died just from knowing me." She glanced around, "Too bad I can't control who this doom affects."

"What're you saying out there?" Lottie asked from the porch.

"Nothing," she answered without looking at Lottie.

"I know you're mourning Josiah," Lottie began, "I know what losing a man is, but young Miss, your attitude about your work is poor."

Inez dropped the basket and turned to look at her. "Poor? Poor? I lost Josiah, I don't have no future, I barely own the clothes on my back, I have to abide by you criticizing me for each move I make, and you call my attitude poor?"

"Now, you listen here, Missy. I run this business—"

"I do all the work," Inez interrupted and thrust both her red, raw hands in front of her to show what the lye soap had done. "You sit around and figure, scratching out numbers on your pad while I do all the washing."

Lottie's face hardened, "That's what I pay you for."

"You don't pay me. I pay you… for food, for boarding, for part of the soap costs." All the resentment Inez had felt for Lottie since her first day in Jerome rushed to the surface of her soul. The bitterness soured in her mouth. "I'm nothing to you but an indentured servant, a slave. By the time you take out what I owe you, my pay won't buy me a bolt of gingham for a new dress. I have to keep wearing the same raggedy dresses because all the washing and mending of other people's clothes don't leave time for me to take care of my own."

Down from the porch with her hands on her hips, Lottie glared at Inez. "If it weren't for me, young lady, you would be on the street begging for food."

"My servitude to you," Inez yelled even though Lottie stood but inches from her face, "my enslavement is over!"

Lottie stepped closer to Inez, exchanging heated breaths like two battling goats. "I should have thrown you out after you shamed this house."

Shocked by the thought that Lottie might know about her night with Josiah, Inez stammered, "I, I didn't…"

"I tried to enlighten your ignorant ways," Lottie continued. "Show you how to be a lady. Help you make something of yourself.

I defended you when the other women talked about how loose and free you acted."

The words ruffled Inez back to rebuttal. "Don't you try to make it sound like you had my interests at heart. You only care about yourself and what you can get out of me. This business can't survive without me, the work-for-nothing slave."

"Missy, you can't survive," Lottie shot back, "without me watching over your ill-bred conduct."

She despised walking away from the stare down with Lottie, but she couldn't take looking at her any longer, so she stepped to the side and stomped up the steps to the back porch. In the house, she threw a few belongings into her bag, then slammed the front door as she stormed out.

Where to go? Inez knew she wouldn't step foot in Lottie's house again. Her pride wouldn't let her. What awful, hurtful, spiteful things that woman hurled at me. "I am intelligent, I am sociable, I am a real lady, and," she marched down the path to the road, "I can take care of myself." Her quick strides down the packed dirt street helped to calm her, even though, she couldn't escape the disapproval of Lottie fast enough. By the time she stopped at the edge of the small community of houses, sweat chilled the side of her face and the wind whipped her hair into her eyes. "Dang it," she kicked a small rock off the road, "I ran off without my bonnet." She wrapped her thin cloth coat tight around her, pulling it up to her ears. The sun crept behind the mountain range, casting long shadows over the valley as the cold wind gusts turned icy fingers to her exposed skin. Only one person she wanted to see: the one who would protect her, the one she loved and loved her. She went to Josiah.

The cemetery perched on the foothills and down wind of the smelter pots of Jerome had a few bare-limbed sumac and brown-needled pinyon pines. Death, sparse tufts of grass, the lonely wooden crosses, the smelter-singed trees, all added up to death. This was the exact place Inez wanted to be. Gathering the wilting goldenrod wildflowers she had left on Josiah's grave a few days before, she bunched them together into a bouquet and sat on the freezing ground and watched the last glow of the sunset dim around her.

"Josiah Caldwell," she began, "I love you more than anyone I ever met. We were married in our hearts, if not by the rules of the mining company. Because of those regulations, I don't have anything of yours. I'm abandoned again."

She set the drooping bouquet at the base of the cherry-wood cross marking Josiah's plot. "I wish you were still here. I need you tonight to help me decide what to do next. Going back to South Carolina would cost too much money, and besides, I don't want to go back there and be nurse-maid to William Grayson and his old mama." Inez traced a circle in the dry dirt at her knee. "Gert probably don't remember me after all these months. Lottie never let me meet many of the other women in town, besides they're all old hags and would be afraid I'd steal their husbands. But honestly," she stared at the wildflowers as if they embodied Josiah's sparkling eyes and wide grin, "I don't want somebody else's husband. I'm not even sure I want a new sweetheart—no man can replace you."

The wind lashed its damp wings over her shivering body, and she gathered her legs up under her so that she wrapped herself completely in her coat, lying over Josiah, whispering to him, confiding her fears and desperation. "I know what we did was right. It wouldn't have felt that way and brought us closer together if it hadn't been true. But, I can't help but feel I did something to cause the Lord to take you away from me. Lottie, the mean ole witch, always said that I didn't understand all the complications of being a good wife, a good woman..." Her tear-filled eyes stung from the whipping drizzle as the wind howled through the dark. "Why? Why did you have to go?" She beat the cold ground with her fists, "Come back. Come back to me." Exhausted and shivering, she clawed at the dirt, "Please, Josiah..."

A pelting, freezing rain woke her. Red mud had formed, then frozen around her hands, hair, and face that prickled her skin as she tried to brush it away and yanked her tangled hair as she shook her head. The night storm still ruled the sky with rare October sheet lightning revealing the distant San Francisco Peaks to the north. Above her, the jaundiced lights of Jerome sputtered against the black mountains. Shivering, she gathered her coat tight around her body and plodded up the hill, not following any established path or trail, over boulders, around prickly-pear cactus clumps, past swaying pinyon pine branches, trudging up Cleopatra Hill.

Few people braved the sharp, bitter weather in the streets of Jerome; that and the late hour prevented Inez from encountering others on her way into town. She had decided that she would continue her laundry career with one of the Chinese laundries located at the end of Main Street. She'd heard some of the men say that the Chinese girls who did the wash lived above the laundry and that Mr. Zhen had new girls on a regular basis. All she needed to do was find a place to clean up, then wait for Zhen's to open and apply for a job. These thoughts occupied her mind until she noticed she had wandered near the cribs of Hull Street.

The lowest of prostitutes used one of the single room shacks lining the street where they would stand in the doorway inviting men in for a quick pleasure. The men, even lower than the prostitutes, walked up and down the street negotiating for the best price. Sam had laughed with Josiah, as Inez eavesdropped on the conversation that the girls probably would have paid the men to go to some other girl if only they'd had the money. Men with names like Bear Billy, Stinky Stan, Extra-finger Emmet, and Hairy Hoyt were laughed about when they discussed the cribs. From her mother's descriptions of Northern cities, Inez knew that diseases, violence, and addiction to spirits bred in these crib rows. But, tonight, the row was quiet like the rest of town.

The only life seemed to be in warm-lighted saloons where even with the door shut to block the howling wind, the feisty music bounced out onto the street. I can't go in there, she thought, teeth chattering with each sharp gust from the storm. From the shadows, she watched a frosty-whiskered man push open the door to the Fashion Saloon. The dank, warm smell drifting out with the music and laughter lured Inez to the window. Inside the Fashion, men leaned against the long bar drinking from icy mugs or small glasses—like thimbles for a giant, Inez mused. A few woman scattered themselves around the saloon, sitting with men at little tables, laughing in high-pitched squeals at the jokes of their customers. She could certainly warm herself by the stove, she reasoned, but as she moved toward the door, she caught the reflection of a wild woman in the plate glass window. The knotted hair, the dirt-smudged cheeks, the wide eyes scared her until she realized it was her own face staring back.

How could I have gotten to this state in one night? I look like a beggar woman, old, worn-out, useless. She searched for someplace out of the harsh night and away from the cruel reflection. "A bit of water and a warm place to clean up is all I need before morning and my search for work," she walked down Main Street checking the buildings for a rain barrel. In a short alley between a milliner and a grocery, she discovered a half-full barrel where she dipped her handkerchief in and rubbed her face clean with the icy water. An advantage of the town being snagged on the side of the hill, Inez found, was that the houses and buildings looked down the chimneys of their down-hill neighbors. She laid a plank from the retaining wall at the end of the alley to the roof edge of the building behind the milliner. Creeping and balancing over the board, she stepped onto the low-sloped roof and huddled between the smoking chimney and the storefront's façade. In the sheltering comfort of the warm brick, Inez fell asleep.

CHAPTER SIX

The harsh wind whistled across the roof, swirling around the corner of the chimney, waking Inez with clammy tendrils. She shivered while searching for any signs of daybreak, but the night sky was as dark as coal, and she pulled her coat tight around her and shouldered close to the brick chimney that had lost its fever.

No noise rumbled from the Fashion Saloon a block away, the wind trailed no scent, the night gave no witness, only damp gusts rolling down the mountain alerted her senses that she still lived—alive and aware. In a low moment, she had hoped not to wake, not to have to contend with the future of taking care of herself. She knew she could join Josiah, no one would miss her, no one would mourn for the girl called Inez. As she contemplated the fact that she hadn't died in her sleep, anger rose in her, tingling her feet and hands and mind—Why not? Why did she have to continue? Fight for survival? Her hot emotions surged throughout her quivering body. She stood and paced around the sheltered corner of the roof, her eyes straining to see where she might go for warmth.

The night sky hid the eastern horizon. The sun must be waking the Carolinas, she thought. Images streamed into her mind: her South Carolina hometown, her mother, the old broken-down house, the familiar people, and the lonely bustle of solitude that had propelled her to take the chance on an advertisement for love and adventure. Love was gone, but adventure survived.

The plank leading off the roof to the alley blended into the night, so Inez knew she was stuck until daylight. On tiptoe, she peered over the façade of the storefront to the street below. A ghostly light bobbed along the street. Inez watched as it drew closer. The outline of a girl emerged through the mist behind a lantern that swung as she walked.

As the girl approached the building, Inez called from the roof, "Hey you, girl."

The girl spun around looking into the shadows for the voice. "Who is that?" she asked in a caution-tinged whisper.

"Up here, on the roof," Inez waved her arm.

"What're you doing up there?" The girl held up her lantern revealing her round teenage face. Her eyes and mouth seemed to glow in the milky light.

"Trying to keep warm," Inez said. "I can't see to get down."

"Hold your horses," the girl circled around the building, climbed the hill to the back wall, then scaled the stone wall with the skill of a goat. She shed light on the plank, and Inez stepped across it to the safety of solid ground.

"Thanks, I didn't want to stay there the rest of the night." Inez stared at the familiar-looking girl. "Don't I know you?"

The girl held up the lantern to peer at Inez. "Hmm," she squinted her eyes, "Yes, ma'am. I'm Pearl. I saw you the day of the mine explosion. Did you find your beloved?"

"Yes, he survived, but was," she found recounting his death difficult, her voice broke, "killed a few days before our wedding."

"Killed?" Pearl persisted. "Someone killed him? In a gunfight? Did he rob a bank?"

"No! No, Josiah wouldn't do that. He went back to the mine, there was another accident."

"Oh," Pearl dropped her shoulders as if she were disappointed in the story. "So, what're you doing here?"

"Good question." Inez moved into the doorway of a boarding house to retreat from the biting wind. "With Josiah gone, I just couldn't go on. Do you know what I mean?"

Pearl nodded.

"Washing, folding, mending other people's clothes didn't mean anything to me when I knew I wasn't saving money for my future. Maybe, that's it. Maybe, I feel like I don't have a future without

Josiah." She and Pearl walked down the street; Pearl, hand on Inez's arm, led the way. "But, I haven't always been this melancholy. I had a lot happen to me in a short time, a lot of death. My father died a few years ago, then my childhood sweetheart came down with rheumatic fever, and my mama died in late spring. The mine accident took Sam," she looked to Pearl to see if she followed her story, "he was the husband of Lottie and best friend to Josiah."

Pearl smiled and walked Inez to a two-story wooden building with a second floor balcony; warm lights glowed inside the windows. "You need to rest and get cleaned up. This is Onalee's place."

Pearl opened the door and began to guide her through when Inez swung out her arms to stop them at the threshold. "I can't go in there!"

"Why not?" Pearl propped her hand on her hip and set the lantern inside the door. "You want to freeze on a rooftop?" She sighed and pulled Inez's hands from the doorframe. "Come on, all the gentlemen have gone for the night. It's just us girls."

With shivering arms and flushed face, Inez stepped into the house. The warm, sweet jasmine and woody tobacco scented air helped to calm her; the sizzle and pop of a roaring fireplace along with the prominent red velvet chaise lounges and divans beckoned her to sleep. She stumbled toward the welcoming hearth.

"Hold on," Pearl called after her. "You don't have to sleep in the parlor. There's an empty room upstairs with a soft bed." She grabbed Inez's hand and escorted her up the steps to a long hallway. "There at the end," she pointed to the last door, "we got indoor facilities—a water closet and sink. Onalee figured out how to pump water to a tank on the roof, and..."

Inez knew she didn't display the excitement that Pearl expected, but the warmth of the house nestled her like a mother's lullaby.

"Okay, we can look at that tomorrow," Pearl said. "This here's your room." She opened a door to a small room with a brass bed, a dresser and mirror, and a washbasin.

Inez's eyes pressed shut as she slouched toward the bed and the seduction of a snug slumber.

A light rapping woke Inez. At first, she didn't recognize the room, but then the memory of Pearl and the whorehouse returned. She sat straight up in the bed. *How will I get out of here? What if someone sees me leaving?*

A gentle tap, tap, tap rolled off the door again.

What if that's a man? What will he want? Can I protect myself?

The doorknob turned and the open door revealed the dark braided head of Onalee. "May I come in?"

Inez swung her feet to the floor. "Yes, ma'am, uh sir."

"How are you feeling?" Onalee, tall and lean in a tanned smock with fringe at the arms, stood before Inez.

"I'm fine, thank you…" Inez confused about what to call Onalee almost said 'Sir,' but that didn't quite fit, although, 'Ma'am' wasn't right either. Onalee didn't dress as other Navajo men in buckskin breeches and cotton shirts; he seemed to favor long shapeless robes, almost like a judge's robe, but in soft suede and Navajo fringed ornamentation. He accented his appearance with rings and bracelets of silver and turquoise and a russet strip of snakeskin weaved into his raven-black braids ending with small dangling white feathers and sapphire beads. Onalee, in her opinion, made a fine looking person—male or female or somewhere in between. She ventured her question to Onalee, "What should I call you: Sir or Ma'am?"

A deep baritone, honeyed laugh erupted from Onalee. "Well, Miss. You can call me whatever you are comfortable with. The girls usually refer to me as 'Mother' or use a female gender with me here in the house—we're all the same here. But, if I need to get aggressive with a gentleman visitor, that's when you see the male side of me emerge. Frenchy always refers to me as 'He' when I'm in a bad temperament. But, you can use what you like."

"Yes, ma'am," Inez said. "You can call me Inez. Thank you for allowing me to sleep here last night. I had a terrible argument with Lottie, who I used to live with. Now, I'm going to look for work at Mr. Zhen's laundry. I hear tell he has a lot of girls working for him, although mostly Chinese girls, but I have experience as a laundress.

Do you think he has a position available?"

"Inez," Onalee sat on the bed next to her, "Mr. Zhen may do a little clothes cleaning, but his main line of work is the same as this house—except he specializes in Chinese girls."

"What?" Inez jerked her head to stare at Onalee. "But that was my plan, to get a job washing and mending. A girl should be able to do something besides whoring. Where can I get respectable work?"

Getting up and walking to the window, Onalee pulled back the lace curtain. "Any work is respectable when you do your best in it."

"Oh, I didn't mean to imply that your work isn't..." She faded out because she knew, and Onalee knew, what she thought.

"Get cleaned up, and I'll make a list of places for you to visit for employment. There is a respectable ladies boarding house on Main Street, south of Jerome Avenue." Onalee closed the lace curtain, then walked out of the room.

Regretting her choice of words, Inez knew she had hurt Onalee's pride. Twice, Onalee and Pearl had come to her rescue, and she intended to make it up to them. She washed her face in the basin on the dresser and straightened her clothes and hair, then went downstairs to find Onalee.

At the bottom of the staircase, the parlor buzzed with activity. Women dusted the mantle and furniture, swept the rugs, washed the windows, set fresh flowers on the tables. Inez wondered: Where do these cleaning women work? They must come in and clean in a swoop, then go on to other places. I could do this.

One of the women, wearing a drab house dress and her hair in a scarf turned to Inez, smiled at her, then ran over. It was Pearl. "Glad to see you up and around. I thought you would sleep all day." She clasped Inez's hand and scurried her over to the other women. "Girls, this is my friend Inez." She hugged Inez and pointed to each of the women. "That there is Molly, Toy, Lois, and Frenchy."

She couldn't tell these women were anything other than house maids in their aprons and frocks with smudges of dust and dirt on their faces. Although some of them were young—about her age,

Molly and Lois looked to be in mid-life, but still pretty in a mature womanly way. Molly's calico scarf corralled her brassy locks into a crown, whereas Lois pulled her gray streaked hair into a bun tied at the back of her head. Frenchy did appear French with a painted mole on her cheek and cherry-red hair, or at least, that's how Inez thought a French woman would look. Toy was small and dainty, just a sparrow of a girl. Pearl's raven hair was tied in a scarf too, but she had a few unruly wisps falling into her face.

"Glad to meet you all," Inez nodded. "I was looking for Miss Onalee." She glanced at Pearl, "Do you know where she is?"

"Mother was out in the kitchen," she pointed through a draped archway. "When we finish cleaning, we're going to dye the gray hair away for Lois. You want to do something with your color?"

Self-consciously, Inez touched her own pallid hair. "Thanks, but I need to talk to Onalee." Through the silk curtains, she found a large dining room, then a door to the kitchen, where Onalee added coal to the stove. "Excuse me," Inez said to get her attention.

She glanced up but kept shoveling coal into the belly of the stove, "Yes, Inez. I have a list for you over there on the butcher-block."

"I want to apologize for implying that this place isn't respectable. I just never had seen one for myself. I always heard bad things from other people, mostly other women." She approached Onalee and gently touched her shoulder. "Let me do that. I have a lot of experience in the kitchen and, like I said before, in washing and mending clothes. I think I could be helpful around here." She took the coal scoop from Onalee and continued the filling of the stove.

Onalee stood up straight and stared at her. "You want to work here with us?"

"Well, I don't think I can do, well you know, that alley cat stuff with a stranger, but I can cook and clean," Inez said.

A smile played across Onalee's face, highlighting her cheekbones and dark eyes. "Hold on. Let me explain a few things to you. All the girls help with the cleaning and cooking, it's part of their job. They don't sit around all day eating bonbons in fancy lingerie waiting for the gentlemen to arrive.

"In this profession," she explained, "there are distinct classes of girls. I run a first-rate parlor house. The brothels aren't as discriminating in their clientele as I am. Dance halls and low class hurdy-gurdy halls are the next step down, and at the bottom of the line are the cribs. Those women are on their own, no protection, no regular meals, no family. Inez, we're a family here, and I can't have one of us thinking she's better than the rest."

Inez felt the blush come to her cheeks, "No, I just didn't understand. Besides, I came to the Arizona Territory as a bride to a man I didn't even know. I was lucky in that he was a kind, handsome, wonderful man, but I lost him in the mines. Now here I am—alone. Probably, one step away from the cribs." She lowered her voice, "I saw them last night; the prospect is scary. But, I'm not sure I can be with a man I don't love."

The comforting laugh came from Onalee again, "I wouldn't ask you to do that, although the money is better. This is officially a boarding house for ladies. The girls pay room and board, plus help with the household chores. At night, we serve supper and drinks to the gentlemen with the company of the girl of their choice for a fee. What is negotiated after supper is between the girl and her gentleman. Unlike, Mr. Zhen's laundry and boarding house, the girls here are free to leave when they want. Mr. Zhen keeps his Chinese girls in debt for their immigration and boarding; a few have been paid out by Chinese rail workers looking for wives, but most can't escape."

"That's terrible," said Inez. She struck a match to light the stove, then set a kettle on. "I understand, but can I work as a maid? I don't think I want to dine with any men."

"Of course you can," Onalee hugged Inez. "You are welcome to move into that same room you slept in last night. Now, let's find you a dust mop and get you working."

Throughout the day, Inez and the other girls cleaned the house and washed sheets, pillow cases, lingerie, stockings, and dresses. Inez took control of the washing detail, which relieved the other girls to attend to Lois' hair color.

In the corner of the kitchen, Toy mixed up a tawny dye to cover

Lo's gray hair. They laughed together and kidded Lois about her age. Onalee sat in a small office off the kitchen, figuring in her books, just as Inez had seen Lottie do.

"Hey, Inez, you're next," Pearl helped brush the dye onto Lo's hair. "I have a recipe for a perfect color for you. It will give you a vivid shine."

"I don't know," Inez hedged. Looking at Lois, she asked, "Has Pearl ever done your color before?"

"Oh, she did mine," Molly shook her curls of brass.

Inez thought her ash-blonde hair to be one of her more pleasing qualities, Josiah had always liked it, but she admitted to herself, it did have that dingy prairie dust look when compared to the ladies of the house; they spent so much time on their hair, face make-up, clothes, and jewelry. Why, I almost look like a boy next to them, she thought.

"Come on, Inez," Frenchy urged. "We can always change it, if you don't like it. Besides, if you are going to be around when the gentlemen call, you need to look your best. Carpet, drapes, food, drink," she counted off, "even the maid must have an air of quality and glamour."

She decided she'd come this far. "Go ahead, Pearl," Inez said.

After the mixing and rubbing on, they waited for the color to soak in. Inez and Lois sat in the kitchen with towels wrapped around their heads.

"I saw that handsome Red Dale," Toy said, catching Inez's attention, "over at the livery and field yard."

"Red Dale that works near Cottonwood as a blacksmith?" she asked.

"Yes, do you know him?"

"He burned a sign for me a while back," Inez said. "Is he a customer here?"

"Oh, no," Toy's light laugh reminded Inez of a bell tinkle. "He doesn't call. Although, I have invited him to stop by on numerous occasions. He just tips his hat and thanks me."

So, Inez thought, Lottie was wrong about the rumors of Red Dale, like she was probably wrong about a lot of other things, too.

Sticking her hand under the towels on both women, Pearl announced that she thought they were done. She rinsed Inez, while Frenchy finished Lois.

A strand of hair fell over Inez's shoulder, "Pearl! It's orange!"

"No, it's not. It will dry lighter." She rubbed Inez with a towel. "I was hoping for a saffron tint," Pearl lifted the towel and frowned.

Grabbing a handful of her hair, Inez pulled it to her eyes. Then she got up and moved to the back porch for more light. "Pearl," she whined, "It's orange marmalade, not saffron."

"Lady Marmalade," Onalee walked in and bowed. "It fits you." Then she turned to the girls, clapped her hands twice, and announced: "Ladies, company's coming."

Molly, Lois, Toy, Frenchy, and Pearl hurried up the back steps to dress. Onalee smiled at Inez. "Lady Marmalade, tonight I'll show you what you need to do. Don't worry, you'll be fine."

CHAPTER SEVEN

As the sun faded behind Cleopatra Hill, the red rocks of Oak Creek Canyon blazed like a wildfire across the valley. Inez sat straight and still in a kitchen chair, watching the distant ridges reflect the last glimmers of the day. She held a *Life* magazine for Pearl to recreate the hairstyle from a Gibson Girl drawing.

"Tomorrow," Pearl said, "we'll have to dye a hairpiece for your Marcel waves, but for tonight, I'll curl your own hair. Don't move, these rods are hot."

Glowing tongs clamped the front locks of Inez's hair, then Pearl rolled it so close to her scalp that Inez thought her head would burn. The faint acid smell of singed hair worried her. "Should my hair put out that odor?"

Pearl fanned a trail of smoke away. "It's just the copper ore I added to your hair dye. That's what's burning, not your hair."

"What?"

"Don't worry," Pearl insisted. "That's why I want to do the hairpiece, so we don't have to Marcel your real hair." She combed the hair high in front and gathered up the back to merge on the top of her head in a bun of coppery waves.

Frenchy carried an emerald gown from the back stairs and over to Pearl and Inez. She held it to the side of Inez and compared the tint of the gown to the color of her hair, "I like this. Onalee said to make you a Gibson Girl, all proper and confident. I don't think this silk is too seductive. Do you Pearl?"

Pearl glanced at it, "No, but you look damn loose in that lingerie and those boots."

"I'm not finished dressing," Frenchy shot back. "Inez, you like this color?" She held the dress up in front of herself so Inez could examine it.

"Yes, ma'am," Inez said. "How long before the gentlemen show up?"

With the gown in front of her, hiding her lingerie, Frenchy peeked out the side window, "They start showing up just after dark." She yelled to someone, apparently very far away by the volume of her voice, "Hey Mildred. What's on the menu tonight?"

The shock of the yell made Inez jump, and Pearl burned her head with the curling iron. "Ouch!" Inez pulled away from Pearl.

"Sorry, but you moved." She turned to Frenchy, "Keep that big mouth shut. You made her flinch; now I done burned her head. Damn, French, you act like you been raised in a barn."

"Maybe I was," Frenchy lobbed the gown over a chair and stuck her nose in the air. "Hey, Pearl, here's what I think of you."

Just as Pearl and Inez looked up, Frenchy bent over, pulled her drawers down, and shook her bare derrière at them.

"That's real classy," huffed Pearl as Frenchy retreated up the staircase.

Never having sisters, Inez didn't know how to take the yelling between Pearl and Frenchy. Certainly, she and Lottie never acted like these women. "You all aren't mad at each other, are you?"

"Us?" Pearl asked. "No, we go on like this all the time."

The door swung open from the back porch and a portly older woman waddled in with a large ham riding one hip and a jug of wine balanced on the other. Her gray hair stuffed into a bonnet and her stained apron hinted to Inez that she was the one who did the majority of the cooking for Onalee and the girls. She went straight to the icebox and dumped the ham onto the bottom shelf, then set the wine on the table with a bang that Inez thought would have cracked the bottle.

Still intent on Inez's hair, Pearl didn't look up at the woman.

"Hello," Inez smiled at the cook.

"Howdy there, Missy," the woman toddled across the floor with her hand out. "You must be the new girl. Onalee said you were going to help serve tonight. I'm Marvelous Mildred." She shook Inez's hand like a man, with gusto. "I cook here." She bent in toward Inez, as if she would tell a secret that Pearl couldn't hear, "I'm the reason the men come here—my cooking. These girls think their feminine wiles draw in the customers, but no," she stood up straight and tall, "it's my recipes. Yes sir, I have some of the best loins and breasts in the territory," she laughed and slapped her watermelon of a knee.

"Hamming it up tonight, I see," Pearl drolled without looking at Mildred.

"Yes, ma'am, Miss Pearl, I am. The gentlemen will get their fill of ham before they get their hammy hands on you." She laughed and popped the cork out of the wine. "Missy, what did you say your name was?"

"She didn't," Pearl said. "You ain't give her time to get a word in edge-ways."

"Inez, my name's Inez. Pleased to meet you Mildred."

Mildred poured herself some wine in a tin cup, then leaned against the counter and looked at Inez with a hawk's eye. "You don't look like any Inez I ever knew."

"Well, damn, Mildred." Pearl stopped working on the Marcel waves and turned to her. "It don't matter if she don't look like other girls you know named Inez, that's her name, and that's what her mama called her. Sorry if she didn't consult the Marvelous Mildred before naming her." Pearl put her hands on Inez's shoulders, "That woman will wear you slap out with her talking. Just ignore her."

With eyes straight ahead, away from Mildred, Inez sat still while Pearl finished the hair styling.

"All I was saying," Mildred grumbled to the pot she pulled from a cupboard, "was that she don't look as plain as an Inez. Maybe a pretty name to help perk her up: Emma, Darla, Julia, Eloise, Athna, Beatrice, Lucille, or could use a flower name," she mused while unwrapping the ham and dressing it with honey and brown sugar. "I was always partial to natural names, like Rose, Lily, Daisy, Iris." She stopped and glanced at Inez and Pearl. "With that there orange hair, I'd call her Copper Kettle," she laughed and held her belly below sagging breasts. "I once worked with a girl with hair that color. She used to be a favorite of a Union Lieutenant—I think he married her after the war. Anyway, he would say that he could spot her as soon as he came into town. Then there was this Quadroon girl that tried to get her hair blond, put all this lemon juice on it, and sat in the sun for hours, well, Miss Inez, her hair turned as orange as yours."

"Is it that bad?" Inez asked Pearl. "Will people stare at me?"

"No, it looks fine." Pearl turned to Mildred, "Will you keep your mouth shut? Inez is a pretty name, and her hair looks glamorous. That's enough of that."

Silence settled over the kitchen except for the occasional rattle of pans and pots as Mildred pushed the ham in the oven, then began cutting carrots. Inez saw her lift a carrot, then stop and look at Inez, but she didn't say a word, she just tapped the carrot on her own head and grinned.

✗ ✗ ✗

The girls appeared as elegant and stylish as any *Life* magazine picture, thought Inez. She peeked around the curtain to watch Lois talking with an older gentleman; he wore a brown walnut-colored suit with a tan waistcoat. His gray hair, short and slicked back, revealed expressive eyebrows that jumped and wiggled as he talked to Lois. She laughed frequently at whatever the man said. Frenchy's beau seemed to be more of a dandy; he sported a spruce-green jacket with a bright rhubarb-red waistcoat. This man was younger than Lois' and more affectionate. His hand rested on Frenchy's knee. There were no miners in the room; these men looked like mine bosses or bankers or lawyers.

"Inez," a soft voice said.

She jumped, then turned to find Toy behind her. Letting the curtain drop back into place, she smiled at Toy, "I just had to see what was happening."

"That's fine with me." Toy's little face gleamed, "I wanted to get a look at Pearl's creation." She surveyed Inez, and Inez stood straight.

She knew her hair looked better at night, the curls and low light softened the color, and the emerald dress had been taped back to give the front a columned look with the layers of silk festooned into a high bustle. With this dress, she had soon realized, she wouldn't be able to sit down. Her leg-o-mutton sleeves highlighted the tight-waist bodice, and her low neckline made her keep touching the gold necklace Molly had loaned her, as if to hide the slight cleavage that Pearl had powdered and rouged. She could smell the jasmine perfume Pearl had squirted on her bare neck. "Onalee," Pearl had explained, "has all us girls use the same perfume so we don't overwhelm the customers."

"You look beautiful," Toy complimented. "When you serve supper, all the men will be looking at you instead of us."

"No," Inez smiled. "No, they won't." She touched the necklace again, "Do you really think so?" The thought of men, several men, giving her attention frightened her and excited her—just a little. She had always been the young mousy girl who faded into the woodwork at social events back in South Carolina. Not until Josiah's attention and love did she feel worthy of the notice. After Toy slipped through the curtain to join the other girls, Inez considered herself in the mirror over the sideboard. Would Josiah think she was a fool for being around these wayward women? Would what reputation she had be destroyed if word leaked out that she worked in a whorehouse—no matter what the task, noble or not? How long would Onalee and the girls allow her to stay before asking her to earn her own way? The woman she saw in the mirror wasn't the mousy South Carolina girl, but a painted lady with a plunging neckline and a curvy silhouette pumped and primed for the excitement and pleasure of gentlemen. Forgive me, she prayed to Josiah, I love only you. You will always have my heart.

Mildred burst through the kitchen door, "Inez, supper is ready. Pull the curtain back and announce it." She wiped her hands on a clean apron.

"How? What do I say?"

"Lord, child, just say 'Gentlemen, supper is served.' Simple as that."

Tugging the heavy velvet drape back, Inez took a deep breath and walked slowly into the parlor. "Gentlemen," her voice cracked, "Ladies," she smiled at Pearl, "supper is served." She swept her arm back to motion to the table, a flourish she had seen in a play once. Playing a part, that was how she had decided to get through the evening—play acting.

"Aren't you a picture?" the dandy said to her as he escorted Frenchy to the table. Inez only smiled and kept her arm out, pointing the way. The other gentlemen nodded to her as they passed. Settling down around the table, more men than women were present. The girls sat between the men, talking and laughing with all the gentlemen around them. She noticed Mildred beckoning her from the kitchen door.

"Now, that they're seated," Mildred explained, "take this pitcher of wine and fill their glasses. Keep track of how many times you refill. The girls' wine is paid for by the customers, keep account of that, too."

Throughout the supper, Inez topped off the wine of the gentlemen, making marks for each time on a drawing she had done of the table and seating. After making her circle around the table, she stood in a far corner by the sideboard, checking her accounting, watching to see if anyone took the last biscuit or slice of ham; the meal was 'limitless' as Mildred had instructed, and Inez was to fetch more of whatever needed replenishment. The girls picked at their food, sometimes hand feeding it to the customers who ate and laughed like farmhands. All men, Inez thought, must act alike, no matter how fancy they dress or how much money they got. Although the girls skimped on their food, they chugged the red wine like water. Pearl's glass was empty every few minutes.

As Inez re-filled Pearl's glass, one of the gentlemen, an Irishman with ruddy cheeks and sharp green eyes, slapped Inez's bottom. "Hey!" she backed away from the table.

Pearl grabbed his hand and placed it on her own chest, "Mr. Walters, she's only here to serve the meal. I'm the dessert."

He laughed and kissed Pearl's hand, as she rolled her eyes and winked at Inez.

Retreating to the kitchen, Inez reported the incident to Mildred.

"Lord, Missy, that ain't nothing. Those men see a new girl and want to try the new merchandise."

"I'm not merchandise," Inez shot back.

"To them, you are," Mildred said. "Pearl and the other girls are the same meat and potatoes these men have every week, but then a new girl shows up and it's like waving some new dish under their noses—maybe a slice of sweetbread with orange marmalade on top." Mildred looked at Inez's hair and grinned. "Just smile and go on. Half the excitement for them is the teasing. They don't really want you; they want a dream, their dream. You might just be the closest thing to that dream—for now."

The thought of playing a part came back to Inez. Acting out the gentlemen's dream, yes, she thought, I can do that. I can be the girl they can't have. The girl promised to another. As her mother had always told her, 'the peach out of reach is always sweeter than the one at your feet.'

Mildred and Inez collected the plates and silverware as the men had slowed their consumption, then returned the dishes to the kitchen, and carried out plates of apple pie for dessert.

Mildred handed Inez a squat wine bottle and whispered, "This is after-supper port. Serve it to all the men—none for the girls, unless the man asks you to. That Pearl will drink the whole bottle if she gets the chance. Pour it in those little glasses we put on the table, only about two fingers worth," she held up two fingers to show the depth. "Keep separate account of these servings."

"Will I have to collect their money?" Inez asked, not wanting to hand a bill to each of the men, possibly dampening their merriment.

"No. Each of the girls collects at the end of the night." Mildred turned to look at the table from their position at the side bar. "Usually, the men eat and drink so much, they fall asleep before getting to the girls," she snickered and winked at Inez. "Hell, Missy, I could be under some of them and they'd never know it."

The heat rushed to Inez's face as those words formed a picture in her mind.

With a pat to her bustled bottom, Mildred pushed Inez and the port wine toward the table and then lowered the wicks on the oil lamps creating a dim, soothing, light in the room.

As the drink requests diminished, the men began to leave the dining room. A couple of the men winked at her, so she smiled back, but stayed near Mildred. One of Pearl's gentlemen settled in the parlor, as the other one led her up the staircase. Frenchy's dandy plunked down on the sofa and pulled her to his lap. She giggled and whispered in his ear. Lois and the older man settled into a corner settee and continued their conversation. Toy and Molly leaned against the banister of the stairs and chatted with their gentlemen. For the first time that evening, Inez saw Onalee enter the parlor. Dressed in a black smock that matched the tint of her braided hair, she took a seat at the piano and began to play a canorous golden tune that entwined the lingering aroma of the honeyed ham and sweet wine with the last whiff of the cinnamon apples. The sensual music snaked through the parlor wrapping around the wisps of the gentlemen's blue cigar smoke and exotic floral scent of the girls' jasmine perfume, and enfolding the golden light of the oil lamps to embrace the innate desires of each foolish soul who heard its melody. Entranced by the scene before her, Inez didn't feel Mildred tugging at her sleeve.

"Missy," Mildred tugged again, "put this apron on and help me clean up. We got a sink full of dishes, pots, and pans to wash. No time to watch the romancing part."

"But..." Inez turned from the curtain between the parlor and dining room.

"I know, but it's time for the girls to get to work and for us to clean up." Mildred tied the apron on Inez protecting the emerald dress from their chores.

By the time the washing was completed, the dishes stored in the cabinets, and the dining room table scrubbed and polished, Inez checked back into the parlor. Onalee still played the piano, but the girls and gentlemen had left. She pulled off the apron and approached the piano, not wanting to disturb Onalee who moved to the music flowing from her hands across the ivory keys. Inez wanted to stand close enough to see her face as the composition came to her without interrupting the process.

Eyes closed, Onalee's slight smile and rhythmic rock implied another facet of the person Inez barely knew. She swayed with the tune she played across the keyboard, her braids keeping time. As the melody slowed, she became still and the smile faded as the melancholy ode pulled the arrangement from desire to longing. The ballad turned to hymn then to lullaby. Onalee opened her eyes and smiled at Inez.

"Oh, don't stop," Inez pleaded.

"I finished. When it's complete, there's no more." Onalee glanced down at the keys and gently ran her fingertips across them without making a sound.

"I didn't realize you played," Inez said. She draped her apron over her shoulder and leaned against the upright piano.

"Oh, yes. When I left the reservation, I made money playing in houses. A few hurdy-gurdies and dancehalls at first, then nicer houses as I learned and listened. You see," she twisted on the stool to face Inez, "music is as much about listening as hitting the right key. I learned that in my childhood education."

The image of a little Onalee at a piano stool amused Inez. "You took music lessons?"

"Not particularly music. I was to be the shaman for the clan, the healer of the family, and as music is part of nature I had lessons in it."

"What? Like bird songs?"

"In a way," she smiled. "Nature has a rhythm: the stride of the ant, the beat of a butterfly wing, the bloom of a cactus, the trickle of a creek. All things teach us how music is formed and flows from one being to the next. The lesson is how to tune into that rhythm."

Inez pulled off the pinching emerald ear bobs. "Life and death, that's a rhythm I can't understand."

"I know your sadness," Onalee reached for Inez's hand and held it tight. "I lost the one I loved, too." The sadness pulled her features into the shadows of the lamplight.

Inez decided to let Onalee's story come as Onalee was willing to tell it, so she simply squeezed her hand in reassurance and sisterhood.

CHAPTER EIGHT

While polishing the dining room table, Inez noticed Lois pacing by the parlor window. "Something wrong?" she asked.

Lois hovered by the curtain, running her hand over the lace. Her dark hair was pulled back into a loose bun, and the sunlight filtering through the curtain revealed worry lines around her eyes and across her forehead. "Well," she hesitated, "yes, Inez, there is something on my mind. Maybe you will understand. The other girls think I'm being silly."

"What?"

"My son is coming to visit." Lois sank into a red velvet chair, "He doesn't know I work here."

"Your son? Where is he?" Inez asked.

"I sent him back to Virginia to go to school." Tears puddled in her eyes. "I haven't seen him in years. He's fourteen now and making the trip to visit me, and I can't have him know I work in a parlor house. I mean, if he was younger, he probably wouldn't understand, but now that he's older, he'll know exactly what I am." She turned away and wiped her eyes.

A tentative pat on the back was all Inez could think to do. "Don't worry," she said. "We can think of something." She sat at the table, elbows propped and her chin resting on her palms. "What does he think you do for a living?"

A short laugh came from Lois. "I told him I worked in a shop... I didn't mention what I sold." A weak smile played across her painted lips. "I don't want him thinking bad about his mother, but this is the only occupation where I can make the money to send him

to a good school. He's going to go to college in a few years and
have opportunities I never thought I could give him."

Inez said it before she thought, "Where's his father?"

The smile stiffened on Lois. "Who knows? It could have been
one of many."

"If he thinks you work in a shop, then we'll get you a job in
a shop while he's here." Inez stood and rested her hand on Lois'
shoulder. Her idea brightened her, finally she felt she might be
able to help these women who had come to her rescue. "What type
of shop do you want to work in? What would impress him? With
Onalee's contacts, I know she can get you in somewhere, at least for
a few days." Ideas churned in Inez's mind. She had a practical side
that would leap into action when summoned. "You'll need a place
to live. How long will he be here?"

"Jared will be here for two weeks, then he said he would meet a
school friend and spend some time in Santa Fe before returning to
Virginia." Lois looked up at Inez with hopeful eyes, "Do you think
we can do it?"

"Don't you worry. I have a plan cooked up."

Inez tucked her marmalade hair under her bonnet and stepped off
Onalee's wagon in front of the little house. She hadn't seen Lottie in
days, not since she stormed out after their argument. Her 'Laundress'
sign hung from its chain on the front porch, and the memories of her
and Josiah flooded back so that she stopped and lightly touched the
sign he had held in his hands. "I'm doing the right thing, Josiah."
Her finger glided over the iron chain. Gathering her courage with a
breath and squared shoulders, she rapped hard on the door.

The squeak of floorboards heralded Lottie's approach, and when
the door opened, the familiar smell of lye and bleach announced her
presence. "You? What do you want?" Lottie held her squat body
straight and rigid.

"I came to get my belongings." Inez walked into the house
without an invitation.

"Your hair..." Lottie started. "What in the Lord's name happened to your hair?"

With a swift tug, Inez plucked off her bonnet to reveal Lady Marmalade hair. "I had it colored."

"Why, why," Lottie stuttered, "you look like some kind of harlot."

Inez marched into her old room, "Some kind," she repeated. Tossing clothes and books into her trunk, she ignored Lottie standing slack-jawed in the doorway. "I want to get my things."

"Good," Lottie said. "That will allow me to get another boarder."

"As to that," Inez stopped stuffing the trunk. "I may have a replacement, at least for a week or two."

"What are you doing with that orange hair? Who did that? Where are you staying?" But before Lottie received an answer, she gasped, "Inez, no! You didn't go to a whorehouse. No, didn't I teach you anything about propriety, manners, behavior? How could you change so quickly? Oh Lord, it must be my fault for throwing you out—"

"I left on my own." Inez corrected her.

"So, it's true. You've become a whore—"

"No," Inez protested. "I work with the ladies, but I don't whore. I help with the cooking and cleaning."

Lottie sank to the bed, pressing her hands over her eyes, rubbing. "Where did I go wrong?" She looked to the heavens, "Josiah, how did I fail you?"

"Stop that!" Inez screamed. "Stop it! This isn't about you doing anything for Josiah. I love him. I always will," she gripped the bedpost and shook it in her anger. "I am surviving for him. You don't know what you're talking about when you call these women whores. They're good people, as kind-hearted and charitable as any Christian woman parading to church on Sunday. They took me in before I froze to death, because a certain respectable woman threw me out."

"You left on your own," corrected Lottie.

A deep breath helped to calm Inez; she needed to be composed for her plan to succeed. "The fact is that I have a job and a place to live. You now have an empty room. I can help you rent that room for two weeks and get two months rent for it."

"No," Lottie, her face drained of blood, stood and turned to Inez, "no whore is going to use this room. What would the neighbors think? What do they think seeing you come in here with your hair all colored up—the color of copper? What are you supposed to be? The Queen of the Copper Mines?"

"Yes, that's me, the Queen of the Copper Mines," she mocked and slammed the trunk shut. Pulling the trunk behind her, she headed toward the door. Lottie's attitude had angered her to the point that she knew there was no use in trying to reason with her and never would Lottie assist her in anything. Their relationship, whatever it had been, was over. She didn't care if she ever saw her again. Rage channeled into her arms allowing her to hoist the trunk, unassisted, onto the back of the wagon.

"Those places should be shut down," Lottie paced next to the wagon, glancing to the neighbor's window, then lowering her voice. "Inez, I know you're a good girl. You just aren't wise to the world. I have a group of ladies at church who help with righteous causes; we could help convert those women to clean God-fearing ladies."

"They don't need your help," Inez said.

"Dear, I'm just thinking about your future. Being a whore is not a path to the rewards of life."

"Good-bye Lottie," Inez could take no more. She climbed to the wagon's bench. "You take your path and I'll take mine." She jerked the reins to send the horse galloping, leaving a trail of dust blowing in Lottie's face.

✕ ✕ ✕

Shucking corn, then breaking the ear in two, Inez dropped the cobs into a bucket of water. She sat on the back porch with Mildred, overlooking the valley below. "There must be somewhere we can get Lois a place to stay while her son is here."

"Missy," Mildred began, "I have numbed my brain trying to come up with a nice place for her to entertain that boy, but I don't think any boarding house will let her in. Everybody in town knows Lois, and if she walked in any boarding house, the women there would run her off. Uppity heifers, they wouldn't know class if it bit them in the ass." Mildred peeled potatoes, letting the skins fall in her lap. "She needs a nice house, something respectable."

"I tried that," Inez said. "But, Lottie wouldn't hear of letting her rent a room. She was too afraid that the neighbors would talk. Like they would think Lottie might be able to entertain a gentleman." Inez grinned at Mildred, "Lottie is not much on looks and even less on personality. It might do her reputation good to have a beauty like Lois staying there."

The back door opened and Onalee joined them on the porch. She absently picked up a corn cob from Inez's pile and began to strip the husk and silks from it. Leaning against the railing, she said, "Inez, you've done very well these past few days. I think you're ready to take on more responsibilities. I need to go to Cottonwood this evening and want you to be in charge of the accounting. Mildred, if any of the gentlemen get out of hand, and I doubt they will, you take my pistol from the office and show them the door. Fetch Sheriff Jim if need be, but I'll be back tomorrow afternoon." Her hair, braided as usual, held a string of silver and turquoise beads, the dress she wore was of the finest doeskin with an intricate multi-color beadwork stripe across the chest and down the sleeves.

"Going somewhere special?" Inez asked.

Mildred's knife stopped mid-potato waiting for Onalee's answer.

"Why, Inez," Onalee began, "I have appointments in Cottonwood from time to time. The girls know that, and I like to keep a little mystery. Just be assured that everything will run smoothly while I'm gone." She tossed the corncob into the bucket.

"Have you thought about Lois?" Inez asked. "Is there anyplace you can get her employed while her son is visiting? Maybe a place to stay?" Inez dropped another cob in the pail and stretched her back from hunching over the corn. "I thought it might be appropriate if Lois had some kind of shop work, maybe the mercantile or a dressmaker."

Onalee smiled, "Yes, I've been thinking about that. Your idea of a dressmaker might be right. Lois always has ideas of new designs for dresses when I have some made for the girls. Of course, Martha makes our dresses, but she doesn't have a shop. Inez, see if you can find a vacant storefront we can rent for a few days. I can set up Martha and Lois in it for a show as dressmakers."

Admiration for Onalee blossomed in her heart as Inez grinned at her. "You would do that for Lois? Create a dressmaker's shop?"

"Of course, we're a family like I told you. I'll do what I can to help Lois."

A sniff came from Mildred, but Inez focused on Onalee. "Can I do anything else for you while you're gone?"

"No thank you. I am impressed by your ability with the accounting and your common sense. Inez, I think you have a head for business." Onalee patted her shoulder, "You are a good woman, Miss Inez. You take a lot of responsibility from me. Now, I have an appointment in Cottonwood, and I must be going. Take care of things. You and Mildred can run this place as well as I do."

Pride streamed in her like a rush of wind from the valley floor. No one had entrusted her or complimented her on her abilities before. "I'll take care of things here," she assured Onalee.

Pearl opened the porch door, "Mildred," she said dressed in her plain white blouse and tan skirt with a flash of her red and gold striped stockings, "Mildred, do you have any wine opened?"

"Hey, Missy," Mildred started, "you can't get into that until the gentlemen arrive. That's for customers, not for a raven-haired floozy." She grinned and winked at Inez.

"Marvelous Mildred," she cooed, "I'd like a drink or two before hand. Those men are so boring. It just helps me get ready—in the right frame of mind."

Mildred looked to Onalee. She nodded back to Mildred.

"Okay, Miss Pearl, but you know we'll charge your account for it." She tapped Inez's chair arm. "Put Pearl down for two bits. The girl is like a trout when it comes to drinking."

Wrinkling up her nose at Mildred, Pearl turned in a flaunt of red petticoats and jasmine perfume to return to the kitchen.

"Onalee," Mildred whispered, "I worry about Pearl. That girl drinks way too much."

"We all have our crutches," Onalee shook her head. "At least she stopped using the opium—"

"Opium?" Inez repeated in shock. "I thought that was a Chinese thing. How'd Pearl do that?"

"That flower pod has been smoked all over the West," Onalee explained. "Although, I think she did start when she worked at Mr. Zhen's. I made her quit when she came here. I will not allow my ladies to go down that road to destruction. I have seen it too many times."

"Well," said Mildred, "that wine bottle is looking mighty destructive for Miss Pearl."

Concern kindled Onalee's eyes as she paced across the porch. "Inez, please watch Pearl. She hides things from Mildred and might conceal them from me, but you are closer to her age and, from what I observe, her confidant. I don't want to distrust her, but she is the type of girl who goes into something with full force. I don't want her to get too deep. Will you do that for me and for her?"

The thought of spying on Pearl didn't appeal to Inez since Pearl had always been kind and open with her, but she knew what the drink could do to a person. She'd seen people in South Carolina too fond of whiskey or moonshine and the mess that desire created for their family. The drink could be a foul mistress for a soul who savored the pungent taste without the will for moderation. Warnings from her South Carolina preacher came to her, and she spoke as if she were a deacon, "I will caution her if she appears to imbibe more than usual."

"Thank you, Inez." Onalee turned to Mildred, "thank you Mildred for noticing and for your concern with Pearl. You two act like cats and dogs, but I can see you do care for each other."

"Now," Mildred stammered, "don't start thinking me and Pearl are bosom buddies. I just don't want her sneaking around and drinking up all the profits."

Smiling at Mildred, Onalee said, "I have business to tend to. I'll be back tomorrow." As she headed for the door, she told Inez,

"Remember to look for a storefront for a dressmaker shop for Lois. If you locate one, I'll secure it tomorrow."

With that, Onalee left them to their tasks. The gentlemen would arrive in a few hours, and supper would need to be started, but Inez hoped to find a place for the shop before Onalee returned. She begged for an hour off from Mildred to conduct her search and convinced Pearl to accompany her; this, she reasoned, would help get Pearl away from the wine cabinet.

The afternoon sun warmed their walk as Inez and Pearl searched for empty storefronts. Gratification, or something like it, gladdened Inez's heart. For as long as she could remember, she hadn't felt this sisterhood, this camaraderie, with any other women. Certainly, Lottie had never offered her a feeling of worth or merit, but Josiah had, and for the first time since his death, her first response to his memory wasn't a tear, but a smile. The sunshine on her calico dress felt like a hug from Josiah, telling her she would be fine and that he watched over her with love.

"What're you grinning about?" asked Pearl. They leaned against a railing below Hill Street with a clear view of the San Francisco Mountains' snow-capped peaks in the distance behind a scarlet-topped ridge that hemmed in the Verde Valley.

"Just thinking how lucky I am." She searched the valley for the buildings of Cottonwood, hoping to see the noble figure of Onalee riding into the town, but the expanse was too great. An opening between buildings on Main Street with steps leading down the slope caught her eye. "What's down that alley?"

"Husbands' Alley," said Pearl. "That's the back way to the cribs on Hull. The more proper gentlemen use it instead of going down Hull Street—less likely to be seen using that alley." She winked at Inez. "Speaking of husbands and alley-sneaking, here comes Sheriff Jim."

Inez saw the tall, broad-shouldered figure of the sheriff swaggering up the hill. The brim of his hat shaded his eyes and a bushy mustache hid his mouth, but she could make out the corners of a grin under the gray-brown whiskers.

"Afternoon, ladies," his voice rumbled with merriment. A handsome square face and sparkling gray eyes revealed themselves when he tipped his hat to them.

"Why, Sheriff Jim," Pearl cooed, "I'm so glad to see you this afternoon. I hate that you caught me in my daytime dress." She swished the harvest-gold skirt coquettishly toward him. "I have a beautiful blue evening gown for tonight."

"Pearl," he drawled, "I'm sure you look beautiful in whatever you wear." The sheriff turned to Inez, "Howdy, Miss."

"Hello," Inez nodded to him. "I'm Inez."

"Yes, this is Inez." Pearl added and grabbed the sheriff's arm to turn him around and escort her down to Main Street. "She just joined Onalee's house."

"As kitchen help," Inez interjected following them down the street.

The sheriff stopped, "Now, Miss Pearl, I can't be seen walking down Main Street arm-in-arm with you; anyway, I was on my way to the barber shop."

She reached up and stroked his bushy mustache, which instigated a chuckle from him. "You look fine to me. You don't need a trim."

The skill of vamping had never been something Inez had witnessed so artfully exhibited as Pearl did with the sheriff. He seemed to melt under her touch and purr like a kitten, this mountain lion of a man. She couldn't be sure, but she thought she saw a blush color his cheeks.

"Anyhow," Pearl continued, her hand lightly resting on top of his hairy forearm. "I thought Inez and I would stop at the Fashion for a drink. Shopping is so much more interesting with a few drinks. Care to join us?"

No doubt about it, he blushed. "Ma'am, like I said, I need to be getting on up to the barber shop. Thank you anyway." He nodded to them both and headed up toward Hill Street.

"Damn," said Pearl grabbing Inez's hand and turning the corner to Main Street. "I would love for that man to come into Onalee's one night. That's my kind of man." She glanced over her shoulder at him. "He's been there before, but never as a customer."

"Pearl! He's the sheriff! He wouldn't be patronizing parlor houses."

"Come on, let's get a drink." Pearl pulled her toward the Fashion Saloon.

"I can't," protested Inez.

"Sure, I'll pay. Just one quick glass of wine, then on with this shop hunt."

"No, I mean I never went in a place like that." Inez twisted out of Pearl's grasp.

"For God's sake, girl, you work in a whorehouse."

"A parlor house."

"Fine," Pearl conceded, "but there's nothing wrong with two respectable women having a drink in a saloon. Come on." She pulled Inez through the doors.

The wooden doors creaked as they entered, and Inez felt like every eye in the saloon was on her. They would know her parlor house association; they would see her marmalade hair beneath her bonnet; they would whisper about her morals; they would gossip about her. But, then the thought hit her: no one here cared. The folks who perched on the slopes of Jerome didn't pay attention to what others did. No one minded if a woman wanted a drink or what color her hair was or what she did to earn money.

Pearl hopped on a barstool and patted the one next to her for Inez to take. "Hey, Carl, give us two red wines down here."

"Dos reales," called the bartender.

Inez turned to Pearl, "What's he say?"

"Quarter of a dollar, two bits," she dug the coins out of her small silk purse she had tied to her waist and clanked them on the polished wooden bar.

Carl, a rather short, balding man with thick spectacles, set the glasses in front of them and scooped up the coins. "You girls aren't working in here."

"Man alive! Carl," Pearl whined, "I don't work in saloons anymore. I'm a customer here, so treat me with a little respect."

"Sorry. I didn't want our girls getting huffed because you're in their territory."

Pearl glanced around the room, "I doubt these cowboys could afford us." She winked at Inez. "Hey, Carl, do you know of a vacant store? We're looking to open a little dress shop."

A smirk wrinkled his nose and wobbled his spectacles to one side, "You taking up a new line of work, Pearl?"

"Just branching out into other enterprises," she boasted. "This here's my friend Inez and we're looking for a store front."

He pushed his glasses up the bridge of his nose, then dug in his left ear with a pencil, "Well, I tell you," he thought out loud, "try up on School Street just before the Methodist church. I think I saw a sign in a window there."

"That would be perfect," said Inez. "Near the school and a church—very respectable."

"Thanks, Carl. We might go take a look at it." Pearl sipped her wine.

"Hey you, Pigtails," Carl yelled toward the door.

When Inez turned to look, she spotted a small Chinese girl huddled with her arms tight around her body, shaking at the entrance.

"We don't allow no yellow sows in here. Go back to Zhen's."

"Hey," Inez spoke up. "That's not very nice."

Carl's face froze with shock. "She's Chinese. They ain't making a habit of coming in here."

Jumping off the stool, Inez went over to the girl and led her out to the warm sun of the street. "Are you alright?"

"Lord, Inez," Pearl followed her out, "leave her alone. Zhen will be after her in a few minutes. She's trying to run away and there ain't no place for a Chinese girl to run."

Tears filled the girl's dark eyes. Her plain cotton dress, sleeves shredded, hung on her like a sack. "I want free," she stammered in broken English.

Inez hugged her close like a mothering hen, "Come back with me. I'll help you."

"No, Inez. You can't take her. She's not a lost kitten," Pearl complained as she walked behind them. "Mr. Zhen will come take her back."

"Over my dead body," vowed Inez.

CHAPTER NINE

The Chinese girl huddled close to Inez as they walked, constantly checking over her shoulder. Her long pigtails swung as she shuffled in her sandals beside the long determined strides of Inez. Complaints issued from Pearl fell from the resolved mind of Inez, who reasoned that this girl was just another version of herself: alone, scared, looking for a better existence, and in need of a helping hand.

"She's the property of Zhen," Pearl said from behind them. "It's like stealing."

Stopping to look at Pearl, Inez said, "No one is the property of anyone else. She's a person, not a wagon. I'm from the South. I know what slavery is, and this is nothing but pure slavery."

"He paid her way from China," Pearl explained. "She has to work off that money. I worked at Zhen's for a while and saw how it's arranged. It's an agreement they have with her family over in China."

"How many of these women pay off that debt?" asked Inez with more of an accusing tone than she meant. "I'm sorry, but it's the same with sharecroppers back home. After the war, Negroes still labored on the plantations under the agreement that they would earn the part of the fields they worked over time, but the owners charged them for everything under the sun, and that was deducted from their pay until they had nothing to put toward buying land."

"I admit," Pearl said, "that's the way Zhen gets his Chinese girls, but what else can she do? Unless one of the Chinamen working the mines or the railroad pays off her debt to be his wife—"

"Wife?" the girl repeated.

Inez peered into her dark eyes, "Wife? You understand? Husband? Do you have a husband?"

"No, me no husband," she said and looked back up the street. "Me want husband. Leave Zhen for good."

"Well, we all want a husband, girl." Pearl leaned against the post in front of the hardware store.

"No, one with hair like you," the girl pointed to a string of coppery hair that had worked loose from under Inez's bonnet.

"Damn, she's specific on what she wants in a husband," Pearl said. "Girl, if I was you, I wouldn't be so damn picky about men." She turned to Inez, "Mildred will have a hissy-fit when you fetch in a Chinese girl. She don't take to Chinese."

The thought of her bringing in another mouth to feed, worried Inez. She knew the house couldn't accommodate another girl and that her arrangement to work in the kitchen may well be sacrificed if they had to pay for this girl's upkeep. She might have to earn money for the house the way Pearl did, and that notion didn't appeal to her. But, as she glanced at the doe-eyed girl, a girl afraid that Zhen would drag her back, a girl that wanted to be married and create a home, she knew she didn't have any choice except to take her where she would be safe and able to get out of the grips of the life in which her family and Zhen had enslaved her.

"I'll talk to Mildred," Inez said.

"No," Mildred yelled. "Ain't no Chiney girl living in this house. She'll run off the gentlemen. Real gentlemen don't want yellow girls, or Negroes, or Mexicans, or Indians. They want clean white girls."

"Onalee is Indian," Inez replied from the kitchen table. She had left the girl on the back porch to finish peeling potatoes so she could talk to Mildred.

"But, Onalee ain't no girl. Onalee runs this place. Other houses can serve up a variety for the men who need something different. Those Chiney girls just aren't clean, and I won't spoil the reputation of this place in one night by having her here."

"But, what am I going to do with her?"

"That's your problem, Missy." Mildred banged a pot on the stove. "We've got supper to fix…" She stared out the window at the girl peeling the potatoes. "She's a hard worker…"

Inez stayed quiet, hoping Mildred would change her mind.

"Well, she can help clean up, but she has to stay in the kitchen and sleep in here. I'll let Onalee decide what to do with her when she gets back tomorrow."

That night, Inez kept the girl in the kitchen to clean the pots and pans. The glasses and plates, Mildred warned, she shouldn't touch because of their expense. Soapy water splashed as the girl scrubbed a stew pot, and she nodded to Inez and Mildred as they hurried in and out of the kitchen with drinks and food. Stopping to tell her how well she washed the pots, Inez patted her shoulder, "Very good."

"Sun," the girl said.

"Sun? No it's nighttime."

"Me Sun."

"Your name is Sun?" asked Inez.

"Yeah, Sun," she said pointing to herself.

"Inez," she introduced, feeling bad that she hadn't even thought to ask the girl's name in the past few hours. Since the idea that Sun had a name and wanted to be called by it had never occurred to Inez, she knew she had treated her like an object just like Zhen had. "You do good work, Sun."

"Me better with the men," Sun bragged.

A blush warmed Inez's face. "That should help you find a husband," Inez teased.

Mildred rushed through the door from the dining room. "Get her out of here quick," she herded them toward the back door. "Zhen is in the parlor looking for her, and he's plenty mad. A couple of the gentlemen are trying to calm him down and get him out."

"Should I fetch the sheriff?" Inez asked.

"No, but I'm getting Onalee's pistol," Mildred waddled toward the little office off the kitchen. She called back, "Take her out the porch and down the hill. I'll signal you when Zhen is gone."

Despite the time in the hot dish water, Sun's hand was cold as Inez led her off the porch and down the steep bank to the street below. They crouched behind a juniper across the street and watched the back porch.

"It will be all right," comforted Inez.

The moonlight gleamed in Sun's coal black hair and pooled in her dark misty eyes. "Me won't go back to Zhen."

"You don't have to. Mildred will run him off."

"He be back. He not give up."

They needed to find a way to pay off Sun's debt to Zhen, then he would have no claim to her. Inez's mind cranked up. Money wasn't easy to earn for a woman, but with the mine producing copper by the ton, plenty of money flowed around Jerome. The mine owners and executives, store owners, doctors, lawyers, all men of wealth and influence could easily pay the debt and not miss the money. "But, how?" pondered Inez.

"Look," Sun whispered and pointed toward the porch above them.

The shadowy figures of Mildred and a short wiry man walked along the porch; she seemed to tower over the little man. Sun slumped deep into the juniper with Inez sliding in next to her.

"It's all right," Inez assured. "Mildred will handle him." The sight of the small man almost amused her because she knew he wouldn't be able to stop her from doing anything. Why, she thought, I could break him like a stick. That little fart of a man shouldn't scare anyone. Nerves rose in her until she was ready to charge up the hill and give Zhen a piece of her mind. She'd tangled with bigger women than him.

As Inez moved from the brush, Sun grabbed her arm to draw her back. "No, not leave me."

"Why, that little piss-ant couldn't hurt anybody."

Sun giggled, but held Inez tight. "Him mean and strong."

"Fine," Inez said. "I'll let Mildred talk to him."

The figures on the porch paced back and forth with mumbled words. Zhen actually laughed at something Mildred had said. They turned and returned to the kitchen leaving silence in their wake.

"We'll wait for Mildred to signal us back," Inez patted Sun's hand that still clamped her arm.

The sound of Sun's breathing filled Inez's ears. A rustling of dry grass signaled the scurrying of some nighttime creature from a near-by pinyon pine. They waited. The kitchen door stayed closed. A light dimmed in Frenchy's room on the second floor. Normalcy seemed to return to the house. But, Mildred didn't come to the porch.

Maybe, Inez thought, she forgot us. No, she dismissed the idea.

The shadow of Mildred moved by the kitchen window, and Inez crept out from under the juniper and peered through its wavy branches.

"You, girl with orange hair," the voice from the road startled her.

She ducked back down.

"I see you. Come out," the squeaky voice commanded.

She knew Zhen had found them. Standing up, she took the toe of her shoe and nudged Sun further under the bush.

"What'd you want Chinaman?" she called out as she stepped up to the road, daring not to look back to where she'd been hiding. She straightened her dress and brushed off dry grass and juniper needles.

"What you do back there? You hide?" Zhen's triangular pale face and slick hair shined in the moonlight.

"No, if you have to know—I pee," Inez mocked his English.

"What pretty girl like you pee behind bush?" he asked, walking up to her.

"When you gotta go, you go," Inez smiled at him. Gauging his size up close, she could tell he wouldn't measure to her shoulder. "Why are you asking a white girl so many questions?" She played on the social structure to try to scare him off.

"No get smart with me. You a whore."

She slapped him, but before she could do it again, he grabbed her arm and twisted her to the ground.

"Hey," Mildred yelled from the porch above them. "You let go of my girl."

His grip relaxed on Inez's wrist, but didn't release her completely. "So sorry, Miss Mildred. She out of line with me."

"Don't make no difference," Mildred marched down the steps from the porch and then slipped and slid on the slope to the road below. "You get your yellow ass away from her. Don't make me tell Onalee about this."

"So sorry," he apologized again and released Inez's wrist. "I thought she might be my girl."

With hands on her ample hips, Mildred cocked her head. "Does she look like one of your girls? I told you we can't help. Go back up Hull and check the cribs or the saloons. No parlor house in town is going to have a Chiney girl."

He stared with cold, lizard eyes while Inez dusted off her dress and assumed the same stance as Mildred between him and the juniper.

"Go on little man," Inez quipped. A quick shake from Mildred's head, let her know that she shouldn't push him any further.

He addressed Mildred, "You let me know if see her. I get her back."

"We both got customers to attend to," Mildred put her arm around Inez while looking at Zhen.

He turned and walked back up the street. They watched him until he disappeared over a hill. Like mother cats, they dashed Sun across the road and up the embankment and to the porch staircase. Sandwiched between the two women, Sun hid as they climbed the stairs and retreated into the kitchen.

The next morning, Inez fixed breakfast for the ladies. As was her schedule, Mildred would amble in mid-afternoon for supper preparation. Inez organized the ladies in the cleaning of the house and allowed Sun to take over the laundry. With Onalee returning in the afternoon, Inez worried about explaining Sun's presence and how they had encountered Zhen and what she expected Onalee to do with Sun. But, Inez herself wasn't sure what to do with Sun. The girl seemed to be happy to be away from Zhen, but the other ladies of the house didn't show any interest toward her, not to the level that they took in Inez. Maybe Sun being Chinese meant something to them, implied some lower status in the West; in any case, the ladies were polite, but distant to Sun as if they didn't want to get to know her. But, Inez asked Sun constant questions about China and how she came to be in the Arizona Territory.

As Sun revealed the story, she had arrived pretty much the same as Inez—a mail-order bride, but Josiah had paid Inez's way. Sun's family had begged Zhen to transport her to America. He had paid her family and her passage to Arizona, but no husband waited for her. No husband met her at the train. No husband confessed his love for her. Like a herd of cattle, Sun and other girls were corralled into a freight car in San Francisco and arrived in Prescott three days later. After a trip by wagon to Jerome, she had been in Zhen's stable of girls for the past two years. Learning a little English and how to please her customers was all the Territory had offered her, but Sun's enthusiasm for her future wasn't dampened by the reign of Zhen over her life.

She laundered the ladies' red-striped stockings, chemises, cotton petticoats, and other unmentionables, plus the sheets and towels. Inez wouldn't trust her with the ladies' finer silk garments or anything with lace, embroidery, or trimmed with ribbons; those, Inez cleaned herself. Pearl, as Inez learned, had trouble keeping wine stains from her gowns, and as Inez scrubbed the spot, Sun offered to help with a pot of boiling water she poured over the stain, then she soaked it in vinegar and rinsed again with the hot water.

"That really helped," Inez said. "Thank you, Sun."

A smiled brightened her face, "Welcome," she bowed a little to Inez.

Inez bowed back.

The back door opened to the porch where they laundered, and Pearl plopped down on a rocking chair. "I finished cleaning. Inez, let's go shopping. I want out of the house on such a pretty day. Won't be long till it's too damn cold to go out."

Holding up the dripping dress, Inez said, "If a certain young lady didn't spill wine all over her good gowns, I'd be done by now, too."

"That man last night was clumsy as an ox with weak eyes." Pearl propped her boots up on the railing and her skirt slid up to her knees displaying her yellow and red striped stockings. "I just dream of a nice man with money and some class. Maybe, a little older, with a wife," she grinned at Inez, "so he's not around all the time. But he would set me up in a nice little house with a monthly allowance for buying pretty clothes, and he would visit a couple of times a week. The rest of my time would be free." She closed her eyes and smiled. "I'd take up painting, and eat a chocolate bon-bon as I surveyed the valley below. Maybe he'd move me to Prescott where I could become an actress."

"You are an actress," Inez commented while hanging the dress on a line stretched from the porch posts. "You act like you love those men and their conversation."

"Me love men," Sun said.

"Bet you do," Pearl opened her eyes to look at Sun, then turned to Inez, "What are you going to do with Miss China? She ain't no pet. She needs to go her own way."

"It ain't up—" Inez caught herself using slang. "It isn't up to me. I want to get her far from Zhen, but I need Onalee's advice on how to do that."

"Speaking of Mother, didn't she say for you to find a storefront for Lois?" Pearl dropped her feet from the railing. "Let's go. I'm itching to get out of here."

"But, Sun..." Inez started. "I need to keep her here, out of sight."

Pearl pushed herself out of the rocker. "Tie her to that post, like a calf. She won't go nowhere."

Sun looked to Inez with terror in her eyes.

"No, no," she reassured Sun. "Pearl was kidding. Made a joke. A funny—ha ha." Jerking her head around to glare at Pearl, Inez said, "Don't say things like that. She'll believe you."

"Who said I was kidding?" Pearl sashayed back into the house.

CHAPTER TEN

The clear, warm afternoon ushered a chilled breeze up the mountain reminding Inez that autumn still immured Cleopatra Hill and that the errant snug day would once again hand over control to the shadow of the coming winter. The wind traced cool fingers through Inez's loose hair, lifting the copper strands, then dropping them to her shoulders in carefree strokes.

Pearl held her arms up toward the gleaming sun, twirling like a dust devil in her fawn colored skirt and crisp white blouse. "Why does December have to arrive so soon?"

Smiling at the freedom and happiness of Pearl, Inez waved her hands above her head and spun around too. "Maybe we can whirl fast enough to reverse the spin of the earth and turn back the season."

Laughing, Pearl stopped and hugged Inez, "You are so silly. Time can't be driven backwards. The present and future are all we got."

Dust bloomed behind a horseman galloping toward them down the sloping street. He sat tall and straight on the gray horse and wore dark trousers and a denim shirt that flapped in the wind. A tan hat shaded his face from their view. As he approached, Pearl bent down to adjust her stockings, raising her skirt to her knee.

"Stop that," Inez grabbed the hem of Pearl's skirt and pulled it back down.

A wicked smile slid across her face and she winked at Inez.

The horseman stopped in front of them, "Howdy, ladies."

The voice sounded familiar, but Inez couldn't see his face. She shaded her eyes from the sun. Auburn hair poked out from under his hat and his open shirt revealed the strong chest and sun-golden hair she had noticed at the Cottonwood blacksmith's barn.

"Why, Red Dale," Pearl fluttered. "How nice to see you in town." She swished her skirt as she talked.

"Miss Pearl, pleasure to see you." He nodded and removed his hat, auburn curls wafted around his face; he looked at Inez, "Howdy ma'am."

"Hello," she said, worried he might recognize her, but then why she worried, she couldn't collect in her mind. Maybe it was that he would remember her as the young bride-to-be, and she'd have to explain how she ended up in Jerome with copper-colored hair and as best friend to Pearl. Probably didn't pay me no mind, thought Inez, and that was a long time—

"You the girl I made the Laundress sign for," he smiled, interrupting her thoughts.

"Yes, sir." She self-consciously touched her hair because she'd forgotten to wear her bonnet.

"Nice to see you again," he grinned.

Pearl nudged her with her shoulder, and Inez stumbled forward a little.

"You still work at the blacksmith?" Inez asked.

"Yes, ma'am. I got some time off, so I came up here for the day."

"Well, Red Dale," Pearl tugged her wind-blown raven-hair out of her eyes, "as long as you're in town, stop by and see us tonight. Mildred will have a fine supper ready, and a strapping young man like you needs a good meal now and then." She fluttered her eyelashes.

"Got some business to attend to," he replied. "Have you seen a small Chinese girl wandering around town?"

Fear clung to Inez's spine. Why was Red Dale looking for Sun? Had Mr. Zhen hired him to find her? Was this what Lottie whispered about? Could he be a bounty hunter? Is that why he left the States for the Territory?

Pearl took a breath and puffed up her chest, "As a matter of fact—"

"No," Inez interrupted. "No, we don't see many Chinese girls. You might try Mr. Zhen's laundry. I hear tell he has several working there." She grabbed Pearl's hand, "We got to be going. We're looking at a storefront up on School Street."

"So long, ladies," Red Dale tipped his hat and urged his horse on down the road.

Inez slapped Pearl's shoulder, "What are you thinking? He's after Sun to take her back to Zhen."

"So? That's where she belongs." Pearl rubbed her shoulder.

"She isn't going back," stressed Inez.

"Well, then she needs to go someplace. Onalee won't let her stay with us," Pearl walked up the street ahead of Inez. "Come on, I see the store with the sign in the window. It looks nice." She hurried up the road with Inez close behind. A two-story pine board building presented a white store front with a large display window and a glass front door. A staircase pitched up the side alley to the second floor landing to the rooms upstairs.

Leaning against the front window, a sign listed with whom to inquire about renting the store. Inez and Pearl found the old man in a house a block away and explained that they wanted to open a dressmaker's shop. The old man's front room smelled of tobacco smoke and cats. His wispy hair had been combed over the top of his spotted head in an attempt to hide the fact that those few hairs were all that still resided there, although Inez noticed he did a good job of sprouting hair in his ears and nostrils. A jovial man, he grinned and shook his head as the girls talked. A yellow, tiger-striped cat purred near his shoulder on a worn blanket folded over the back of his chair.

"That there store is a gem, a true gem," he reached up and pulled the cat off the blanket and to his knee. "Come here Tom." He patted the old cat's head. "You got husbands that I can talk business with?"

"No sir," Inez said. "We can talk business with you as well as a man. The shop needs to be cleaned and painted before we could move in." She hoped to get him to come down on the rent, even though the place would be perfect for Lois since the rent included an apartment above the shop.

"Miss, that last tenant left some straightening up to do, but I can do that."

Inez thought and rubbed her chin, "How about we clean and paint, and in exchange for our renovation, you cut some off the rent?"

He patted the cat and stared off into the corner of the room. "Tell you what ladies," he began, "I can let you have it for twenty-five dollars a month. That includes the rooms above too."

Pearl sat up straight in her excitement over the low price, but Inez put her hand on Pearl's arm.

"Now, Pearl," she frowned at her trying to get her to play along with her negotiations, "I know that is more than we can pay, and there's no sense in walking out. You sit still and let me talk with this gentleman." Onalee had said they could pay up to 50 dollars a month to get a place for Lois. "I really can't do much more than ten dollars a month since we have to clean and paint."

The old man frowned.

"You see we have to get fabric and a sewing machine and threads of different colors," Inez listed. "And all those things cost money."

"Can't do it for less than twenty dollars," he muttered. "That is the price I'd give my own daughters."

Inez studied her skirt, and tried to make her eyes water so he'd think she was crying. She sniffed and leaned into Pearl's shoulder, then without looking at him, she choked out, "We just can't."

She let the silence spread across the room, shepherded by a small sob. She knew that a man would have been able to deal with him, but he was bound to think that two girls would pay a higher price.

Clearing his throat in a rough cough, the old man asked, "How about fifteen dollars until you get going, say for three months, then up to twenty dollars after that?"

A sniff and a swipe at her eyes and Inez smiled at the old man. "Could you clean the place for us? We'll paint it."

With a long sigh, the old man stood, letting the cat leap from his knee. "Alright, but you girls need to pay me the first month's rent by the end of the week."

"Yes sir." Inez shook his hand. "Thank you."

As they walked down the street, Pearl complimented Inez on her negotiation. "You played that old man like a harp. We will have enough money to rent the place for several months. Maybe Onalee could open another house there."

"On School Street?" Inez asked, surprised by the thought. "That's a place where children pass everyday, and there's churches just down the road."

"We don't work during the day," Pearl reminded her.

"No, that will be a dress shop. Maybe Martha can really use the shop for her sewing, and Lois would help design some of the dresses. With the rail road being extended from the Junction to here, more and more ladies will be going to the Opera House in Prescott. They will need fancy dresses for that." Inez rattled off more ideas, "Christmas and New Year's Eve are just around the corner and dresses will be needed for that. Oh," she twirled around and grabbed Pearl's arm, "I heard talk about opening an Opera House here for shows." The prospects grew greener with each step she took. She knew that with a little work, they could make a success of the dress shop.

As they turned the corner toward the parlor house, Inez saw Onalee standing on the front porch, waiting for them. The stern expression on her face told Inez that she had seen Sun and waited for an explanation.

"I know you wanted to help her," Onalee paced the front parlor, stopping at a side table to adjust the position of a carved great-horned owl fashioned from a piece of cottonwood root. "This has upset plans," she perched next to Inez on the sofa, "a strategy to assist Sun."

Confusion swept over Inez, and she rubbed her eyes to help clear her mind. "Sun is free. She's back in the kitchen." The open windows aired the house of the previous night's stale cigar smoke and spicy roast beef meal, and Inez watched a swirl of dust settle in a sunbeam.

"I realize your intention, but Sun doesn't understand the ways of the Territory, and at times, you don't either." She walked to the front window and closed it for privacy from the people walking along the road. "Men like Mr. Zhen are here to make their fortune; some come to pick the copper veins of Cleopatra Hill, others to get their share from the miners by providing for their needs." The corners of her dark lips hinted at an apologetic smile, "I have my motivation for being here too, but I try to be honorable and kind both to the women who work here and to our customers. Mr. Zhen wants to make as much money as fast as he can without regard to the women he uses." She glanced at Inez. "He will use a girl until she is no longer profitable, leaching her like slag smelted from the copper ore."

The image of the mounds of dark, hardened slag dumped at the bottom of the hill haunted Inez. She could see that black waste as the lost and damaged souls of the girls entertaining the men of Jerome. Was this what would become of Pearl? Lois? Toy? Frenchy? Molly? Maybe, even her? "But you don't do that to girls," she pleaded to Onalee.

"I hope I don't," Onalee said. "I try not to."

From the first time Inez had met Onalee, she knew that this person was pure and good-hearted. A spirit of kindness, not a user, not a profiteer, not an exploiter. "So, how do we keep Sun from Mr. Zhen?"

"That's one of the reasons I traveled to Cottonwood yesterday. I have been working with a man who wants to marry Sun, to take her away from Jerome, but our plans have been cut short by Sun running away. I had a deal to offer Zhen to pay off her import fees, but now that Sun is with you, we'll have to take her back to propose the offer for her legal payment." Onalee shook her head, "I know he will think we tried to steal her, which makes his cooperation all the more difficult."

"A man wants to marry Sun?" The connections clicked as Inez asked the question. He had been looking for her, not as a bounty hunter, but out of personal concern. "Red Dale?"

"Yes," Onalee smiled. "Do you know him?"

"Pearl and I just saw him. He asked if we had seen her."

"What do you mean? Is she not with you and Pearl?"

On reflex, Inez jerked her head to stare at the kitchen door. "She's not here?"

Onalee sprang from the sofa and strode toward the kitchen with Inez following. "Molly told me about Sun and about Zhen's visit here last night, then she said you and Pearl had gone looking at storefronts..." She swung open the kitchen door and surveyed the room. "I came through the kitchen earlier, but no one was here." She looked at Inez, "I thought Sun had gone with you."

"No, we told her to stay here." Inez rushed to the back porch, but Sun was gone.

✗ ✗ ✗

Sheriff Jim rested his arm across the back of the sofa, Onalee sat next to him with a tablet of paper and her pencil making notes of what was said, Red Dale straddled the piano stool, Pearl reclined on the chaise, and Inez paced in front of them recounting how they had seen Sun at the Fashion and wanted to help her, how she had insisted that Sun come back with them. Mildred leaned in the doorway of the dining room and added her encounter with Zhen.

"Did she have any other place she might try to go?" Sheriff Jim asked Red Dale, then looked to Inez to extend the question to her.

Red Dale rested his hat on his knee and scratched his head, "She never got out of that place to know anyone else."

The sheriff's gray eyes focused on Inez. She pushed Pearl's feet from the edge of the chaise and settled there.

"I don't think she knows much about the town. She didn't seem to know her way around," Inez said. She wondered if she was right, Sun didn't say much about her daily life at Zhen's, but then Inez never saw Chinese girls walking along the streets. The West wasn't a friendly place for the Chinese, so they pretty much stayed together. "Maybe," she ventured, "she went to that Chinese camp on Diaz below the Chinese restaurant."

"I checked there," Red Dale said. "No one claims to have seen her, but they might be afraid to say anything."

"I hate to suggest this," the sheriff said while looking at Red Dale, "but she might have gone to find another man she knew, another regular customer who might have offered her marriage."

Red Dale raked the rug with the tip of his boot, "I thought about that. I know what profession she's in, and I know I weren't the only man—"

"No," Pearl interrupted. "No, that girl had one man on her mind, and one man only that she wanted to get to and to marry. That man had hair this color," she leaned forward and lifted a lock of Inez's hair. "She made sure we knew that was the man for her. Red Dale, that girl loved only you."

At times, Inez thought, Pearl could be the sweetest, most good-hearted girl in all the West. She reached over and patted Pearl's foot, smiling at her.

"Thank you, Miss Pearl," Red Dale said. "That's comforting to me."

"So," Onalee pulled her dark braids back behind her broad shoulders and glanced at her tablet, "the Chinese camp has been checked, Zhen's laundry and boarding house are off the list. Sheriff, you inspected the cribs on Hull Avenue. The hurdy gurdy houses and the saloons probably wouldn't allow her in, but they need to be asked."

"What about Zhen?" Mildred asked. "He ain't sitting around waiting for that Chiney girl to show up on his doorstep. He probably got his rice-eaters out looking too."

Pearl glanced over her shoulder at Mildred. "Marvelous Mildred, you got a way with words. I'm surprised that you're not the Mayor's wife."

"Listen here, Missy—" she began before Onalee held up a hand for quiet.

"You two settle down. Mildred has a point; Zhen is looking too, and I'm afraid what he'll do if he finds her first."

"He better not hurt her," Red Dale stood and paced Inez's path in the rug.

Sheriff Jim pulled himself up from the sofa, straightening his tall frame, and in two strides met Red Dale halfway across the floor. He placed a hand on his shoulder, "Don't worry about that. I have warned Zhen on disciplining his girls. I'd just as soon haul his ass into jail as look at him." He glanced around the room, "Excuse my French, ladies."

"Hell," Mildred laughed, "around here, we use harsher words than that during Sunday supper."

He looked to Inez, and she felt the heat come to her cheeks. "Thank you," she smiled, glanced down, then back to meet his eyes still on her. His gray eyes, canopied by bushy brows, seemed as soft and gentle as velvet on her skin. Self-consciously, Inez looked down, then to Pearl to see if she'd noticed.

She had. Pearl raised one eyebrow as if to challenge Inez to make a move, not to let the sheriff's interest wane. But, Inez didn't know the art of flirtation like the other girls of the house, so she just smiled back at Sheriff Jim.

Apparently, Onalee had noticed too. She stood and handed the tablet to Inez. "Go sit over there and make sure we have a plan together." She took the place next to Pearl on the chaise, so Inez sat on the sofa.

Sheriff Jim returned to sit next to Inez, and Red Dale went back to the piano stool. Inez sneaked a look at the sheriff's profile as he talked.

"I'll send out one of my deputies to ask around the saloons. Red Dale," he instructed, "you stay in Cottonwood. I don't want you tangling with Zhen, and Sun might find her way down there looking for you, so it's best that you be at the blacksmith barn if she shows up."

He turned to Inez, his smile and eyes lingering a little longer than necessary, then looked to Onalee, Pearl, and Mildred. "You ladies watch for her. She knows this house has gentle women in it who would help her. She might be back." He focused on Inez again. "You come by my office if you see her or if you hear anything that might help us." He grinned and dimples appeared at the edges of his bushy mustache, then he pointed to Red Dale, "That goes for you too. If she shows up, don't you two run off. You come to me. We have to get this settled legally with Zhen, otherwise, I'll be obliged to come after you both."

Mildred checked the clock on the mantle, "Lord, all this Chiney stuff has put me off schedule for cooking tonight's supper. Come on Inez, we got to commence baking. Sheriff and Red Dale, you are welcome to stay for some food and entertainment. The girls would be glad to have your handsome faces here."

"Now, Mildred," Onalee said. "The sheriff and Red Dale know they're welcome to dine with us any time."

"Thank you both," the sheriff stood and placed his hat on his head, covering his short coffee-colored hair. "I need to get back to the office, then home for my own supper."

"What's the wife cooking tonight?" Mildred asked.

Wife? The sharp word sliced into Inez, so quick and clean, surprising her with its sting.

CHAPTER ELEVEN

Molly and Lois swiped beige paint on the walls of the dress shop as Toy inched her brush across the front window to block out precise lettering. Frenchy mopped the pine floor and Pearl supervised the progress. With her pad and pencil, Inez checked off items on her list: two bolts each of green silk and cobalt-blue silk, three bolts of midnight-blue damask, one bolt of scarlet, two bolts of gold, four bolts of black wool; she had bought out all the luxurious fabric at the local mercantile. As she inventoried thread, lace, and beads, Inez pointed out to Pearl where the sewing area and the fitting rooms would be constructed.

Jedediah, a cornstalk of a man, was a regular customer of Toy's and had agreed to construct the walls for the fitting rooms and build work tables, counters, and wardrobes. Pearl instructed Jedediah on the plan and offered her opinion on his work. "Miss Pearl, I been building things most of my life, and I think I know how to build a table."

"But," Pearl frowned, "I want it wider. Martha will have to lay out her patterns on there, and some of these society women will require a lot of fabric. Just imagine one of Marvelous Mildred's dresses laid out."

Frenchy stopped mopping and laughed. "Better make that table a heap bigger."

"You ladies might be right," Jedediah said. "I ain't built no dress-making tables before, but you want to be able to reach across the thing."

Hearing their conversation, Inez decided to settle the dispute.

"Pearl, go see if Martha can come over here to tell us exactly what she wants. It's her table; she should be the one to design it. Jedediah, can you finish those wardrobes and cabinets today? I want to be able to get the fabric put away so it stays clean."

"Yes ma'am," he said. "That there's a good idea to get Martha. Like my daddy always said, 'go to the horse's mouth.'"

Pearl shook her head at him, "Don't you let Martha hear you calling her a horse or she'll sew your mouth shut."

He chuckled and started measuring a cabinet for a door. "You ladies are fun to work with. Men don't cut up like this."

Toy climbed off her bench, "Jed, you are the one who's fun to work with." She flashed him a smile, then turned to survey her lettering. "It's hard painting these letters backwards. Frenchy, go outside and tell me if they look right."

Onalee had suggested the name for the shop: Jerome Dressmakers. She said it would give the place a sense of belonging to all of Jerome and bring in the local women who saw Martha sewing in the front of the store.

"Keep painting," Frenchy said as she came back in the shop. "The letters are straight and spelled right."

With careful strokes, Toy finished the letters with her gold paint, then after they dried, she outlined them with black. Inez stepped out onto the street and assessed the progress. Amazed at the talent of the women and of their hard manual labor, she grinned at the people walking by.

She glanced around, wondering if Sun could be near. Maybe, she's just a street away, thought Inez. Could she be hurt, scared, hungry? Would anyone help a hapless Chinese girl on the streets of Jerome? For the past three days, thoughts of Sun had plagued Inez; also the specter of Sheriff Jim haunted her thoughts. Why? She couldn't reason. Just a man; a kind, handsome, strong, secure man, but just a man still. The gray in his hair and the laugh lines around his eyes hinted that he could be twice her age, but was it, she thought, a courtship she desired or fatherly security? The question tumbled over and over since she saw him last. He had a wife. What a silly, little-girl obsession. Her consideration of the subject would stop—now. She focused back on the storefront and the progress they had made in the two days of work.

A mother and her small girl stopped to look at the shop. "When will it be open?" she asked. The girl, about five years old, tugged at her mother's hand.

"We hope by next week," Inez said. "Our dress maker specializes in evening gowns for special occasions. She's made dresses for women in Boston and New York before moving here," Inez made up the facts as she went. "Jerome is growing so fast, that she decided to bring her skills here to help the local women display an air of sophistication and class that the town deserves." This she had heard Frenchy say. "I mean, we can't be going to the Prescott Opera House in calico."

"You're right," the woman said. "I would love to have a new dress. Everyone's seen my one gown."

"I tell you what," Inez began. "You look through *Godey's Lady's Book* or *Vogue* or *Harper's Bazaar*, and we can make any thing you find." As the little girl struggled to free herself from her mother's grip, Inez added, "We can even sew mother-daughter dresses for Christmas service."

"Oh, that would be perfect," the woman said. "I'll come back next week with some ideas of what I'd like."

☒ ☒ ☒

A few days later, with the renovations completed, Martha lined up spools and bobbins of thread close to her sewing machine. Her small age-spotted hands arranged the wooden spools in shades of dye, then she hooked her spectacles over each ear to peer closer at the tints of the blues. "Inez, where'd you find all these colors? The mercantile never had this much variety when I stop there."

From the storage room, Inez juggled an armload of fashion magazines. She dumped them on a table by the front window. "That young man, who works with the textiles, said he could get me any color I could imagine, so I told him to get us every one he could find." She leaned against the counter across from Martha. "I think he went to Prescott to get them," then she added, "but if he thinks I'm going to entertain him for going to so much trouble, he's got the wrong girl."

"That's right," Martha nodded her small gray head. "You stay sweet and pure. Them other girls can entertain. You are too smart for that. Why, it would be a waste for you to end up like them."

Inez glanced around to make sure the other girls hadn't arrived at the store yet. The hour of day was still too early for them, so she and Martha were the only ones at the shop to open the doors. "I like planning and organizing. This shop has been the most fun I've had. I really believe we can make a success of it."

Martha started to say, "But—"

"I know," Inez said. "I know we are doing this just to make a show for Lois' son, but I tell you Martha, the women in this town are excited. They're excited to see something besides coveralls and mining equipment in the windows of stores." She walked to the front window where two dress forms stood, torsos of bare cotton batting balanced on wooden stick legs. "I snatched some of your prettier gowns from Toy and from Pearl, things they don't wear a lot because they're too delicate. I thought we would put them on the dress forms to show what you can do."

"Let me take a look at them," Martha said pushing herself up from the sewing machine, accidentally stepping on the foot pedal causing the machine to whine to life. "Shut up, you contraption. Sometimes, I think I could sew by hand quicker than getting that thing set up and ready to go." She lifted one dress of gold gossamer satin. "You think this might be a bit too..." She shook her withered chest in a mock seductive gesture and winked. "You know too... fancy for the front window?"

"Well," Inez inspected it with a new look as Martha held it draped over her shoulder; a shoulder that Martha wiggled to make the dress dance and shimmer in the morning light. "Well, it is a little gay for the average woman. Maybe, we can hang it back near the fitting room, so customers will know we can do something a little more daring if they want." Inez smiled at Martha. "You never know what goes on in respectable homes."

"Ain't that the truth," Martha moved close to Inez as if to confide a deep secret. "I hear tell that Stella, Sheriff Jim's wife, may be spending too much time visiting with her sister in Prescott. I ain't ever heard her mention a sister, but neighbors say she goes over to Prescott about once a month." Martha frowned, wrinkling her brow, "And once the narrow gauge is finished to the Junction, she could go and be back fast as lightning."

"You don't think she has another man there, do you?" Excitement raised Inez's voice almost to a shrill, but then she calmed herself. Why do I care? He's married: happy or not. "Gossip, pure gossip," she said. "Sheriff Jim is a good man. That woman would have to be out of her head to cheat on him."

"If a man ain't at home to tend to his wife, sometimes she strays." Martha inspected her apron and sat back down at her sewing machine. "Of course, the opposite is true too, or Onalee would be out of business." A short sharp laugh escaped from her. "Now, seriously, I keep my man occupied at home. He's almost too old to keep working the mines, so I have things to keep him busy, hobbies to keep a roving eye from finding another old woman." With a pale pink tongue, she licked the end of a black thread and angled it from the mounted spool through a steel eyelet above the needle, then to the needle's eye. She lifted a small steel door below the needle to check the color of thread on the bobbin. Rocking the metal foot pedal back and forth, started the machine's whine and the needle nodding. "I ask him to patch up things around the house; I tell him how important he is; I fix him good meals; I don't nag; I perform my wifely duties when he wants." She lifted the end of her own apron and ran a quick stitch across a loose hem. "Men ain't complicated, Inez. It's easy to keep them happy. The problems come when both man and wife just plain lose interest in each other." She snipped the thread and inspected the repaired hem.

Had Sheriff Jim's wife lost her fancy of him? Had he lost his in her? The thought quickened her heart, but she reeled reason back in. "Well, no man and wife can keep the honeymoon going. They turn into friends," Inez said. "My mama and daddy worked the farm together for years. Oh, they had a few spats, but nothing big. They needed each other to survive, to put food on the table."

"How many children did they have?" Martha asked.

"Three. But, I'm the only one still alive. A baby girl was born dead to Mama when I was barely a year old. Mama always said that the baby had come too soon after me. Sometimes I felt it was my fault for taking too much of Mama from that baby and she didn't have the chance to grow strong."

Martha reached over and patted her hand, "Honey, that ain't your burden. That baby weren't meant to be."

"Then my brother, two years older than me," Inez continued, "died at the age of eight. I barely remember him. A mule kicked him in the head." Visions played in Inez's memory of her parents hovering over her brother's bed, crying and begging the doctor to save him. Her father leaving the house for two days after the boy passed, caused her mother to bear the grief alone with only a six-year-old Inez to comfort her. "You know, Martha, I don't think men are strong with feelings. They can fight and build and farm, but when something breaks their heart, they crumble like a dried cactus. I think that was the one time when Daddy let Mama down, after my brother died. She needed him to be strong for her, but losing his only son crushed him. They were fine later on, but Teddy's passing sure tested them."

"Are they still together?"

Smiling at the thought, Inez said, "Yes ma'am. In heaven." She kissed the top of Martha's head. "That was nice to talk about them."

The dresses she had taken from the parlor house still draped the table, so she sorted through them and picked out a sapphire blue silk gown with leg-o-mutton sleeves and a long slim waistline for one of the window dress forms, then a sage green velvet dress with puffed shoulder ruffles and tight sleeves for the other to show the different styles of Saint Louis and New York. Matching millinery emphasized the overall fashion that Inez created; these feathered felt hats were hung over the dress forms with string extending from the ceiling. She strived to give the impression that two invisible, but very fashionable women stood in the front window, and the effect worked. As Inez strung up the second hat, a woman entered the shop, jingling a bell Jedediah had fastened to the door.

"May I help you?" Inez asked.

The woman stood tall and thin glancing about the room, "I'm interested in having a dress made." She wore a simple cloth coat, embellished with a rabbit fur collar and pearl buttons.

"Do you have a notion of what you'd like?" Martha joined Inez in the sales presentation. "We have several dresses here," she motioned to the table, "as models or you can pick something from a magazine."

"Yes," Inez said. "You have a lovely shape. The slim, tapered style is all the fashion back East."

"Thank you," the woman said and folded herself into a chair to flip through a *Vogue*. "I don't ever get to see fashion magazines, so I fall behind in the styles. That green dress in the window is beautiful. Do you think you could do something like that for me?"

"Of course," Martha sat down next to the customer and pointed out dresses of similar style in the magazine.

Leaving the customer to Martha, Inez finished hanging the hat, then arranged the dresses on the table so the customer could see them all. The bell jangled again as the door opened.

Sheriff Jim, broad shouldered and grinning, strode in with his hat in his hand. "Miss Inez, the place looks grand." He nodded to the customer and Martha, then approached Inez at the table near the fitting room.

"Hello," she smiled and almost stumbled over one of the dresses draped over her arm. "I didn't expect to see you here, but I'm glad you stopped."

"Just wanted to see how our newest business was doing and offer my assistance if there's anything you need." He learned against the table, his gun holster skewed to the side.

The presence of this man excited Inez in a way she hadn't experienced since meeting Josiah at the train station so many months before. Although with Josiah, they had a set relationship, set before they had even met, and luckily for them both, they had been matched to perfection. But Sheriff Jim wasn't her future husband, not a man who had waited for her arrival, not a man with marriage intentions and a future mapped out for her. This man just happened to see her and want... What did he want?

"Need?" Inez repeated his word. Yes, she could think of things she needed from him, but then she felt her face flush from thoughts that Pearl had whispered in her ear about Sheriff Jim. "No, sir. I think we're fine here. Lois' son will be arriving next week. We have a nice place upstairs for her and Jared."

"Lois is a good girl," he said. "I'm not crazy about this scheme to hide her profession, but I guess a mother does what she feels she needs to do."

Inez moved away from the table and laid the gowns over a chair back. "Sun," she turned to him, "have you heard any news about her?"

"No ma'am. She's bound to be hiding out somewhere, and since I ain't heard from Red Dale in over a week, I suspect she's with him." He walked over to Inez, "And that's another reason I came here. I was hoping you would go to Cottonwood with me to talk to Red Dale and Sun, to help convince them to come back and settle things with Zhen."

"But," Inez stuttered, "I... What can I do?"

"I reckon Sun trusts you. I bet Red Dale trusts you too, and in matters like this, sometimes a woman's touch is needed."

She wanted to help, and she knew Onalee wouldn't mind, in fact she would encourage it. Any favors done for the law could only help the house. Besides, the prospect of spending time with Sheriff Jim made her head swim and fingers tingle, despite the call for reason, propriety, and reserve coming from her mind. "Yes, I would be glad to help," Inez smiled at him.

"Thank you, Miss Inez." He grinned back at her and placed his hat on his head. He leaned in close to her and whispered so that the customer wouldn't hear, "I'll stop by to see Onalee to make sure you can go with me tomorrow morning. I don't want to get you in trouble with your boss."

The heat from his breath lingered on her cheek. She stared into his gray eyes, hypnotized by the play of light in them.

He winked at her, then turned and left, tipping his hat to Martha and the customer as he ambled out the door.

CHAPTER TWELVE

While the afternoon shadows grew long and the sun slumped behind the black hills, Inez left Martha at the shop. She knew Marvelous Mildred would be waiting for her to help get supper started for the gentlemen's evening visit. The first day of the Jerome Dressmakers shop had snagged three commissions for gowns. A cover or not, Inez thought, that place will do well. Nobody in this town caters to women. We struck a vein.

She realized, as she left School Street, that she was thinking in mining terms and a smile graced her lips. Someone ahead of her on Main caught her eye—a woman whose hair shone like a summer sunset. She inspected the woman—not a Jerome girl, she would have remembered that hair. Pearl's intent for Inez's hair had been that sunset color, but instead she was Lady Marmalade, a bit faded, but rightly orange. Still, the woman seemed familiar, her manner of poise, the way she held her head high. She wore a fitted silk periwinkle blue skirt with a matching jacket trimmed at the collar and cuffs with black fur, bear fur Inez guessed. Her wine colored hair swept into a tight bun topped by a blue hat with more fur trim and a feather plume. Any other person on the street would have regarded the woman as a sophisticate maybe from the East or San Francisco, but Inez spotted the signs of a sporting woman. First, to be dressed so nice, she would have been on her way to a social occasion, but she was unescorted. Secondly, her hair wasn't a natural color, not that Inez could say that would mean a woman fallen, but as a rule, respectable local women didn't dye their hair. Finally and most importantly in Inez's mind, she was talking to a street prostitute, a woman who worked from the cribs.

As if they had spotted her at the same time she had seen them, the women turned to stare at Inez. A recognition of sisters in sin, Inez thought as she pulled her bonnet lower on her head and tried to stuff her orange hair under it. Just because I have dyed hair, Inez fumed in her mind, they think I'm one of them. She had to pass them to get to the house. She switched to the other side of the street and hastened her pace.

"Hello there," the fancy woman nodded to Inez as she walked past.

Inez nodded in response, but kept walking with a quick glance at them.

The prostitute, dressed in a ragged once-white but now yellowed gown and scuffed boots, flashed a gap-toothed smile at Inez. Her coarse features reminded Inez of a teenage boy, but her eyes held the weariness of an old woman. She whispered something to the elegant woman, then walked down the hill toward a Mexican saloon.

"You there," the fancy woman walked toward Inez. "Don't I know you?"

She couldn't ignore someone talking to her, but Inez didn't slow her pace. 'Show respect for your elders,' her mother had always said. 'Be kind to strangers' was another lesson imparted on her. She stopped and turned to find the woman catching up to her, amazingly quick considering the high heeled boots the woman wore.

"No, ma'am," Inez said. "I don't think we've been introduced."

The woman cocked her head, the feather plume jerking on top of her hat. "Yes, yes, I do think I remember you. A young girl on the train alone. You got off at the Junction."

The woman from the train, the one who had given her perfume to freshen up for Josiah, Inez couldn't remember her name. "Yes, ma'am, I believe I do remember you."

"My name is Linda," she nodded to Inez.

"Yes, Miss Linda. My name is Inez." She hadn't seen this woman since her first day in the Arizona Territory, and she wondered why she saw her now. "I need to be getting to my job," she backed away from Linda, not sure why she felt the need to leave her company. "I have to get supper begun. Good-bye."

"Good-bye, Inez," Linda said, then added, "I come to town from time to time. If you need work, let me know."

Inez just waved her hand without turning around. So, she has some of those crib girls working for her, Inez thought. The revelation surprised her mainly because she had believed that horrible men did that to girls, she couldn't believe that a woman would make girls work in the cribs. How desperate those women must be, how alone, how hopeless, how destitute, Inez slowed her gait, then stopped. "Miss Linda," she called.

She had been walking in the same direction as Inez and soon caught up to her. "Yes, Inez?"

"A friend of mine," she started. "A Chinese girl named Sun is missing. Have you seen her?"

Linda smiled. "I know a lot of young Chinese girls, don't know them all by name, but maybe I know this one."

The comment confused Inez. Why was she so shifty about if she knew Sun? "I was just asking," Inez said, "because we think she might be in trouble."

"You said 'we.' You and who else is looking for this girl?"

"Well, ma'am, uh," dang, Inez thought, this woman is forward. "Miss Linda, I don't reckon it means a lot who is looking for her with me. I just want to find the girl." She considered bringing in Sheriff Jim's name, but then thought better of it. Talking about the law might scare her away.

"The girls I know," Linda glanced around the street at a couple of miners walking up the road toward them, "like to keep a sensible distance from people who ask too many questions. Honey, this ain't no social club. These girls are working to feed themselves and to have a roof to keep the cold away." She peeked around her shoulder again at the approaching miners. "Honey, it's payday for the boys. I need to get them to my girls." She turned to sashay toward the miners, one young and one old, then she stopped and said to Inez, "Now, remember, if you need employment, let Miss Linda know. I come to town every two weeks same as the payroll."

The next day, Inez prepared for her trip with Sheriff Jim. Onalee had said it would be helpful for Inez to ride down to Cottonwood with the sheriff, but she had warned, "Don't get too involved in finding Sun. We want to help her, but it's not our fight. Let the sheriff do his job. We want Sheriff Jim to know we will assist the law any way we can."

So, with that, Inez put on a slim juniper green skirt and a tailored white blouse. Pearl braided Inez's hair and twisted it into a bun, then she placed a black cowboy hat on her head. "Women wearing men's hats," Pearl instructed, "shows we can be as practical and smart as them." She winked at Inez. "And it looks decadent on you."

"That's not good," protested Inez. Most women wore fashionable hats or bonnets; if they did sport a wide-brimmed sunhat, it was more girlish than manly. But this was a cowboy's hat, worn by the wranglers and herders of the West. What would Sheriff Jim think of it? Pearl handed her a felted wool bolero trimmed in golden cording. "What are you trying to make me into? A boy?" Inez asked as she slipped on the short, soft jacket.

"No, ma'am," Pearl smiled, then crossed her arms as she scanned the new look for Inez. "You are my idea of the modern western woman."

As Inez gazed in her mirror, she did have to admit she liked the clothes. They were comfortable and warm; the hat bestowed a more serious look and toned down the color of her hair. She felt and looked older, more mature. She wondered, Would Sheriff Jim notice?

A knock on the bedroom door announced Onalee. She always respected the girls' privacy and knocked before entering their rooms. Her braids hung across her broad shoulders and the simple doe-skin robe fluttered beaded fringe as she walked. "Inez, you look remarkable."

"Is that good?" Inez asked.

"Of course," Pearl slapped Inez's bottom with a playful swat. "I told you, you are powerful in those clothes."

"Yes," Onalee agreed and sat on the edge of the bed. "You have changed so much since Pearl brought you in here all those weeks ago."

The memories of losing Josiah, her argument with Lottie, and the cold lonely night huddled on a Jerome rooftop trying not to freeze came flooding back to her. Then, the warm kindness and assistance that Onalee, Pearl, and the other girls had shown her pulled a smile to her lips. "Onalee, I don't know how I would have made it without you. You are a blessing to me."

"Thank you," Onalee stood and hugged Inez. "You're a big help to us. I hope you think of me and the girls as family."

The sweet smell of sage surrounded Onalee as Inez let go of the hug. "I sure do." She grinned at Pearl, then glanced back at Onalee. "So, you think I look alright to go to Cottonwood with Sheriff Jim?"

"I'm proud to have you represent us. Now, go downstairs. Mildred has your and the sheriff's dinner in a basket for the trip." She turned to leave, but stopped. "If you find Sun, and I think she's there with Red Dale, don't try to force her to come back. Let Sheriff Jim handle things. He knows what's best."

Inez knew that Sheriff Jim would do the right thing. His kind words and thoughtful dealings always took into account the people behind the actions. Sun only did what she had to. Red Dale loved her and would get her away from Zhen—lawful or not. And Sheriff Jim understood that, at least Inez believed he did.

In the kitchen, Mildred packed a basket of fried chicken, biscuits, and baked apples. She handed Inez a jug of water, "Now you behave yourself with that man. I seen how you been eyeing him. And that there outfit is made for teasing."

"Mildred, why would you say such a thing? He's married and the sheriff and…" She tried to think of more reasons to deny the thoughts she had for him.

"Never mind," Mildred folded her plump arms across her ample chest. "I know how young girls get stars in their eyes. He's a good man and under the watch of every nosey so-and-so in Jerome. Why,

I can already hear the tongues wagging when people see you riding down the hill with him."

"Are you saying I shouldn't go?" Inez shot back in a tone harsher than she had ever used with Mildred.

"No ma'am," Mildred stood up straight and pushed the basket across the table at her. "Onalee said for you to go. I don't cross her. I just give you my say and a warning to behave."

Inez opened her mouth to protest the implication that she wasn't a good girl, but Mildred beat her to it.

"Inez, you and me been working in this kitchen side by side for almost two months, and I know you ain't loose with yourself like the girls upstairs, but," she turned away from Inez and grabbed a handful of pea pods and started popping out the little green orbs into a bowl. "But, women got needs just like men and you ain't been attending to yours like the girls do."

"Why Mildred," shock tinged Inez's voice. Pearl always talked about her men and how she enjoyed her work, but that was Pearl. Mildred was old enough to be Inez's mother, and here she was talking about men and women and animal instincts.

Mildred turned to glance at Inez. "It's nature Honey. We all knows it. Sometimes you got to let propriety go and set your mind on what's really happening."

"I understand what you're saying," Inez said. "I'm not going to throw myself at him. I got more control than that. I reckon I do fancy him, like any woman would, but my mama raised me right and I'm old enough to know better." She knew Mildred was only trying to be motherly and give her some advice on being around an attractive man. "Thank you for the warning. It's comforting to know you're looking out for me." She kissed Mildred on the fleshy cheek and grabbed the basket from the table.

Her intent was to walk over to the jail to meet Sheriff Jim, but when she opened the front door, a black buggy attached to tawny mare waited at the porch. Sheriff Jim jumped down from the bench seat and took the dinner basket from her.

"I was just getting ready to knock on the door," his grey eyes sparkled in the morning light. "What's this?" he hefted the basket onto the back of the carriage.

"Mildred made us dinner for the trip." Inez set the water jug on the floorboard, under the bench. Before she could step up in the buggy, she felt the sheriff's strong hands wrap around her waist and lift her up.

"Let me help you," he said placing her easily in the seat.

"Thank you," she managed to squeak out and scooted across the seat to make room for him.

"You're looking might pretty this morning," he said climbing up to the bench beside her. "That's a real practical hat, like mine." He tipped his hat to her. "Most ladies like lacy bonnets or hats with big feathers, but these here hats keep the sun and rain off you."

"Yes, sir," Inez said.

"Now don't start calling me sir. Jim will do." He slapped the reins against the flank of the horse to get her moving. The carriage wobbled down the rutted dirt street toward the road to Cottonwood.

"This is a nice buggy," Inez said. The heavy black fabric of the canopy shaded them from the sun and the eyes of the townspeople as they rode along. The sheriff would tip his hat to the ladies as the carriage rolled past, but Inez saw them whisper and stare at their sheriff and the strange girl.

"Well, Miss Inez," he started, "I didn't think it was fitting for a fine lady like you to ride a horse down to the valley and back, so I borrowed this buggy from the mayor. I told him, I said, 'Mister Mayor, I got official business in Cottonwood and I need to take a young lady with me, a fine young lady from the East, and I need to borrow that carriage.' He said, 'Jim, I think that's a grand idea.' Yep, he was all for it. The mayor is a good man. Drinks a lot, but it just makes him jolly."

So, Inez thought, I'm riding in the mayor's carriage with the sheriff. I wish haughty Lottie could see this. They rolled out of the town and began angling down the switchbacks that traversed Cleopatra Hill to the Verde Valley floor.

"Look over there, those red rocks," the sheriff pointed northeast. "That's where Oak Creek comes out of the canyon. It's might pretty over there. And there's some good fishing up in the canyon."

"I've never been there," Inez said. "Although, I can see the rocks when the sun hits them in the afternoon."

"There's a few families living around the creek. I go on fishing trips up there in the spring and summer." He pushed up the brim of his hat and scratched his forehead. His smile reminded her of Josiah. That habit of grinning when other people talked always impressed her, like he listened and liked what he was hearing. Josiah had it and so did the sheriff. He wore a canvas jacket with his sheriff's badge pinned over the breast pocket, and he would tap the toe of his boot as he talked as if he had a song in his head.

"I used to love to fish back in South Carolina." Inez found conservation with him easy and comfortable, like she'd known him for years. His eyes would glance at her while she talked. "My father would take me to the Catawba River and we'd fish. Sometimes, we'd borrow a little boat and go way out in a cove to get the big fish."

"Oh, this ain't no boat creek, it's too small. I should take you fishing some time."

"I'd like that," Inez said.

Sheriff Jim shook his head, "What am I saying? You're a young lady. I can't go off taking you fishing. Your young man would have my hide."

"Oh, I don't have a young man. At least, not anymore."

"I'm sorry to bring it up. Onalee told me about your intended, but I thought a pretty girl like you would have been swooped up by another young man in town."

"I don't meet many marrying men at the house," she said. "They aren't there to find a wife." Then she felt embarrassed for implying the workings of the parlor house. "I mean, they come to have fun and a good meal."

The sheriff laughed a loud belly laugh that scared the mare and caused her to speed to a gallop then he had to rein her back down to a slow trot to make the curves in the trail. "I don't mean to hoot at that, but I know what goes on there."

She shifted in her seat. She didn't want to tell him anything that would get Onalee and the girls in trouble. She had been talking too freely. Lottie had warned her about that habit. Now, here she had brought up the subject of the parlor house's operations with the law. Pulling out the water jug, she offered it to the sheriff. "Here, Jim, have a drink of water."

He grinned at her and took a swig from the jug. "I think you're trying to change the subject of our talk."

"No, it's just not that interesting working in the kitchen at Onalee's."

"Is that all you do?"

The question caught her off-guard. Was he implying she was one of the girls? Was he going to arrest her, then go back and take the girls and Onalee to jail? She knew she would be too free in her talking to him. Was he was using his charm to trap her? She got mad at the thought.

"Yes, Sheriff," she tapped out her voice. "I work in the kitchen and clean up. It's better than starving to death on the streets of Jerome. You know, there isn't any vocation for a woman in the Territory. We can't work the mines, we can't farm alone, how do we survive? Is there a law to protect us and give us a way to provide for ourselves? Do you have any lady deputies?"

He laughed again, "Hell, Inez. A woman can't be a deputy. She couldn't handle the outlaws."

"Well, then," her mind calmed and she reasoned, "what am I doing on this trip? There are times when you need a woman to help out. When other women are involved, when you need someone who won't ask the wrong questions, questions that might embarrass a lady."

"Did I do that?" he asked. The sparkle had escaped his eyes.

"Yes," she admitted. "But I guess I should expect that, working at Onalee's. Honestly, I only work in the kitchen. I don't entertain."

"Onalee is a good person," he said. "She wouldn't make you do anything you didn't want to. That's why I let her alone. The law just don't apply to her and the girls—unless something gets out of hand. That Pearl can be a mess if she gets too much wine in her, but the other girls are more settled."

"Yes, but she has a good heart," Inez watched a rabbit hop across the trail ahead of the horse; its white tail just a flash going behind a rock.

"Miss Inez, I didn't mean to embarrass you. I apologize."

"Thank you," she said. How could this man, a man she barely knew, cause her emotions to swing so far and so fast? She assured herself he was only a man like Josiah, a little older, a bit more mature, experienced in the ways of the world that Josiah hadn't been, but still he brought out feelings of excitement, anger, pride, sorrow, and anticipation that she hadn't had in the months since Josiah's death. But this man was married. And he was the sheriff, a public official who talked with the mayor. What was she, an abandoned mail-order bride, having such feelings about this man? As Lottie would have said, 'Who do you think you are?'

CHAPTER
THIRTEEN

The buggy rolled across the valley and into Cottonwood. Inez liked the tone of the town, wood plank sidewalks to keep the people from walking in the dusty street, the bustle of commerce, a little girl holding her mother's hand as she crossed the avenue to a dry goods store.

She peeked around the carriage's canopy to peer at someone who brought a familiar twinge, a pang of discovery, the stitch in her moral failings. Lottie's stout frame plodded down the pine walkway in front of the post office. As the buggy came up behind her, Inez sat back so that she wouldn't be recognized, but her movement only caught the eye of Lottie because she turned to look straight at Inez. In an instant, Lottie's face changed from interest, to the narrow eyes of detection, a confused brow of the situation, then a satisfied grin of conclusion. Inez knew Lottie had jumped to a finish that had her receiving her due in the custody of the sheriff. The old busybody, Inez thought, she would love to think I am in trouble with the law. She didn't even consider I might be with him for a good reason. The thought of yelling out, 'Howdy Lottie, this is the mayor's carriage and I'm on official business with the sheriff' occurred to her, then faded. The act would be too fresh, too bold, but she smiled at the thought of setting Lottie straight.

The sheriff turned a corner and brought the buggy to a stop outside Red Dale's blacksmith barn. "Let me help you," the sheriff jumped down and offered his hand to Inez.

She smoothed her skirt and straightened her cowboy hat. Pearl had been right, she liked the clothes and the outfit made her feel capable. The thought of Lottie's stare fell away as she marched across the soft dirt behind the sheriff, her boots kicking up dust. Control, yes, that's what she felt. She knew that Sun would come with her and that Red Dale would listen to her reasoning.

They entered the dark barn and she let her eyes adjust to the dim light. Red Dale worked by a fire and anvil, banging out a door hinge. A quick glance around confirmed that Red Dale was alone.

"Howdy there, Red Dale," Sheriff Jim bellowed. "Me and Miss Inez have come to talk to you."

Red Dale looked up with a flinch as if he had been absorbed in his work and hadn't noticed them coming in. "Well, howdy there Sheriff... Miss Inez." He nodded to them and set the glowing flat piece of metal back in the fire. Sweat glistened on his bare chest and Inez felt herself blush as he pulled up the straps on his overalls to cover himself. "What do I owe the pleasure of your visit?"

"We wanted to ask a couple more questions about your young lady," the sheriff meandered over to a bench and sat down. "This Miss Sun that we are all looking for," he scratched his head, "well, we just can't figure out where she's gone." He glanced at Inez and then nodded at the place beside him on the bench. When Inez took a seat, Red Dale did too. The sheriff continued, "She's a right smart girl, that Sun. But I can't figure how she could stay out of sight for so many weeks."

Red Dale sat quiet looking at the sheriff. His eyes didn't wander from Jim's face. Inez watched. Maybe he's being polite, she thought, because the sheriff hasn't really asked him anything yet, he's just talking about Sun.

"Some people say," Sheriff Jim tapped his boot heel on the packed dirt floor, then inspected it with great interest. "Some people say that Sun has found a cohort, a friend to assist her in getting away from Zhen." He let the statement settle in the warm air of the barn like summer dust.

Getting up to grab a flannel shirt, Red Dale didn't look at them while he buttoned it. He sat back down and smiled at the sheriff. "You implying that I might have Sun hidden someplace?"

"Just repeating what I heard," the sheriff said.

Inez wanted to say something, but she didn't want to interfere with the sheriff's plan. She glanced at Jim, then back to Red Dale. Neither one seemed ready to break the silence.

The tension grew thick, so she stood without saying anything and walked to the shelves of candlestick holders, stove lids, irons, and other practical items the blacksmith made. The men still sat there looking at each other, rubbing their chin or scratching their head as if the next one to speak would spill everything he knew.

In the midst of the copper, iron, and silver, a glint of scarlet red caught her attention. A lantern of tin had been fashioned and covered with red paper, strange scrawled writing was on the paper with a picture of a frilly lizard. She knew a Chinese lantern when she saw it, but that didn't prove Sun was there. Maybe he created it to give to her when she was found. But, reckoned Inez, who drew those Chinese symbols on the paper?

She heard the men murmur a few more sentences to each other, but kept looking around the barn. She knew Sun was there, somewhere. Red Dale had stopped coming to Jerome looking for her. Those were not the actions of a man who'd lost his love, if she wasn't here, Red Dale would be out looking for her, not banging out door hinges. She heard the men laugh, then the smell hit her. Languid and thick, the air felt heavy like summertime in South Carolina, but this was November in the Arizona Territory, and Inez knew someone was cooking beyond the door in the corner, boiling gains of rice. The same smell she associated with the Chinese Corner of Jerome. A quick glance back at the men confirmed that they still talked. She eased the door open. On a small stove, fire splashed around an iron pot. Opening the door more, she saw no one in the tiny room; a wash basin and cot lined the opposite wall. To the left, a door stood open to the cold autumn air.

Inez rushed to the door, "Sun, it's me Inez." She looked in the alley behind the barn, but didn't see anyone. "Remember?" she asked the dead weeds and brush that surrounded the alley. "We want to help you get away from Zhen for good. He won't be able to lay claim to you—ever."

From behind a sugar bush, a small voice answered, "Ever?"

"The only way to settle this legally," Sheriff Jim explained, "is for you to pay Zhen the money she owes him for her ship ride here." He and Inez sat across from Red Dale and Sun, trying to convince them to let Sun go back with them.

"That sounds real simple," Red Dale said. "The only hitch is I ain't got the money. Besides, why can't you arrest Zhen for what he does to these girls?"

"Dale," the sheriff began, "Do you have any idea how many houses there are in Jerome?"

Red Dale looked down at his boots and jerked his head toward Sun and Inez.

"Well," Jim seemed to catch on, "of course you don't. But let me tell you, there are a lot of them." He leaned back, "I can't enforce the law on one house and look the other way on the others. Anyway, Zhen has them girls in a legal contract." He scratched his head; "I don't think any judge would..." he faded into thought.

Inez considered the predicament. Sun owed Zhen money for bringing her to the territory from China. He made her work in the house to pay the debt, but with what little he paid her and the expenses he deducted, she would never satisfy her obligation. Catching onto the sheriff's last statement, she understood his notion. "A judge," Inez repeated looking at Jim.

"Yep," he winked at her.

"What?" Red Dale asked.

"Well," Sheriff Jim tapped his foot. "If we told Zhen that Sun wasn't going to pay and wasn't going to work for him, his only course would be to bring out that signed contract and take her to court. And Judge Billingsley over in Prescott ain't going to be happy with the way Zhen works the girls."

Sun looked to Red Dale, then to Inez.

"I think Zhen would be more afraid of appearing in front of the judge than letting Sun go," the sheriff explained. "His illegal activities would be exposed."

"Me no go back to Zhen," Sun protested.

"No," said Inez. "You stay here, and we'll," she motioned to herself and the sheriff, "we'll make things right."

"No more Zhen?" Sun asked.

Red Dale grinned. "No more Zhen, and no more money to raise."

"I hope we can work it out this way," Jim said. "Zhen doesn't give up easy."

Inez watched the way Sun looked at Red Dale. Her eyes would go wide when he talked and she smiled and nodded with what he said.

Sun glanced back at Inez. "Married," she said and smiled.

"You two are getting married?" Inez asked.

Sheriff Jim studied Red Dale, then Sun. "You found a preacher that will marry a white man to a Chinese girl?"

"No, not yet," said Red Dale.

Noticing the look in Jim's eyes, Inez knew that would not be an easy find. The churches above everyone else, didn't like to see a white man marry outside his race. But, that didn't stop most men. Usually, no church wedding was provided. No legal documents could be written for the relationships that the miners, farmers, and trappers established with the companion of their choice. She had seen white men with Indians, Mexicans, Negroes, and Chinese. These things didn't bother her. The thought of the churches refusing to recognize the love between two people was a direct contradiction to what her mother had taught her about Jesus. The churches, even in the Territory, had drifted from the real meaning of love to encouraging differences and pitting people against their neighbors.

"If you can't find a preacher," Inez offered, "Onalee could marry you. She's a Navajo shaman."

Sheriff Jim grinned at her. "That sounds like a fine idea."

"Miss Inez," Red Dale began. "Do you think Zhen will let Sun go?"

Impressed that he had asked her opinion, she sat up straight and said, "He had better, or I'll have half of Jerome after him."

After assuring Red Dale and Sun that they would talk with Zhen, Inez began to climb into the carriage when she heard her name called.

"You there, Inez," Lottie's voice burned through the chilled air.

The thought of ignoring the call crossed Inez's mind first, then she stopped and turned to meet the pumpkin face of Lottie. "Miss Lottie, how are you?" sweetness dripped from her words.

Lottie's eyes scanned Inez, her outfit, then the sheriff. "Oh, Inez," she shook her head in dismay, "how could you come to this? I have prayed for you because I knew you were a working girl up in Jerome. Now I see the sheriff has you in his custody." She rubbed her jowls and her eyes hardened, "A sporting woman is no life for a girl such as yourself. That's what I told the ladies at church—about your downfall after leaving my influence."

"Women with idle hands and minds tend to have overactive imaginations," Inez said. "The sheriff and I are on official business. Something I can't discuss with a known gossip. Excuse me." She took Jim's hand and stepped up into the carriage.

The redness increased in Lottie's face, "Sheriff, why haven't you closed down those places instead of cavorting with harlots?"

Jim turned to look at Lottie. His cold gray eyes locked on her round face and her grim tight mouth. "Ma'am, I believe you have the impression that you enforce the laws in this county. That's a mistake. It is my responsibility to keep the peace, not yours. Also, there's a law against slander. You need to keep your opinions to yourself."

Jim tipped his hat to her and climbed into the carriage beside Inez.

The past relationship with Lottie was a topic Inez didn't want to discuss, so she just kept quiet. The sheriff only winked at her and reined the horse toward Jerome.

After leaving the town of Cottonwood, he looked at her and said, "It's past noon. I know a nice place by the river for a picnic. Are you hungry?"

"Starved," answered Inez. The morning, despite Lottie, had been exciting and being with Sheriff Jim made it more so. He was a man she admired. His sensibilities on how to handle the people he encountered displayed to her a man of thought and emotion. Not many people she'd met had that capability. Usually, all thought or all emotion ruled a person, but Jim had a balance.

He steered the horse and buggy down a slight slope to the river's edge. Under an autumn-bare sycamore, he helped her down and took the lunch basket from the back of the carriage. A flat rock near the trickling water served as a bench for their meal. Inez began to unpack the basket Mildred had loaded with food.

"Do you think Zhen will be too afraid to take Sun to court?" Inez asked.

The sheriff chewed on a chicken leg, then answered. "It's the best way I can figure to get her away. But," he bit into a biscuit, "if word gets around that she just run and he didn't do anything, all his girls will take off."

"Good," Inez said. "They can all get away from that monster."

"Well... That may be the righteous way, but Zhen ain't the type to let his business walk out the door."

Zhen would lose all the girls if the intimidation of a signed contract was taken from him. Inez considered him as a business man, a horrid business man, but still the girls were his livelihood. "He'll fight it. You're right, he won't let her go because all the girls will go."

Sheriff Jim chewed and tapped his foot while watching the river slosh across some boulders. Inez noticed a few floating branches caught against rocks, corralling autumn leaves into a tiny dam.

"Why doesn't he run his business like Onalee?" she asked.

"Not enough profit," Jim raked some baked apples onto his plate. "He takes everything the girls make."

"What if," Inez ventured, "he took part and gave them part. Maybe they would stay as real employees, not as slaves. I know back home, after the war, some of the Negroes stayed on as paid workers at the farms and plantations. At least that's what mama said. Women in the West are just like the Negroes in the South," she stood and walked to the water's edge. "There's little opportunity to make it on our own."

The sheriff nodded his head in agreement, but said nothing.

"I mean, I came out here because I had no prospects in South Carolina with my family all gone. Then I lost Josiah." She faced the river. The thought of Josiah still hurt. "Onalee and the girls took me in and gave me a job in the kitchen," she turned back to him. "That's all, I never entertain the gentlemen. I can't do that. My mama brought me up in a Christian way. That stuff is for people in love, not for recreation."

He nodded again.

"But, for a woman alone, she can't survive. I know the parlor houses aren't the best place for a woman to be, but Onalee is good to the girls and to me and Mildred. And those poor Chinese girls have even less opportunity than us white women. Why do people hate the Chinese so?"

He rubbed his chin, "They're different. They got odd ways to us. Too, they took a lot of jobs on the railroads."

"That's just because white men were too lazy to do it, or they thought they were too good for it."

"Now, you can't put us all in one bucket," he defended.

She laughed, "I didn't mean you. You are beyond most men. In fact, I don't think there's another man in the Territory that can compare to you."

Color flowed to his cheeks at the compliment. "That's a mighty nice thing to say," he said and studied his boots.

She walked back and sat down close to him on the boulder. "I mean it."

He looked up and the brim of his Stetson brushed the edge of her hat. She smiled. Jim tilted his head to the side and leaned in. His lips barely touched hers. His mustache brushed the side of her mouth. A breath closer and she met his light touch, pursing her lips to make contact with his again. His smile raked his mustache delicately against her mouth again. She smiled too, then leaned in for another light kiss.

CHAPTER FOURTEEN

Inez jumped up from the boulder. "I, I just, I'm sorry," she stammered. "Didn't mean to, I just," she turned from the sheriff to stare at the river. What had she just done? Kissed a married man? And after explaining about her upbringing and how she was not what Lottie accused her of being. Acting like a common harlot, she condemned herself.

"Now, Miss Inez," Sheriff Jim's voice soothed her. "It's my entire fault. I got caught up in the moment. You're a nice young lady, and I'm just a big old clumsy bear." He walked to where she stood at the water's edge. "Forgive me."

Her mind raged over the past few seconds. How did she go so wrong? You must take responsibility for your actions, she reminded herself. "Sheriff," she turned back to him, "it wasn't your fault. I think I said things to you that were too familiar. We don't know each other that well and, so," she tried to think of what to say next.

"You and me," Jim said, "we are both fine people, but just got caught up." He laughed and slapped a bare tree limb of the sycamore. "I mean this is such a romantic place down here at the river with the dead leaves clogging up the water."

She straightened the collar of her jacket. "Well, I reckon it's time to head back up the hill," she thought it better to not say much more about the kiss. But, talking about it and thinking about it were two entirely different things. As Jim helped her into the buggy and loaded the lunch basket on the back, Inez watched each action he made. The gait of his walk and the twitch of his mustache enthralled her, and when he climbed up beside her, he winked at her then urged the horse forward to the Jerome road.

"So," he broke the silence that had settled between them. "You like Onalee a lot don't you?"

"Yes. She's been kind and helpful to me."

"How much do you know about her?"

The question caught Inez by surprise. Onalee seemed to be open about things with her and the girls. Should she be talking to the sheriff about Onalee? Did he have other motives than just making conversation after their awkward moment by the river? "Onalee and me have talked some about her past. Like how she used to play the piano in houses and how she's a Navajo. And I know she's a berdache. What was the name she used?"

Jim nodded. "Some call them Two-Moon. The Diné call them Nádleehí. And you know what that means?"

"Yes, Onalee is a man, but he has qualities of a woman." That was about the extent of her knowledge, but she wondered where Jim was headed with the questions.

Rubbing his mouth as if not knowing where to start and trying to keep the words in, he looked at her and shrugged. "Onalee is a good person. The Diné were rounded up and put on reservations years ago. Onalee was young and had a mate, a brave called Cha-Gee, Blue Jay in English." He steered the buggy around a rut and guided the horse up the meandering road to their town perched on the side of the hill. "On the reservation, the Navajo ways were not like they used to be." He frowned a bit. "You see, Inez, white men and their Christian traditions condemned some things that no Navajo gave a second thought. I mean," he seemed to reflect on things, "just things that are between two people and really aren't anybody's business."

The sun warmed the buggy as it climbed the hill. Adjusting the brim of her hat, she kept the glare out of her eyes. She had been raised in the church and knew people who used the Bible as a sword, attacking things they didn't understand in the name of the God. "The Navajo had their own religion, didn't they?"

"Oh yes ma'am," Jim said. "A fine religion that related all things in their world. You know how the seasons and the animals and man all connect? It was that. Now, I'm a Christian man, but I got eyes and I got a heart. I know there are different ways to live in peace and," his voice softened, "in love."

Was he talking about her and him or about Onalee and Blue Jay? Inez wondered.

"My way of thinking," the sheriff continued, "and I believe the way that Jesus wanted it, is to let folks be folks and love who they love. He didn't restrict who you love, it just happens and it's nobody's business."

The talk of love sent her mind jumping. The rumor that Martha had recounted about the sheriff's wife not being around and not being the kind of wife he deserved almost brought tears to Inez's eyes. His consideration of others and kind heart were more than any woman could want. How could his wife stray? She glanced at him. His eyes stayed focused on the road as the buggy climbed the hill. What did she really know about him? He seemed fair to everyone. He accepted people and their situations. He was going to help Red Dale and Sun, something other lawmen might not have pondered too long on before dragging Sun back to Zhen. He was a friend to Onalee.

"Do you know where Blue Jay is?" she asked.

"No, but I wish I did. I know Onalee would like to find him. I had heard that he was with the Yavapai Apache, but no one has seen him in years. I think that's why Onalee is in Jerome—just in case he shows up at the reservation down the hill."

A wagon turned a bend in the road ahead of them, so Jim steered their buggy to the right side as far as he could. "Howdy, Nathan," the sheriff called to the driver of the wagon.

"Sheriff," the man waved. "Good to see you." The wagon pulled up beside them and stopped. "Just going down to Cottonwood to fetch Lizzie's mama." The man looked at Inez and tipped his hat, "Howdy ma'am."

"So, your mother-in-law is going to stay with you for a few days?" Jim asked.

Nathan sighed, "Yeah, but I'm thinking about staying at the Grand View while she's here. It would be worth the money." He laughed, then slapped the reins to get his horse moving down the road. "Keep it between the ditches and the wheels on the dirt," he called back laughing.

The sheriff chuckled, "That Nathan is a character. He complains about his wife and her mother, but I assure you they're everything to him."

"Is your mother-in-law nearby?" she asked.

"No, Stella's mother passed away a few years ago." He reached up under his hat and scratched his forehead. "Since then, Stella has been right distant. She goes to her sister's house in Prescott for visits, but I can't figure out what will make her happy."

Some man in Prescott, Inez thought. She quickly pushed the catty thought out of her mind. Here Jim was telling her about his wife and she was thinking of gossip instead of focusing on the facts. "I know losing my mama was the hardest thing that ever happened to me. I mean, a person's mama is the one person in the world that will always take care of you, the one that will love you no matter what. I left not long after she died. Sometimes I long to see her grave," tears welled up in her eyes, "just to touch the ground where she is."

Then Josiah came to her mind and how she wished he was still around, but her memory of him wasn't as strong as it had been. They had only known each other for a short time. The shock had softened, but the hurt was still as hard as ice. Losing him had stunned her. Was that devastation lessening? The thought of him or sound of his name still ushered in pain, but memories of him didn't come as often as they had.

The sheriff glanced over at her. "It must be lonely for a girl like you here."

"Sometimes," she admitted. "But like I said, Onalee and the girls are good to me."

The crunch of rocks under the wagon wheels replaced their conversation. Josiah and the sheriff engaged her thoughts. Josiah the man who had asked her to come to the Territory, sight unseen, ready to make her his wife, and build a life with her. Then there was Sheriff Jim, married to a wandering woman, a steady and caring man, but married. She kept coming back to the marriage. Red Dale and Sun wanted to marry, but probably couldn't find a preacher to do it. Onalee and Blue Jay would never be able to marry in the ways of the white people. Now, a marriage that seemed to be over, but still intact by the ways of the territorial government, kept her at bay from Jim.

She breathed in the cool air and glanced at Jim. He hummed as he guided the horse and carriage up the road like he was the happiest man alive and just driving that old brown mare in the right direction was the most important thing in his life. They settled into silence until they saw the first buildings of Jerome.

"What are you going to say to Zhen?" Inez asked.

The sheriff shook his head, "Still figuring on that one. Red Dale don't have the money to pay her debt. Zhen won't let it go. I reckon the best thing to say is that he would have to take her to court to enforce the agreement, but remind him that the judge will find out what he makes the girls do to repay their expenses, and he'll end up in jail." He thought for a moment. "It would be best for Red Dale and Sun to leave this part of the Territory."

After they arrived in town, Sheriff Jim stopped the horse and buggy at Onalee's front door, then helped Inez down. "Thank you Miss Inez for making the trip with me. You helped me find Sun and talked some sense into Red Dale. Now, I just got to handle this the best I can."

She wondered if he would bring up the kiss. Standing so close, she wanted to touch him, maybe a handshake, a hug, something to say good-bye. But, then she didn't want a good-bye, she wanted him to stay there, to spend more time together. She held out her hand. He looked at it, then took her hand in his and raised it to his lips. He gently kissed the back of her hand.

He winked at her, "Saw that once in a play. That's how a gentleman says 'so long' to a lady."

A short laugh was Inez's response. She couldn't find words to reply, so she picked up the lunch basket and water jug and headed to the door. She stopped and looked back at him: the tall, handsome sheriff grinning at her, one boot resting the buggy step. "Sheriff," she called, "it was my pleasure." She had heard Pearl say this to a customer once. "Now, you come back and see us real soon." It was her best flirt, a little bit southern belle and a smidgen western parlor house. She closed the door behind her, then collapsed on the sofa.

"So, what happened next?" Pearl pried more details from Inez.

"Nothing," Inez smiled. "But it was perfect. I mean, he is considerate and handsome and..." She faded off into the memory of the kiss by the creek.

Pearl bounced off the bed and began brushing her hair. "The next encounter is all important," she said. "Play it coy, but don't let him forget what happened. That hand kiss should be required next time he sees you. When you say good-bye next time, offer your hand to him." Pearl turned around and grabbed the ties to her corset and shook them at Inez. "Help please."

"Breath in," Inez instructed and she pulled the strings tight.

"Make them secure, but easy for the gentlemen to get loose," Pearl laughed. She slipped her satin dress on over her head, then brushed her hair again.

Already dressed for supper, Inez smoothed out Pearl's bedspread and adjusted the oil lamp wick to lower the light. "I need to get back to the kitchen. Now, don't go repeating what I told you. Mildred will have my hide if she knows the sheriff kissed me."

Pearl turned and smiled at her.

"He did it, didn't he?" Inez asked Pearl. "I mean I didn't dream it, did I?"

"No, Miss Inez, you done hooked the sheriff." Pearl kidded her. "Now, if it had been me down there by the river with Jim, that kiss would have led to other things." Wicked eyebrows wiggled at Inez. "Things that a good man like the sheriff has never imagined."

"Oh, stop it." Inez giggled. She started to open the door, then hesitated. "Like what?"

CHAPTER FIFTEEN

"Company, ladies," Inez announced. She stood at the bottom of the staircase as the girls made their entrance for the evening. Lois descended the stairs first, a regal woman greeted by the admiring nods of the gentlemen. Following Lois, Molly shimmered in a gown to match her brassy curls and attitude. Toy wore a simple dress, almost child-like in her appearance and that was her appeal—a waif of a girl who would charm the toughest of men into purring kittens. Inez had queued them in this order to provide variety and add drama for the gentleman. Subdued to flashy to childlike, then to exotic Frenchy; a cigarette dangled from her lips as she sashayed down the steps. A tight skirt and low-cut ruffled blouse revealed her European persona. Just as Pearl demanded, she would be the last girl to make a grand entrance. Pearl stood at the top of the staircase, one hand on the railing, the other on her hip. Her long black hair gleamed in the lamp light, and the ruby satin gown hugged her curves and its wide sloping neckline revealed the alabaster of her breasts. With each step down the staircase, Pearl's chest jiggled in the push-up corset. Inez watched and worried that the contraption they had created to add the bounce might be too much and that one of Pearl's breasts might actually pop out of the dress. Inez had fashioned two clock springs under a felt liner to lift and liven each breast. Now, the lift seemed extreme and Pearl's chest was too lively. Although Pearl descended the staircase without incident, Inez knew her new contraption required more work. Several gentlemen flocked around Pearl and her vivacious breasts. The other girls talked with the men and began pouring drinks and lighting cigars.

The accomplished laughter of Lois cued Inez that the men were settling in and choosing their girls. Lois could laugh at a gentleman's joke no matter how stale or humorless she found it—a true skill for a girl. Men appreciate women who find them entertaining and delightful, she had told Inez. So that was Lois' method, flattery and imparting an air of importance on the gentleman.

Going into the kitchen, Inez assisted Mildred in preparing the beef roast. Mildred tested the carrots and potatoes with a fork.

"Mildred?" she called to get her attention.

"Yes, Miss Inez," Mildred didn't turn her bulky frame from the oven.

"How old is too old for a parlor house girl?"

"Child, them girls work till they can't give it away." She slid the roast back in the oven and looked at Inez. "Why do you ask?"

"Lois," she began, then reconsidered bringing up the subject with Mildred. Not that Mildred was known for repeating conversations, but she tended to blurt things out without thinking. Inez didn't want Lois to know she had noticed how the gentlemen acted. "Well, never mind."

"No, now you got something on your mind about Lois and her age," Mildred added more coal to the oven. "In my time, a girl knew when to move on or quit. Lois hasn't been here that long. Yes, she's older than the other girls, but she's still fairly new to the gentlemen in these parts."

The smell of the roasted beef and vegetables in the warm kitchen relaxed Inez. The cold November wind rattled the windows as it swirled up Cleopatra Hill. "Maybe it ain't a thing to worry over," Inez said. "But, I noticed that Lois is usually the last girl picked. She's so sweet and kind-hearted—"

"That ain't what them men is looking for," Mildred interrupted with a short laugh. "Hell, a girl can be as mean as a striped-ass snake, but if she's pretty, she gets customers. Take your friend Pearl. She gets them lined up for her."

She knew the women would not always stay together, new ones would arrive and old ones would go, but the comfort of Onalee's family was something Inez wanted to preserve. "Where would a girl go if the gentlemen no longer showed an interest?"

"Another house, maybe," Mildred said. "Usually, the older ones move down the order where the men ain't so picky: parlor house to saloon to hurdy gurdy house to the cribs to the street."

The thought of any of the girls having to work in a saloon or hurdy gurdy disheartened Inez, but the thought of one of them in a crib or on the street terrified her. "Marriage," she blurted out. "A girl could get married and leave the house."

"I been here for twenty years," Mildred pulled the roast from the oven and slid in two apple cobblers. "Not once have I seen a parlor house girl marry a customer. Now, when the town was young and so was I," she winked at Inez, "girls was scarce as hen's teeth. That's when the men wanted wives and would take a soiled dove. But, look at yourself," she waved a dripping spoon in Inez's direction. "Why, that young man of yours sent all the way to South Carolina for you instead of marrying one of the sporting girls. Men likes 'em untouched, or at least not one where his mining buddy was a former customer of his new bride."

Inez stood by the chattering window and pressed her forehead against the cold pane, hoping to dull her worries. How perfect it would be if the girls all found husbands to take them away from this work, she thought.

"You got a headache?" Mildred called.

"No, ma'am."

"Then get over here and let's start serving the customers."

As the men dined and the women ordered more drinks, Inez noticed the man next to Lois. A new customer to the house, he wore a nice jacket and had his hair trimmed short, but an oversize mustache gave him a bit of an unkempt look. What caught her eye was the lack of attention he was paying Lois and the amount of attention he focused on her. Customers in the past had asked for her, but Onalee made it known that Inez worked only in the kitchen. The new gentleman would discover that fact too.

Beckoned with a raise of a wine glass, Inez approached the table and filled Frenchy's goblet. Then, she went back to her station in the corner and noted the order in her book. The gentlemen drank well; the girls even better. The talk and laughter at the table increased

as the meal completed. Mildred brought out the apple cobbler and
Inez scooped ice cream over each serving.

Just as she served the mustached man sitting with Lois, he leaned
back and slapped her bottom. "How about you for dessert, Missy?"
he laughed.

"No sir," she backed away from his reach.

"Honey," Lois took the man's hand, "Inez is our kitchen help."
She placed his hand over her heart and smiled. "I'm all the dessert
you need."

He laughed again, "You're a sweet thing, but just a bit stale. I'd
like that fresh young girl."

One of the regular customers with Toy spoke up, "Look here.
Miss Inez ain't available," then he stood up from the table, "and I
reckon you need to apologize to Miss Lois."

Tugging at his hand, Toy tried to get him to sit back down.
"Whitney, that's alright. Everything is fine."

Mustache Man pushed back his chair, almost turning it over and
rose to his feet. "Sir, this is not your affair."

The men stared at each other as Inez backed into the corner. She
caught a movement from the corner of her eye as Mildred pushed
open the kitchen door with Onalee following.

"Gentlemen," Onalee's baritone voice boomed through the
dining room. She walked over to the mustached man and offered
her hand. He looked at the size of Onalee's hand—larger than his,
then reluctantly took it. She guided him into the parlor, and Whitney
left his place with Toy and followed.

The dining table resumed its merriment. Neither Toy nor Lois
seemed upset by the men challenging each other, but Inez wandered
over toward the curtain separating them from the parlor.

"I will not have arguments in this house," Onalee's stern voice
stated. "The available girls are presented, and no other staff is
offered."

Inez heard no other voices. The men were being awfully quiet.

Onalee continued, "Mr. Ridley, you have two options: go back
into the dining room and continue your evening after apologizing
to Lois and to Inez, or I will collect your bill and send you on your

way."

"Now wait a minute," the mustached Mr. Ridley said, "I ain't finished. I intend to get upstairs."

The rustle of Onalee's deerskin smock passed close by the curtain and Inez stepped back to keep from being discovered.

"My girls," Onalee said, "work only with gentlemen. You need to prove yourself to me and to the girls, otherwise," her voice became deep and threatening, "I will handle you myself."

Inez fought the urge to look through the drapes, Onalee sounded like a man, a threatening man, and she wanted to see if Onalee had physically transformed. Onalee was no longer 'Mother' as the girls liked to call her, but an aggressive male protecting his family.

Silence settled behind the curtain. Then mustache man stammered, "Alright, I reckon I was out of line. I should apologize to the ladies."

Whitney, Toy's customer, spoke up, "That's the least you could do. Miss Lois is a fine woman and you insulted her. You probably scared little Inez half to death grabbing her. This ain't no whore house, it's a fine establishment. Why, it's a second home to some of these men. You treat it as a home."

"That's settled," Onalee's voice calmed to its normal tone, soothing and melodic. "Now, let's join the ladies and act like gentlemen. Since we are," Onalee assured them, "all gentlemen."

Moving away from the drapes and busying herself with her account book, Inez waited for them to re-enter the dining room. Onalee pulled the curtain back, allowing Mr. Ridley and Whitney to enter first, then she followed and stood next to Inez as the men took their seats.

Ridley tapped his wine class with his fork to gain the attention of the table. "I'd like to apologize to Miss Lois and Miss Inez for my actions. They were completely uncalled for. Miss Lois is a beautiful and gracious lady. Miss Inez," he looked to her, "I'm sorry to have rough handled you."

Unconsciously, Inez leaned into Onalee, then she felt Onalee's arm move around her shoulder. Warmth and security filled her as if both her parents were there to protect her so far from her childhood home.

✕ ✕ ✕

"I'm so nervous," Lois paced the rooms above the dress shop. "Inez, will you go with me to the Junction tomorrow to fetch Jared? His train pulls in about nine o'clock." She picked up a vase of flowers, searched the room for a more appropriate place, then set them back in the original position. Her simple house dress fit her well, but was far more modest then the gown she had worn at the parlor house the night before.

"Of course," Inez said. "I look forward to meeting him." She finished dusting the rooms they had turned into Lois' home while her son visited. A parlor, two bedrooms, and a small kitchen had been fashioned from the storage area over the shop. The winter sun streamed through the front windows helping the coal stove warm the space. The slight hum of Martha's sewing machine downstairs stirred the air. The shop had become quite busy since opening; they had several gowns to make and women continued to come in to be fitted for new dresses or to have Martha alter existing ones. The slight, stiff scent of dye hung in the air from the bolts of new fabric stored in a back room.

"We should cook something in your kitchen tonight," Inez suggested. "Just to give the place a lived-in smell."

A creaking of wood from the outside stairs alerted them. Lois opened the door to Onalee.

"I'm glad we finished carrying furniture up those steps," Onalee said almost out of breath. "Your place looks inviting. Now, Lois, I want you to relax and enjoy your son's visit. The house can get along without you for a few days. You can help Martha with the shop so Jared can witness your profession as a dressmaker. If you need anything, send Martha to the house for us." She turned around and inspected the finished rooms. "Looks like you are ready to be mother of your own house," she winked at Lois.

"Thank you," Lois said. "I'd like to have Inez ride with me to the train station tomorrow, if that's okay?"

"Yes, of course," Onalee said. "I should have suggested it myself." She patted Lois on the shoulder, then as if giving the action a second thought, pulled Lois to her in a hug. The deerskin sleeves of Onalee enveloping Lois' deep blue calico intertwined cultures and lives.

Tears welled up in Inez's eyes. This is family, she thought. Helping each other, even in a charade to fool a son about his mother's life. But, she considered, it's just for a short time and the truth can hurt a young boy.

The house customers, shop clerks, delivery men, and even Sheriff Jim had bought into the plan.

Lois was officially a dress shop girl. No one would say different.

CHAPTER SIXTEEN

Inez slapped the reins against the flanks of the mare, driving the wagon up the hill.

Beside Inez, Lois sat and fiddled with the ribbon of her bonnet. "I hate wearing bonnets," she said. "They make me feel like an old woman."

Inez glanced at her and had to admit that Lois looked older in the plain dress, heavy coat, and wide-brimmed bonnet. Amazing, Inez thought, what a notion clothes place on a person. From regal parlor house girl to dowdy mama with just a change of clothes.

The attire Inez had settled into since her trip with Sheriff Jim consisted of her cowboy hat, a long skirt, and now a denim jacket that had belonged to Josiah. The jacket smelled like juniper and tobacco smoke, scents she associated with Josiah and his little plot of land, and she loved wearing it even though she had to roll up the sleeves. It kept the chill away on early mornings.

The sun peeked over the mountain chasing away the shadows. As the morning broadened, the top of Mingus Mountain glowed as the sunlight slid down the steep slope. Rolling over the road, climbing Cleopatra Hill, Inez welcomed the sun to warm them on their journey to Jerome Junction. The prospect of meeting Jared intrigued her. She had never thought of Lois as a mother, so she was curious to see what kind of boy he was. Did he have his mother's looks? Was he kind and gentle? Would she be able to see hints of his father?

"How long has it been," Inez asked, "since you last saw Jared?"

Lois pulled the collar of her coat up to her chin. "A long time. I reckon two years—why, he's almost a man. But, we write to each other every week." She glanced down at her lap and let the conversation wane.

A young coyote trotted across the road ahead of them, his bushy yellow-brown tail held down in cautious study of the approaching wagon. Watching him watching them, Inez wondered what he thought of the two women traveling up the mountain: her in a cowboy hat, boots, and a man's coat, and Lois in her 'mother' outfit of gingham and calico. Almost as if they were both playing roles meant for others. But, Inez felt stronger, more in control of her destiny. Being asked to accompany Lois on the trip to the Junction thrilled Inez. She wasn't just a little girl who didn't know the proper way to act or speak—as Lottie had told her so often, but now she was a valuable and important part of the lives of these women.

The young coyote skulked off into a thicket of dead manzanita. The sun's rays met their wagon as they topped the hill and continued up the mountain. The smelter's smoke had strangled most of the saplings and brush above Jerome, now the larger junipers and pinyon pines drooped in pallid sighs.

The copper mines brought them jobs and each other, but at the same time decocting so much life from the people and land. Josiah's life had been claimed by the mines, so had Lottie's husband Sam. The images of the mine accident that took Sam still haunted Inez. She thanked the Lord that she hadn't seen Josiah pulled from the mine, crushed and lifeless. The dying vegetation along the road only brought back those memories of death. She wiped her eyes with the rolled up sleeve of her coat.

"You alright?" Lois asked her.

"Just a little road dust in my eyes," she explained. She wanted to get her mind off death and all the troubles that clung to it, so she focused on the rising sun and the ravens floating on the warming gusts from the valley below. "Jared will be tired from riding that train so long. I remember coming out here on the train and I was plum worn out by the time I reached the Junction, then I had to meet Josiah. It's a wonder that he didn't take one look at me and walk on by, get in the wagon, and never look back," she laughed.

Lois rolled her eyes, "Now, Inez, that Josiah wouldn't have done that. I'm sure you were the prettiest thing he'd seen in years. You know, you could make some good money at the house."

"No," Inez shook her head. "My mama taught me that stuff is between a husband and wife."

"Honey, it's not just for making babies," Lois patted her on the knee and giggled. "Why, sometimes it's right enjoyable."

Thoughts of Josiah came back. She had worried about that night in his tent, but now she was glad she had stayed with him. That memory kept her sane at times, she considered them married since they were committed to each other and the marriage was planned. Just no official certificate to prove their love, no legal document to allow her to collect his death pension, no piece of paper to allow her to own that sacred plot of land where they had dreamed of raising a family. The old coat and his memories were all she had left.

"...then some are so sweet," Lois talked on. "Once a gentleman brought me flowers and chocolates like we were courting. Oh, I get gifts of lacy undergarments or other provocative attire, but those are really for the gentleman. The flowers and chocolates were mine, just for me with not a thought about himself or his own pleasure." She leaned back on the bench of the wagon, gazing at the blue sky, "It's not a bad life, Inez. There are nuggets of gold in them copper miners. Of course, we work in a nice house that draws in gentlemen. I once worked in a hurdy-gurdy down in Bisbee. That was an enlightening experience. We'd dance and dance, then some of those big ol' bumbling ranch hands and miners would try to dance with us. Well, my feet never had been stomped so much. I got so that as soon as one of them boys came toward me with a skip in his step, I'd pull him off to the bartender to buy me a drink," she raised her pointed-toed boots up and inspected them. "That saved my feet and made some money for the place."

Lois talked on about the men and her friends she'd made at different jobs. Onalee's house was by far the nicest place she'd worked. They rounded a bend in the road and saw the small scattering of buildings that made up Jerome Junction. Several wagons assembled at the train station waited for the train's arrival.

"Now, Lois," Inez warned, "our subjects of conversation need to stick with dress making, fashions, local gossip about the respectable ladies, and Jared's schooling. You are a dress shop girl, not a parlor house lady."

"I know, I know. It will be so wonderful to see him. Last time, we met at my aunt's house in Saint Louis. Before that, I'd make my way back East to visit him at school or at my sister's house."

"I wasn't aware you had a sister," Inez realized how little of Lois' family situation she knew.

"Yes, two sisters and my old aunt are still alive. They don't know what I do either. We never discuss it."

They stopped the wagon at the watering trough to let the mare drink, and the ladies went into the station to check on the train's schedule. As Lois talked with the man at the ticket window, Inez walked about the station. She opened the door to the platform and looked down the tracks, no train. She glanced in the other direction and saw a small wiry Chinaman. Wind and dust blew across the platform, stinging her eyes. Squeezing them shut and open again, she focused on the little man. A chill shot through her. The sausage biscuits she'd had for breakfast threatened to climb back up her throat. Ducking her head back in the station, she prayed Zhen hadn't seen her. What was he doing here? Would he remember her and Lois? Would he call her a whore like he had that night when they saved Sun from his grasp? What would Jared think if he saw Zhen staring at them? She searched the station for Lois and found her admiring her image in a mirror at the door.

"I just saw Zhen out on the platform," Inez managed to say while calming her rapid breathing.

"Still yourself, Honey," Lois stroked her shoulder. "That crazy Chinaman is here?"

"Yes, ma'am." Inez pulled Lois to a corner. "We just need to stay clear of him."

Lois sighed and patted Inez on the shoulder, "Look at us. We don't look like Onalee's girls. He'll never recognize us. Besides, he won't give us no trouble, he's a Chinaman. These men," she motioned to the ranchers and mine company men around the station, "would tar and feather a Chinaman that lifted a hand to two white women."

She knew Lois was right, but the prospect of a quarrel with Zhen didn't appeal to her, especially with Jared arriving. "I wonder what Zhen is doing here?"

"Probably getting a load of rice. I never seen people eat so much rice as those Chinese." She sat down on a bench and patted the place beside her. "Come sit down Inez, you're making me nervous."

She took the seat next to Lois, sighed, and watched the door to see if Zhen would come into the station. Then, she pulled her long braid of hair from under her coat and inspected the color. Pearl had braided Inez's hair for the ride to the Junction and had commented on the color fading. The orange marmalade had paled to corn meal yellow, but streaks of orange remained. Pearl offered to re-dye it, but Inez wasn't sure if she wanted to take the risk. What would she be this time? Orange, lemon, strawberry, or grape? She contemplated Pearl's skills as a hair dresser as she studied the end of the braid.

"Inez," Lois took the braid out of her hand, "your hair looks fine. It feels a little stiff, but that's just from the dye. We'll wash it with beer when we get back, that will help soften it."

The door opened from the street, and a tall man with shiny black hair, slicked back behind his ears, entered the station. He held his hat in his left hand, and his right hand thumb hooked on a low slung gun belt. His confident swagger and invading stare caused Inez to lose her attention on her braid and watch him move across the station.

"That man," Lois whispered, "is a man who could teach even me a thing or two about the art of love."

The man's eyes stayed on them and he nodded a respectful 'hello' as his pace never slowed across the floor to the ticket window. He seemed a man with a purpose, an important intention. The gun belt set him apart from the mine company men. He didn't possess the worn and sun-weary look of the ranchers, but he wasn't a merchant. The prospects ran through Inez's mind as she watched. She watched to see what he would do next.

"He's a handsome one," Lois nudged her.

"Interesting," Inez said. "I see people like that. You know, people that don't seem to fit the place they're in. And I wonder about them. Where did he come from? What was he thinking when he picked that blue shirt to wear? As cold as it is, where is his jacket? Why did he look at us?"

Lois interrupted, "Cause we're pretty ladies. Miss Inez, are you fascinated by that man?"

"No," she said. "It's just a game I play to pass the time. I see someone like him, someone unlike the other people, then I wonder about what makes him different."

As the ticket agent talked, the man looked toward the door that led to the trains, slipped the agent some money, but didn't receive a ticket back. He walked out to the platform without another glance around the station.

"I'll be right back," Inez told Lois. A dusty window revealed the man talking to Zhen. What does he have to do with that crazy Chinaman? They talked, and Zhen motioned toward the railroad tracks, then back toward the road to Jerome. She wished she could hear what transpired between the man and Zhen. It wasn't the gun belt or his association with Zhen that bristled Inez, but the power the man emanated. She had seen plenty of men wearing guns, but usually they were young and trying to impress girls. Few men really needed to carry guns on their hips. Most had a rifle on their saddle or kept one on the wagon, more for wild animals than for shooting people. Sheriff Jim wore a gun as lawmen do—wore it like an extension of himself. That was the difference here, Inez decided, this man was familiar with his gun just like Sheriff Jim. The gun was both expertly and often used. She could tell by the way the man ignored it. Most men would be nervous, touching it all the time, glancing down at it. Zhen was doing that now, stealing a look at the holster and gun as they talked. I wonder, she thought, if he's a lawman? She dismissed the idea because she knew Zhen wouldn't associate with the law.

Both men turned toward the track. Inez heard the train whistle, then the rumble of the engine.

Lois joined her at the window. "That's Jared's train. I'm getting jumpy. Do I look alright?"

Inez reassured her, "You are pretty as a picture. Jared will be so happy to see you."

The women went out to the platform to wait for the train to arrive. Inez led Lois to a far post away from the mysterious man and Zhen, but she watched them as best she could from her position. As the train neared, Zhen turned to catch Inez looking straight at him. She quickly glanced away, but observed him from his reflection in the station's window. He said something to the man and they both turned to look at Inez and Lois. They didn't continue talking, but just stared.

Zhen couldn't recognize them, she figured. Her in her cowboy hat, Josiah's jacket, and long skirt, and Lois in her calico and bonnet, but he continued to scrutinize them as if they meant trouble.

The train rumbled into the station and the brakes squealed it to a slow stop. The conductor jumped from one of the passenger cars and set a wooden step at the door of the car and began helping people off the train.

Zhen and the man walked to the conductor, said a few words to him, and waited by his side. Then, Inez saw what they had come to collect. Two young Chinese girls nervously stepped off the train. Immediately, Zhen took each one by the hand and jabbered something in loud Chinese. The girls kept their gaze down, but nodded. He handed the conductor some money, then with the mysterious man leading the way, they started for the station.

"There he is," Lois pulled on Inez's sleeve.

A tall, thin boy stepped down from the train. His gray wool jacket seemed a little too large for him, and his black trousers stopped short of his ankles as if he had grown several inches in height since the pants were hemmed. Gangly arms carried two canvas bags, while he jerked his head back to the left to throw a lock of coffee-brown hair out of his eyes.

Lois waved and hurried toward him, "Jared!"

That's when Inez saw the resemblance. He broke into a large smile when he saw his mother and his eyes sparked, just as Lois' did when she became excited. The bags dropped to the platform floor and he hugged his mother with teenage enthusiasm and lanky limbs.

Sniffing back a tear, Inez knew she was emotional today, missing Josiah, now missing her own mother. The sight of the boy and his mother, reunited, happy to be in each other's presence, delighted her, but she stood back to let them enjoy their hellos.

Lois held out her hand to beckon Inez to their reunion. "Jared," she said, "this is my friend Inez."

He nodded, "Pleased to meet you." He gazed her up and down, before turning back to his mother. "Does Inez work with you?"

"Yes," Lois said. "We work at the dress maker's. Although, Inez has a couple of jobs. You might not see her there often." She hooked her arm in his while he grabbed one of his bags. Inez picked up the other. The smoke from the idling train puffed across their path and coated them with the odor of cinder. Lois coughed and waved her hand in front of her face as she would when a gentleman would light a penny cigar in the parlor.

Ahead of them, Zhen and the man corralled the Chinese girls into a buggy. The man mounted his horse and followed Zhen down the road toward Jerome.

Lois and Jared continued talking while Inez placed his bags in the back of the wagon. "Oh," Jared noticed Inez struggling with one of the bags. "Allow me. You shouldn't be lifting that."

"I can get it," she insisted, but he was up in the back of the wagon moving the bag before she could finish. "Thank you. You are quite a gentleman."

He blushed a bit and looked at his mother.

Lois giggled, "Yes, he's always been a helpful boy."

"Mother, I'm not a little boy anymore." He stood up straight and towered over Inez.

"Excuse me, kind sir," Lois bowed. "He's a helpful young man."

He glanced at Inez with a shy grin, then jumped off the back of the wagon to help his mother up to the bench. Inez hiked up her skirt and stepped over the seat to sit next to Lois. Claiming his place to the left of Lois, Jared reached for the reins just as Inez did.

"I can handle the wagon," she said trying not to sound too bossy, too much like Lottie.

"I wouldn't hear of it," he said and gently pulled the leather tethers toward him.

"No, thank you. The old mare is used to my direction," Inez explained. "I'd rather lead her." The less than subtle implication that as a woman she shouldn't be behind the reins irritated her. She tugged back.

"Now, children," Lois held up her hands. "No need to argue over this. Jared, let Inez take control, she knows the mare and the road."

He released the reins with a long sigh, "Alright, but I feel peculiar letting a girl steer the wagon."

Inez stuck out her chin and whacked the leather leads to get the horse going with a jolt. She had two reasons for wanting to take the reins, first to show Jared that she was capable and to allow Zhen and the man to get far enough ahead so that there would be no unexpected encounters on the road to Jerome.

CHAPTER SEVENTEEN

"He must have something to do with those poor Chinese girls," Inez sat across from Sheriff Jim. The sheriff had his office in the front of the jail, and it consisted mainly of a pine desk, a gun cabinet, and shelves stacked with papers.

"Strangers come to town all the time," Jim explained, "for mine work, gambling, drinking, and women. Just because he met up with Zhen at the train station doesn't mean he's a slave trader."

She knew she had reached a conclusion that not everyone would make, but she hoped Jim would be more concerned about the mysterious man from the station. Since they had returned to Jerome, she hadn't seen him or Zhen again. But, she and Lois had taken Jared to the apartment over the dressmaker's shop, and that wasn't a section of town that Zhen frequented. The nagging sensation of building trouble ached in her head. Tension seemed to fill every encounter. Was it just her? Was she supposing more dramatic situations than what really existed?

"Jim." She leaned in toward the desk to keep the conversation confidential, since one of the deputies worked in the back room, "I honestly believe that man is a danger. If you had seen him... and you will, you'll have the same reaction. I mean the way he carried that gun and the strut in his step... That man is cocky. He's got the confidence of a gun fighter." She said it, the worry she had. Slave trading of the Chinese girls, that was Zhen's vocation, but the man he met at the Junction was in another business, a business to settle scores. And Inez worried that Zhen had plans to reclaim Sun.

Leaning back in his chair, Jim scratched his head and stared at the wall.

Inez waited for his thoughts.

"It wouldn't surprise me," he began, "that Zhen hired a bounty hunter to find Sun. Now, all this is speculation. Neither you or me know anything about this man." He looked at the same place on the wall across from his desk—his 'thinking spot,' Inez guessed.

His grey eyes shifted from the wall to Inez. A tremble traveled down her body from the intensity of his stare. She kept her gaze on him, but said nothing. He didn't blink. The seconds ticked away on the wall clock, but the time seemed to stall for Inez. She studied his short dark hair with flecks of grey mixed in, his mustache trimmed slightly above his lip, then the memory of kissing those lips and the tickle of the mustache brought a smile to her.

Her movement must have brought him out of his contemplation because he blinked and then rubbed his eyes as if just waking up.

"I need to meet this man, but I want you to stay away from him and from Zhen," he stood to open the door for Inez.

"But what about Sun and Red Dale?" she whispered to keep the secret of Sun's location. "If we found her with him, surely a bounty hunter would look to Red Dale first."

"That's why I'm heading to Cottonwood," he retrieved his hat from the peg by the door. "After you, Miss Inez." He bowed as he held the door for her.

"Let me go with—" she started.

"No, ma'am." He placed his hand gently on her back as they walked out the door. "You stay away from this. If I need your assistance with," he lowered his voice since they were outside on the street, "that certain lady, I'll come fetch you."

As she walked back toward Onalee's house, she wondered about Zhen and the man. She stopped at the corner of Main Street and Jerome Avenue, looked down the hill toward the Chinese district, then she checked back to see if Jim was within sight. I'll walk by, she thought, just to see whatever there might be to see.

Like all of Jerome, the Chinese district clung to the side of the hill with a few rickety buildings selling goods specifically for the foreign clientele, a whitewashed building housed a restaurant with harsh smells billowing from the back door, then there was Zhen's place, by far the nicest structure in the district. Zhen's two-story business was built of wood like most of Jerome, but a brightly painted sign on the front announced "Mr. Zhen's Chinese Laundry" in English. The other Chinese businesses had signs written in their own language. Inez could only guess their trade by looking at what was displayed in the windows.

In Zhen's window, a couple of girls scrubbed sheets in a big wash tub. Drawn curtains concealed the windows of the second story. No customers entered or left the building, for mid-afternoon, not much laundry business transpired at Zhen's.

She pulled the collar of Josiah's coat up around her ears to abate the brisk wind. Still scrubbing in the window, the girls seemed to work hard. They weren't as efficient or thorough as she and Lottie had been with their laundress duties, but then, Inez reminded herself, this was not the girls' primary means of making money.

A little Chinese man passed by keeping his eyes down; his hair, braided into a long pigtail, swung back and forth with his quick stride. The population of the Chinese district seemed to be men of all ages and girls. She didn't notice many older women or women with children which reinforced Jerome being a working town more than a family place.

Searching the people on the street, Inez tried to locate the man from the station or Zhen. They must be inside, she thought. Did she want to go into Zhen's place? What would she say to them? Officially, the business was a laundry, so she could take something to be cleaned. How, she considered, could I find that man and discover what he knows about Sun?

Across the street, a white man came out of the door of Zhen's place, and Inez stepped back close to a storefront to help hide herself. His suit jacket looked pressed, but he glanced around as if embarrassed to be seen leaving the establishment. It wasn't the potential bounty hunter, but one of the mine officials. The girls in the window with their wash tub stopped scrubbing and waved good-bye to him as he hurried down the street.

Leaving the Chinese district, she wondered how many girls

Zhen had in there. Were they all enslaved or did some of them stay because they liked the work? She decided to concentrate on Sun then worry about the others later. One thing at a time, her mother had always said when Inez became too distracted with what life had to offer her. She climbed the hill back toward Main Street and glimpsed Sheriff Jim riding down the road toward Cottonwood. A step back to the safety of a doorway hid her from possible discovery. He hadn't seen her coming from Zhen's, for which she was glad. Zhen and the mysterious man had a plot going, and she ran potential evil designs through her head each time coming to a conclusion where the sheriff foiled their efforts. He was a hero, her hero. As she turned the corner on Main Street, she heard a horse's gallop slow to a trot just behind her.

"Miss Inez," the sheriff's voice startled her, "you stay away from Zhen's place."

She turned to find Jim looking down at her from his mount on the horse. "How'd you get around here so fast?" she asked, amazed he had gone around the block so quick.

"Never you mind that. Now run on home. I got work to do and I can't be worrying about you getting into trouble." He winked at her.

"Okay, I was just walking," she sashayed her best imitation of Frenchy's walk toward Main. "Can't a girl stroll down the street without the county's deputy sheriff harassing her?" She turned to him and raised one eyebrow to emphasize the question.

The horse trotted up next to her. "Well, ma'am, most girls can, but some are known to be feisty and think they are deputies themselves and try to rid the town of bad men."

"The only bad man I know is following me," she flirted.

He laughed and bent down from the horse to say in a quiet voice, "If we weren't in the middle of town right now, I'd kiss you." With that, he straightened up, tipped his hat to her, and spurred the horse to a gallop up the street.

Stunned, she just stood there and smiled.

✗ ✗ ✗

"Inez," Martha beckoned from her sewing machine. "Please bring me some of that blue silk. You know, the damask."

Still in a giddy fog from her encounter with Jim, she didn't hear Martha. The people walking past the dress shop window intrigued her, or was she really hoping he would ride by on his way back from Cottonwood? Either way, she felt warm and settled there at the front table of the shop.

"Inez?" Martha asked again.

"Oh, her mind's gone off somewhere," Lois stopped pinning a paper pattern onto a piece of olive green velvet. "Jared," she called, "fetch out that bolt of blue silk with a rose pattern in it."

Jared emerged from the back room with the bolt of fabric riding on his shoulder. He placed it on the table next to Martha. "I finished the storage room. Can I go roam around town now?"

"I don't know if I want you alone in a town you don't know," Lois said.

"Oh Mother," he plopped down on a chair, long legs splayed out in despair. "I traveled across the country to see you. I think I can walk around this town on my own."

Lois threw a thimble at Inez to get her attention. "Dream girl, you want to show Jared around town?"

"But you need me here," Inez said and shuffled a stack of orders.

"Go on," Martha urged. "I have plenty to keep me and Lois busy, but if we get a flood of customers this afternoon, I'll send up a smoke signal to bring you back."

"Yeah, come on Inez," Jared stood and grabbed his hat.

Inez figured there was no reason to expect to see Jim ride by. School Street wasn't on the route back from Cottonwood to the Sheriff's Office, but she hoped he might come by to inform her on what he had found at the blacksmith's. Were Red Dale and Sun still there? What were their plans? Had Jim found a way to legally get Sun released from Zhen?

Bounding out the door of the dressmaker's shop, Jared loped down the street with Inez trying to keep up. "So, what's there to do in this town?" he asked.

"Slow down, you're like a puppy just let out of the house."

He stopped at the corner and surveyed each direction. "Hey, there's a saloon. Let's go in."

"No," Inez scolded. "You're too young for that."

"I'm fourteen and training to be in the military," he said. "How old are you?"

"Seventeen and a widow. So I know that you're too young for the saloon."

He sulked a bit, "I want to see a gun fight."

She laughed. "Hold on, I'll get a gun and shoot you. Are you silly? There aren't gun fights on the streets; that's the stuff of dime novels."

"Well, hell," he kicked a rock and it skidded across the street. "What's there to do in this town?"

"Work. There's a play or a show from time to time or a dance in the town hall." But, as she thought about it, Jerome didn't have much for young boys to do. Older boys and men could find plenty to keep themselves occupied: drinking, gambling, fighting, women.

"Well, then," he thought, "I want to see the mines. See if I can find some copper or maybe a bit of gold."

"That's a business, I don't think they let people just walk in and start mining," she looked out across the Verde Valley. In the distance, the San Francisco Peaks dazzled in the sunlight with their caps of snow. "Bet you ain't seen mountains that high back in Virginia," she pointed at the peaks.

"Who's that?" Jared almost tripped over his own feet as he left the corner to follow a girl who had just walked out of the saloon.

"Pearl?" Inez muttered and tried to catch up with Jared. His enthusiasm combined with his belief that he was a grown man began to aggravate her. She'd forgotten how irritating boys could be. Here he was following Pearl down the street. He wouldn't have any idea, Inez thought, what to do with her if he caught her.

"Pearl!" Inez called.

She stopped and waved, then came toward them. Jared, looking a bit alarmed, glanced at Inez then at Pearl.

Inez wanted to head off anything Pearl might say, especially since she had been in the saloon and probably had a few drinks. "Pearl, this is Jared, Lois' son. You know Lois; she works with Martha at the dressmaker's."

"Oh, yes. I'm so charmed to make your acquaintance." Pearl batted her eyelashes.

Speechless, for the first time Inez had noticed, Jared just nodded.

"What's a handsome young boy like you do for fun?" Pearl asked pivoting from one foot to the other so that her skirt swished.

Raising her eyebrows in a warning to behave, Inez took Pearl by the arm to settle her swishing and flirting. "This young man," she explained while squeezing Pearl's elbow, "is on a break from school and is visiting his mother. We thought we would walk around town so he could see the sights—"

"Well," she interrupted, "I'm the best sight you'll see all day."

Attempting to move on with her tour for Jared, Inez said, "Pearl, it was a pleasure to see you. We must be going."

Jared tipped his hat as Inez led him down the street.

"She sure was pretty," he managed to say after they left Pearl. "Is she a dance hall girl?"

She stopped suddenly, inadvertently kicking up a puff of road dust. "What do you know about dance hall girls?"

"I know they're young and pretty and work in dance halls to entertain the men."

Not knowing if she should pursue the subject, she wondered how much this boy really understood about the life of women in the West. Was his complete understanding from dime novels and newspaper serials? "How do they entertain the," she chose her words carefully, "audience?" She hoped using a general description for the men at the halls would steer his mind away from the man and woman nature of the establishments.

He stopped to look in the window of a hat maker's shop. "Oh, those girls sing and dance up on a stage; they put on a real nice show. Just like the shows up in New York, London, and Paris. You know, one day, I'm going to New York."

"What's in New York?" she asked.

His eyes widened with excitement, "It's the gateway to the rest of the world. There's a Statue of Liberty in the harbor that France sent over. It welcomes immigrants, but I want to go the opposite way. I want to go to see Europe, Arabia, Africa. There are so many different people and places in the world, and I want to experience them."

The lure of adventure hadn't snagged her, or had it? She considered her life at Jared's age. She and her mother had just buried her father and knew they would have to survive on their own. In the small South Carolina town, many folks stepped in to assist after a death in the family, especially when a woman was widowed with a child. Inez became the main focus of her mother. Everything the woman did, she did to benefit Inez.

"My life is about you," her mother said one spring day while they hoed chick weed from the string bean plants. "With my husband and son gone, you are all I have left. Oh, life is hard, Inez. I never thought I could go on without Andrew, but I knowed I had to take care of you. You're my reason for living." The woman leaned on the hoe and surveyed their garden.

Saying nothing back to her mother, Inez continued working and thinking. She didn't want to be a burden, to keep her mother from marrying again, to be the only reason for her existence. She missed her father too, but she knew there was more to life than their little house on the hard red dirt. She watched her mother chop a thistle from the row of potato plants. A woman still in her prime, she could re-marry. Inez tried to think of local widowers. With her mother not bothered with Inez, and focused on a new husband, that would allow Inez more freedom. She loved her mother, but a mother's love can smother. Inez craved some independence.

In just these few years, independence had been forced on her.

Now, she saw that same longing in Jared, to be rid of school, to experience the world, to not have family fussing over every step. "Jared," she said, "you'll make it to New York and Europe, just give it time."

Finishing their walk around the town, Inez pointed out places like the mine company's gentlemen's boarding houses, the hospital, the Baptist church, the Mexican church, a cigar store (where Jared insisted on buying tobacco and cigarette paper), and the school.

They arrived back at the dressmaker's shop to find a finely dressed woman talking to Martha about a gown. Jared headed to the back room to roll and smoke his cigarette, and Inez asked Lois if she could help with anything before she had to get back to Onalee's for the evening.

"That woman," Lois whispered and nodded at the lady talking to Martha, "wants a dress to wear to the opera in Prescott."

"Oh," Inez said, "I would love to see the opera house and all those people in their nicest clothes, so elegant and sophisticated." She watched the lady talk to Martha. What a fine figure she had, Inez thought. The woman's back was to her, but she could see Martha's face as they talked. As the woman looked through *Godey's Lady's Book* and *Vogue* and pointed out styles and patterns, Martha caught Inez's attention with a nod of her head toward the woman. She kept doing it each time the woman studied the fashion magazines.

"What is going on with Martha?" Inez asked Lois.

"Oh, she's trying to let you know that's Stella."

"Who's Stella?"

Lois sighed, "Stella is that woman Martha was telling you about who runs around on her husband—you know, Stella is the sheriff's wife."

CHAPTER EIGHTEEN

So, Inez thought, there she is. Jim's wife stood just a few feet from her browsing through magazines to select a style of dress. A dress she would wear, if the rumors were true, to rendezvous with another man. Stella's high-collared, fitted jacket accented her long neck and tapered waist. Her hips were full and round. Or maybe, Inez considered, she wore a bustle.

As it was late afternoon, Stella's chestnut hair was pulled into a tidy knot on the top of her head. But, Inez could imagine her dressing for an evening at the opera house and curling her hair into Marcel waves, then pulling on a dress from *Vogue* magazine.

Inez lowered herself into a chair next to Lois, and watched, and waited for Stella to turn around so she could get a good look at her face. She had to admit she was very curious about the woman Jim had married.

Stella finalized the pattern for her new gown, and Martha couldn't contain her excitement about the object of rumors being in the shop. "Girls," Martha escorted Stella around the table to where Inez and Lois sat. "Look at this beautiful gown she decided on." She held out the magazine, but Inez couldn't take her eyes off Stella.

She was beautiful. Inez shrank down in her chair. Large almond-shaped eyes caught the lamp light with twinkles of fire, and her ivory smooth skin held the sheen of silk. Stella's movements seemed slow and calculated, even to the smallest detail of flipping the page of the magazine. Her eyes led the direction of her head. First she would scan her eyes to the left, then as if she approved of what she saw, she committed to turning her head to look. That was what captured Inez's attention, that odd way of movement, cat-like, but then almost mechanical, like a marionette in a little theater. Maybe, Inez thought, when you are beautiful, you feel as if you're on a stage and being observed.

"Stella," Martha said, "this is a stunning dress. Will you need a satin-lined mantle to keep the chill off in Prescott?"

Her eyes moved toward Martha just a second before her head turned to face her. "Why, yes." She purred the words. "That opera house can be drafty this time of year."

"I always wanted to see the opera house," Inez said waited for the feline movements of Stella to focus on her.

Again, Stella's eyes slid to Inez just a moment before she turned her head. This produced a smile from Inez. The ability to find a quirk in a seemingly perfect person alleviated her apprehension of them. "The opera house produces a variety of shows. Do you think Jerome will build one? It seems to be all the gossip." Inez baited her with the word 'gossip,' but Stella didn't notice, maybe she was unaware of the rumors about her and another man.

She stretched her neck and looked out the front window as if she bored of the conversation, "Jerome will never have the refinement that graces Prescott."

Then, Stella's face drooped a bit and ashen-gray pallor clouded her expressions.

Glancing out the window, Inez rose from her seat as Sheriff Jim dismounted from his horse. There was the man who threatened to kiss her on the street just a few hours before, Inez straightened up her hair, and now his wife stood next to her. Who is he intending to find here?

He opened the door to the four women lined up in front of him. Stopping midway in the entrance, hand still on the doorknob, he nodded to each woman: Martha, Lois, Inez, and Stella. "Good evening, ladies." His eyes lingered on Inez, then on Stella.

"Jim," Stella began, "what are you doing here?"

"Just making my rounds," he said. "And what about you? Buying another gown?"

Martha held out the *Vogue* magazine, "It's a beauty, Sheriff Jim.

You two will be the talk of the town."

The tension in Inez increased. She squeezed her hands into fists so tight her fingernails bent into her palms. She busied herself with threading bobbins at the counter. She didn't want to hear what went on between Jim and Stella, conversations as man and wife, public, yet intimate details of their daily lives. That made her feelings for him too sinful. But, what was sin to her? She had relations with a man who had yet to become her husband. She worked in a parlor house, assisting the girls in exchanging money for carnal pleasures. She harbored ill feelings for Lottie, a woman who had taken her into her home and given her a job after Josiah's death. The list added up in her mind as she wound the thread on the bobbins and placed them in a wooden box for Martha. A deep breath helped settle her thinking and her opinion of herself improved. She stacked the bobbins by color, then unwound one and rethreaded it. She had done nothing shameful with the sheriff. A kiss between friends, that was common. Sun's life was better because of her actions, so were the lives of the girls at Onalee's house. Lois seemed happy with Jared seeing her working at the dressmaker's and that secret stayed secure. The shop door clanging shut broke into Inez's thoughts. Stella walked down the street, leaving Jim standing at the door with his hat in his hands.

"Miss Inez," he said. "May I talk to you privately about that matter in Cottonwood?"

With Jared in the storage room, Lois and Martha occupying the shop, there wasn't a private place to talk. "We can go up to Lois' rooms," she suggested and led him out the side door and up the stairs. Once inside, they settled on the divan, she wanted to ask him about Stella, but waited for his news about Sun.

"At the blacksmith's barn, I found Red Dale. Again, he didn't acknowledge Sun being there, even though we all know she's still staying with him," he leaned back and rubbed the stubble on his chin. "We talked about the man you saw at the Junction with Zhen. Dale recollects that a strange man had come into the barn asking some questions, less to do with blacksmithing and more about women. A tall man, nicely dressed, that appeared odd to Dale since most of his customers are ranchers."

"He didn't say anything to him about Zhen or Sun, did he?" she asked.

"You know how closed-mouth that Red Dale is. He just kept on working and let the man talk. Now, I told him that he and Sun needed to get out of town, just to let Zhen get over losing her, but that boy said he had obligations here. He wouldn't elaborate on what those obligations are..."

Inez sighed, propped her elbows on her knees, and rested her chin on her palms. Finger tapping her cheeks as she thought, she asked, "What could be more important than getting him and Sun away from Zhen? Unless, he ain't afraid of that crazy Chinaman." She glanced over at Jim to gauge his reaction.

He reached over and patted her back then let his hand rest at the nape of her neck, rubbing it a little. "You might have something there. Dale don't let many things bother him. And that can be dangerous to a man."

Although the front room trapped a chill in the air, Inez could feel heat rising from his touch, a cooling mist of sweat formed on her forehead and she reached up to wipe it away. His hand remained there as if it were the most natural thing in the world, him touching her. Wanting to look at him, to gaze into his gray eyes, to study the angles of his chin, Inez feared that turning toward him would be giving permission for him to kiss her. Although, a kiss would have been fine with her earlier in the day, now she had met his wife, and while she didn't particularly like Stella, she couldn't deny that she existed. With great strength of character, or so she told herself, Inez stood, pulling away from his touch, walked to the window where the shadow of Mingus Mountain stretched across the valley as the setting sun sunk to the west.

"It was a pleasure to meet your wife," she said without turning back toward Jim.

"If there's a place to shop, you'll find Stella there," his voice was strong, confident, and jovial, not a hint of remorse, anger, or unkindness. "She has her interests, things that make her happy, keep her occupied. I know living in this town isn't easy for her," his tone mellowed. "Why she married a deputy county sheriff, I'll never understand."

"Maybe," Inez ventured without turning to face him, "she loves you."

Silence rooted the room as Inez waited for his response. The quiet grew, wrapping tendrils around her thoughts, threatening to strangle her for daring to approach the subject. The thud of his boots across the bare wood floor hacked through the thicket of her notions. His hands gripped her shoulders and gently turned her to face him. The cool gray eyes had warmed. "No," he said simply, "she doesn't."

He let his hands drift down her shoulders to grasp her fingers. He held them for a moment, then lifted her hands to his face. His mustache brushed across them with a soft kiss. Without another word, he turned and left her alone in the apartment over the dress shop.

⚔ ⚔ ⚔

As she worked that night, serving supper and drinks to the ladies and their gentlemen, she kept thinking about Jim and what he had said. Some of the regular gentlemen attended that evening, and she wondered if they felt their wives did not love them. Was this the reality? Did the gentlemen visit Onalee's for companionship, respect, and attention more than for what commenced in the bedrooms upstairs? Inez stood in the corner with her order book, noting the drinks for each girl and customer.

From her vantage point, she listened to the conversations of work grumblings, boasts of great deeds, sharing of local gossip, and a few intimate whispers. Nothing held her attention because her mind kept drifting back to Jim. She wondered what he was doing at that very moment. Had Stella prepared supper for him? Was he relaxing in his favorite chair, reading a book? Day and night, he spends his time in service to this town, Inez thought, and I bet she doesn't realize that his life is in danger every time he walks out the door.

Gathering up the supper dishes and replacing them with dessert bowls and pouring port for the gentlemen and ladies, Inez and Mildred began the last of their chores. The girls took their customers to the front room, and Inez closed the curtain between the dining room and the parlor.

She heard Onalee begin to play the piano. As she folded the table cloth and set it aside for washing, Inez stopped for a moment and listened to the melodic lines of the waltz Onalee performed. The meter of the music lifted her spirits and she began to sway with the three-beat rhythm. Mildred strutted into the dining room, set the silver on a side table, then grabbed Inez's hands and twirled her around the large dining room table to the step of the music.

"If them men don't take advantage of this dancing music, Marvelous Mildred will," she switched directions and led Inez back around the table. She stopped and plopped into a chair, "Woo," she fanned herself, "I ain't as nimble or as light on my feet as I used to be." She held up a finger to Inez, "Don't get old and fat. It ain't as fun as it looks."

"I just love to hear Onalee play the piano," Inez said, lingering by the curtain.

"Come on and help Marvelous Mildred out of this chair," she held both hands out toward Inez. "We got dishes to wash and put away."

With the kitchen chores completed, Mildred said her good-nights and headed home. Inez assisted in the bookkeeping, and settled in Onalee's little office room to transfer her numbers for the evening to the ledger. Not as glamorous as working in the front part of the house, but the tasks that Inez performed satisfied her feelings of usefulness and supporting the ladies in what they did best.

The night grew old and weary. The ladies collected their money, and the gentlemen wandered home. Onalee continued playing the piano, but her tune had slowed and hushed to a lullaby. As had become her habit, Inez joined Onalee at the piano bench, resting her head on Onalee's broad shoulder as the music trickled down to a series of chords with no melody, just chords of mood; the doeskin sleeve felt smooth and soft against Inez's cheek and the tensions of the day drained away.

"You have something on your mind," Onalee stated.

"I met Sheriff Jim's wife today at the dress shop," she said as casually as she could, trying to make the event seem of little importance.

Onalee continued to pick notes from the keyboard. "Ah yes, Stella."

Lifting her head to look at the dark eyes of Onalee, Inez asked, "Why do you say it that way? What about her?" She thought for a moment, "No? Stella wasn't one of the girls, was she?"

"No," Onalee laughed. "She claims to be from a prestigious family from the East. She lived in Prescott most of her life. Stella has a discontented spirit."

Inez waited for more, but she had learned Onalee would give only what she felt she needed to say, no more or no less.

Finally, Inez asked, "What do you mean by a discontented spirit?"

Continuing to play her moody music, Onalee smiled. "Like most people, what she desires is not what she has. Many would be content with her life. Many would be content with our life. So many people have less and struggle. We are fortunate to be warm and well-fed, but our spirits aren't satisfied."

"Well," Inez reasoned, "as those basic needs are met, a person looks for more. Love, respect, gratification all comes after feeling secure. I know that after I left Lottie's house where I had shelter and food, I felt I might die. But," she laid her head back on Onalee's shoulder, "you and the ladies took me in and gave me security. Now, I want more. Do I have a discontented spirit?"

"You, my child, have a loving spirit. Stella seems to be remote, as if living outside herself, searching for significance in possessions and other people. I knew Stella several years ago."

Inez waited for the explanation, hoping that wasn't all Onalee had to say. "What happened?" Inez prompted.

"From the old times, I have a mate."

Remembering what Jim had told her about Onalee, she whispered, "Blue Jay?"

"Why yes," Onalee nodded her head, but didn't ask for the source of the information. "Blue Jay, like his namesake, can be a bully or a force of vengeance. When the Diné were marched to Fort Sumner then relocated back to our tribal lands that became the reservation, many were not at ease. Blue Jay and I were born on the reservation, but the buffalo and other game were gone. The land wouldn't support us. As we grew and took our place among our people, Blue Jay wanted more. He craved what our grandfathers enjoyed before the whites came. He left, and soon after, I followed, searching for him." Her chords changed to a slower and more bass tone. "In the white world, money is a god. You must have it to survive. I had the gift of music and could perform it on this instrument," she nodded toward the piano. "That created opportunities in saloons and parlor houses," she produced a short sad laugh, "some of the whites liked to call me Professor Owl. My Diné name is Listening Owl. Somehow, that was translated to Onalee. Anyway, it became my white name. Several years ago, I was enlisted by Stella's parents to teach her and her sister how to play the piano. Her father frequented a saloon on the Square where I worked. She was indifferent as a musical student and was more concerned about her appearance than learning the spirit of the instrument. Who can expect more of a young woman of that age?"

Inez reached up to Onalee's hands on the keyboard and took them in her own. "Where is Blue Jay?"

"I wish I knew. I have procured several people to look for him. Money drives the search. After all this time, I don't know if we are still one, mates for life." She became lost in her thoughts for a moment.

Inez patted her hands, then released them.

Onalee kissed Inez's forehead and resumed her seemingly random chords on the piano. "Back to my story about Stella, she knew about my search for Blue Jay and claimed to have an acquaintance that had seen him with some Apaches in Wickenburg. This friend of Stella's traded whiskey to the Apaches in exchange for information on Geronimo's location. Stella claimed Blue Jay was one of Geronimo's warriors, helping him elude General Crook."

The adventures of the Apache leader seeking revenge for the

slaughter of his family by the Mexican army had become legendary in the newspapers even in South Carolina. Inez knew of him and his rampages across the Southwest. "I thought Geronimo was in prison in Florida."

"Yes, he is now," Onalee said. "But, Stella's friend was a young man looking for adventure and fame, qualities that I'm sure attracted young Stella. He claimed more than he knew, and in my quest to find Blue Jay, I paid a large sum of money for his information. When I traveled to Wickenburg, I found nothing. Stella and the young man had taken the money and run away. Her parents blamed me and threatened to have the county sheriff arrest me for whatever reason they could produce." The music died and she stared at the keyboard. "Being a Navajo and a berdache in a white man's town ensured few rights in their legal system.

"I left to track down Stella and her young man. They hadn't traveled far, and I enlisted the assistance of several of the Yavapai Apache warriors. We tracked them to Spruce Mountain, just east of Prescott. In the darkness of night, the Yavapai surrounded their campsite." She smiled at the memory, "I began with a few low owl calls, then the warriors added wolf and bob cat cries. The firelight flickered and shadows danced. The young man stumbled around in circles waving his gun in an effort to protect Stella from the wild animals that were closing in on them. In a frantic state, he pulled Stella onto his horse and they both rode off into the night leaving their belongings and Stella's horse. We followed and herded them back to Prescott.

"Those two young people wouldn't leave the safety of town again."

"That young man wasn't Sheriff Jim, was it?" Inez asked.

"No, Stella didn't meet Jim for several years later. Actually, I think they have only been married for a short time. Stella hasn't changed much since those days, still looking for adventure, romance, excitement... She's never content with what she has."

Onalee but her arm around Inez's shoulders. "Young one, you are wise beyond your years. Don't let complications send you on the wrong path. Now, go get some rest."

The wrong path that Onalee mentioned played discords in Inez's mind. Did she refer to her budding relationship with Sheriff Jim or maybe her involvement with Sun's escape from Zhen? Then there was her plan to deceive Jared about his mother's occupation. And her own plight from the propriety of Lottie's world to working in a parlor house, which path was the wrong one? Or were they all not the place for a young girl to be? She began to ask, but Onalee had focused her attention back to the piano, playing a soft lullaby that brought echoes of South Carolina and Inez's mother.

Inez kissed Onalee good-night and went upstairs to her room. Again, the images of Onalee's story about Stella brought a smile to her. Combing out her hair, she wondered if Jim saw more to Stella than just the beauty. Visions of Indian warriors, a scared Stella, and an avenged Onalee filled her head as she drifted off to sleep.

CHAPTER NINETEEN

"Relax," instructed Pearl as she slopped hair dye on Inez. "This will take care of the streaks showing through and give you a more natural color."

The mixture smelled of a combination of wet dog and scorched lard. "Should my head be getting hot?" Inez started to reach up to her hair, but Pearl slapped her hand away.

"Let it be," scolded Pearl. "Don't go messing up my masterpiece. Your hair will be better than ever."

"Lois said we should wash it in beer," Inez said. "That will make it softer."

Standing back with her hand on her hips, Pearl surveyed her handiwork then wrapped a towel around Inez's head. "This time," she assured Inez, "we won't leave it on so long. Yep, that was the problem last go round. We got to talking and didn't rinse soon enough."

The solution tingled on Inez's scalp.

"How long should we wait?" she asked.

"Oh, another few minutes," Pearl inspected her fingernails and began to push her cuticles down with her thumbnail. "Toy and Frenchy say the dress shop is making money."

The tingle increased to low throbbing.

"Is it time yet?" she asked.

"No, not yet. Is Martha actually making and selling dresses? How will she have time to make ours if she's doing all these other women's? I just don't know if I like this situation. I need a new gown, and Martha can't be distracted by some dowdy housewife's

Christmas frock." She looked up from her cuticle work. "Are you listening to me?"

Inez pulled the towel away from her head. "Pearl, it's awful warm. Come check it."

She sighed. "My dress will be the best yet, scarlet satin with pearl buttons, cut low to show my 'creamy breasts.' Did I tell you a gentleman told me I had 'creamy breasts?' I felt like I was being inventoried: raven hair, piercing eyes, creamy breasts." She rubbed her fingers under the towel to test the progress of the hair dye, "Too much is coming off; it needs more time. Anyway, this gentleman fancied himself a poet. We got up to my room and he wants to look, that's it, just look and write in his notebook. Which," she leaned toward Inez, "is fine with me. Some of these ole boys are so tiring. It's nice to have something different once in a while."

Inez touched her hair to see if the dye had dried enough.

"Now, speaking of something different," Pearl continued. "That Jared is kinda handsome. I mean he's all gangly arms and legs, but he's young and can be taught," she winked at Inez.

"Why Pearl, that's Lois' son," she scolded.

"He has to learn somewhere. So, why not with a woman of experience instead of some scared little girl in the back of a barn?"

Pulling the towel off, Inez said, "You get that out of your mind. Jared is too young and he's like a nephew to us."

Pearl inspected strands of Inez's hair then bent her over the sink to rinse the remaining dye out. "Lois mentioned that man from the train station. A big good-looking man with a gun strapped low on his hip, now that sounds like an adventure to me."

"An adventure?" Inez asked bent over the sink.

"Yes, an adventure in love." She filled another pitcher of water from the faucet and poured it over Inez's head. "Something about a dangerous looking man makes my heart flutter. 'Course you know about that," she paused for effect, "Sheriff Jim ruffles my petticoat every time I see him. I can't imagine what he does for you." She guided Inez up from the sink and wrapped a clean towel around her head. "You have the opportunity that a lot of us girls have pursued. Sheriff Jim barely gives us the time of day, but you... Well, let's just say he's ripe for the picking."

Leaning against the kitchen counter, Inez rubbed her hair with the towel to help dry it. Although the kitchen was warm with a fire in the stove, a cool breeze rattled the windows and brought a chill to her damp scalp. "Jim has a wife," she stated it as the bare fact it was.

"Stella? Hell, she's no wife." Pearl crossed her arms over her chest. "That woman is never home, and when she is, she pays him no attention."

"She is a beautiful woman," Inez admitted. "But, that can't be the reason he married her, could it?"

"Many a man is caught by an attractive figure, a coy smile, or creamy breasts," Pearl laughed. "If they weren't, we'd be out of business."

He wasn't the type of man to have his head and heart turned by a pretty face. Although Stella was a beautiful woman, and probably when they courted, an attentive companion, she just seemed mismatched for the sensible and compassionate Jim. Of course, Inez told herself, I don't know the woman; everything I know has come second-handed.

Sitting her down at the table, Pearl began to brush Inez's damp hair. "Perfect," she appraised. "Yes, ma'am, I got it perfect."

A strand of hair rested across her shoulder. Inez inspected it. Definitely saffron, not orange marmalade. The color of Arizona sunsets, she was pleased to see.

"Back to that man you and Lo saw at the Junction," Pearl began to wrap locks of hair around a curling rod, "where do you think he's staying? He wouldn't stay over at Zhen's place, would he?"

"That's the only place I know of."

"Maybe, we should take a walk and do a little shopping," Pearl suggested.

"I told Sheriff Jim I'd stay away from Zhen's place. And, he's right; we shouldn't get mixed up in whatever is going on."

"I don't care what Zhen does," Pearl said. "I just want to catch a glimpse of the new man in town."

The prospect of actually finding the man again and studying his actions appealed to Inez. Maybe, she was wrong in her assumption he was a bounty hunter, but he had called on Red Dale. The sheriff hadn't given her enough information about what transpired in Cottonwood, and he would have gone to the man himself, if he knew where to find him. Yes, she thought, that's what he needs to do; just go up to the man and say 'What's your business here?' The sheriff would have that right.

"Yes, Pearl. Let's do a little shopping," she said.

"Good, I need to get out of this house for a while." Pearl continued to brush and curl Inez's hair until she was satisfied with the look. She twisted her hair into a loose bun that she secured with tortoiseshell combs leaving a few ringlets to frame her face. "Much better," she appraised. "Curly hair is a sign of a sweet temperament. But, just a few curls is a sign of a woman who may change her mind. That's a bit more exciting to the gentlemen."

They dressed in their usual daytime outfits, Pearl in her white blouse and long tan skirt with her yellow and red striped stockings 'to give a bit of color' as she would say. Inez favored her fitted skirt that reached to the top of her boots and her felted wool bolero trimmed in golden cording, the day was warm enough not to require a coat, so the short jacket was enough. With her new hair color and style, she also declined her usual cowboy hat. She had a womanly confidence in her appearance, no more Lady Marmalade of the Kitchen.

As they strolled down the street, avoiding mud puddles and droppings from horses, Inez decided that the ladies deserved a sidewalk in front of the dressmaker's shop. Jerome grew too fast to stop and consider anything as mundane as a sidewalk to keep the women's dresses from dragging through the mud, but Inez thought that a nice wooden sidewalk in front of shop would be appreciated by the ladies of the town and would probably draw in more business. A simple boardwalk extending from one end of the building to the other, but then she considered asking the shop next door to extend the boardwalk past their business. She knew Onalee would help finance the project. She shared her idea with Pearl.

"A sidewalk would be a grand addition," Pearl said. "We would have to put one in front of the house too. Maybe that would keep the gentlemen from tracking mud and manure on our rugs." She took Inez's hand and pulled her toward the Fashion Saloon. "One drink?"

"I don't know. It's awful early," Inez protested.

"Come on, Zhen's man might be in there." Pearl tugged her through the door. A gust of sour cigar smoke and a whiff of stale beer greeted them as Pearl guided Inez to a table in the corner.

The bartender approached, a bit of a waddle in his step, wiping his hands on a towel. "Pearl, you know my girls don't like it when you come in here." He pushed his thick spectacles further up the bridge of his nose.

"Carl, I ain't ever intruded on your heifers. I work in a respectable house, not saloons. Besides, I only stop by during the day. I'm a customer."

Standing straight and slicking back the few strands of hair left on his head, Carl retrieved a pad and pencil from his pocket. "Alright, ladies, what can I bring you?"

"Two wines," Pearl slapped two bits on the table.

With the smoothness of a garter snake, he slid the coins off the table and into his pocket. "So," he eyed Inez, "what are you two ladies doing this afternoon?"

"We have errands," Inez said.

"Yes," Pearl added, "but we wanted to stop in at the Fashion to see who was here and catch up on any gossip."

He raised one eyebrow, skewing his spectacles and giving his round face the look of a sliced cherry pie.

Realizing where Pearl was headed, Inez asked, "I saw a tall man at the Junction the other day with Zhen; do you know anything about him?"

"Why do you ask?"

"He sounded handsome," Pearl said. "And like he might have some money to spend for entertainment," she winked at Carl.

"There's plenty of men with money in their pockets without you messing with that one." Carl tapped his pencil on his order book, "Now, I'll get you those drinks."

"Wait a minute," Pearl grabbed his apron. "What do you know?"

His eyes sparkled behind his glasses as if he relished having something to share with the girls, a bit of information they wanted to hear. He glanced over his shoulder at the almost empty saloon. The bar stretched from one end of the long space to the other with tables splattering the rest of the room. A dusty cowboy sat at the bar with one of the girls. In a far corner, three girls sat together cleaning beer mugs and wine glasses. Nearby, two older men played poker with a whiskey bottle at their side. Carl turned back to Pearl and Inez, apparently satisfied that the environment was safe to talk.

"You know Miss Linda?" he asked. "She has most of the cribs down on Hull Street and a house by the Mexican Quarter."

Inez made the connection: the woman she had met on the train on her way to Jerome, and again on the street just a few weeks earlier. "What about her?" she asked.

He pulled up a creaky pine chair and plopped down next to Pearl, "Miss Linda travels about, visiting her different businesses. So, she ain't here all that much. Well, the way I heard it," he continued slowly as if to build the girls' anticipation, "and this is just the rumor, I didn't get it first hand—"

"Damn it, Carl," Pearl fumed, "get on with it."

"This man you're asking about. Well, he shows up at the Mexican house. Looking over the girls, you know Miss Linda has a little bit of everything there, Mexicans, Negroes, Chinese, Indians, maybe even a white girl. Not that I have ever been there," he added.

Pearl tapped her fingers on the table.

"Well, he didn't find any girl from the selection to fit his fancy. He asks to talk to the Madam of the house. Miss Linda wasn't there that night, so he grabs the Mexican girl in charge and pulls her into one of the rooms. She's yelling and he's slapping her around, real violent like. The little Negro girl runs up the street to get some help and brings back some of the Mexican miners. By that time, the man is gone and little Rosanna is beat half to death."

"Why didn't they fetch the sheriff?" Inez couldn't believe the man was still roaming the streets.

"The girls didn't want to get no trouble going with the law, you know houses like that like to stay low and not get noticed." He pushed himself up from the table. "Let me get those drinks for you."

Inez looked to Pearl who watched Carl pour the wine at the bar. "Can you believe that? I wonder what set him off."

"Happens all the time in those lower class houses," Pearl said. "The girls have to fend for themselves if a customer gets out of line."

"He can't get away with that. Sheriff Jim would lock him away in jail if he knew," Inez started to get up, but Pearl pulled her back down.

"No, I been through this type of thing before. The girl would have to complain, then the law would have to look into it, then she would be in the papers as a prostitute, and the people in town would just say she deserved it for what she was doing. It's hard to be protected by the law when you break the law," Pearl cast her eyes down to the battered table.

She appeared older and a bit defeated in her lot in life. Inez knew the situation wasn't fair and that if this had happened to some other young girl, maybe the daughter of a mine official or of a merchant, the man would be in jail and the town would be thirsty for blood. But, a poor Mexican prostitute didn't mean anything in most people's view.

Carl set the wine glasses on the table, and Pearl drank half of hers in one gulp. He returned with the bottle and left it at the table without saying anything.

After a couple more drinks, Inez's head felt a little hazy, but light as if her concerns didn't weigh as much. She didn't drink as a general rule, maybe a sip here or there. This reprieve from her worries over the mysterious man and the Mexican girl, Sun and Red Dale, Sheriff Jim and Stella was a welcome state. Apparently enjoying the same boost in morale, Pearl laughed at her own jokes and had Inez amused with stories of the local mine officials, one of whom always asked the girls to dress him in a corset. With the bottle empty, they left Carl a few coins and waved good-bye.

Back on the street, Inez checked one direction then the next, "Where were we going Pearl?"

"Damned if I know," she leaned on Inez's shoulder and inspected a strand of hair. "Your hair looks real natural. I did a fine job on it."

"If you ever tire of dressing men in corsets," Inez whispered in a bit of a slurred tone, "you can always fix hair for a living."

"Shopping," Pearl blurted out as if someone had pinched her. "That's our destination. I knew it would come to me."

They linked arms and headed down the street toward the mercantile at the corner. A cool breeze traveled up the hill with the afternoon sun, and the aroma of freshly baked wheat bread filled the air as they approached a bakery.

A large woman barreled out the door just as they passed, almost knocking them down. "Beg your pardon," she mumbled, then stopped and turned toward them. "Inez?"

She recognized Lottie's rotund figure and pumpkin face immediately. A sobering chill ran through Inez, and she wondered what she had done to deserve another encounter with this woman.

With a quick, but obvious inspection of the girls' outfits and hair styles, Lottie wrinkled her nose and straightened her stance with righteous pride. "Why Inez, I knew my worries were valid. First, I see you escorted by the sheriff through the streets of Cottonwood, now here you are in the company," she looked at Pearl, "of a harlot."

"You fat cow—" Pearl balled up her fist.

"Hold on," Inez stepped in front of her.

"Lord, oh Lord, I take this as all my fault. But I tried," Lottie hugged her sack of bread close to her body. "I tried to teach you right from wrong, how to be a lady, how to act proper, which people to associate with and which ones to avoid, but I failed."

Pearl placed her chin on Inez's shoulder. "So, you're that old cow that threw Inez out of the house."

"Hush, Pearl," Inez said. "Lottie, all you taught me was to be snooty, to look down on people who were different. You judge by appearance only." She took a breath, "There is more to people than appearance, and a person of real character knows that and looks deeper to find the good in everyone."

"Is that alcohol I smell on your breath? You're drunk," she accused. "All your Christian upbringing has been lost to the decadence of this town. You need to get back to church. I'll send the reverend. Maybe he can save your soul."

"I'm more of a Christian now than you have ever been. You are a vicious, manipulating," Inez stepped toward Lottie, "sad, old busy-body who has nothing in your life to do, but eat, sneak bourbon in your coffee, and belittle other people in an effort to feel good about yourself."

Lottie's face ripened to a deep red as she glanced around to see if other people were listening. "I will not stand here on the streets of Jerome and be verbally accosted by two harlots."

"Cow," Pearl sneered.

"I don't understand why the righteous women of this community let harlots like you walk the streets. The sheriff needs to be held accountable for the illegal activity that goes on right under his nose," her eyes darted about to assess the passersby who had stopped to see the commotion. "You good ladies of Jerome," she motioned broadly with one chubby arm while the other held tight to her bag of bread, "why let drunken women of ill repute roam the avenues of this fair city?"

An old man with a scraggly beard spoke up, "I say we need more of them." The small group laughed and began to wander off to their errands.

"I think the old bag is running for public office," Pearl said to Inez.

Lottie turned to them, "You say I don't have anything in my life? Well, I have decency and I have respectability. Things you will never have living the life of a," she smeared the word with coarse contempt, "whore."

Nothing registered in Inez's mind but searing light that flashed through her eyes until she was able to focus again and saw Lottie holding her red cheek. The sound of Pearl's laughter gradually increased to a roar in her ears. A stinging throbbed in Inez's palm. Lottie bent down to pick up her sack of bread, and when she straightened up, Inez saw the hand print across Lottie's fleshy cheek.

CHAPTER TWENTY

"Y̶ou slapped her into next week," Pearl laughed as they walked down the street. Lottie had stormed off in the other direction without another word. With a throbbing palm, Inez rubbed the side of her skirt trying to get her hand to stop hurting and attempting to understand what she had done.

"How could I have hit her? I don't think I ever hit another person in anger," she looked to Pearl for condolence.

"If a body ever deserved it, that one did. Why, that old cow said things to you no woman in her right mind would say." She slipped her arm around Inez's shoulder as they walked. "You had every reason to slap some sense into her. Maybe, she'll think before she opens that big mouth and gives her opinion."

Stopping in front of the mercantile, Inez leaned against the rough planks of the storefront, head down, worried. "You don't understand. Lottie has a fondness for causes, the more righteous the better. But, instead being a suffragette or a missionary, she fancies herself a protector of the Cult of True Womanhood."

"What the hell is that?" Pearl asked.

"Oh, I had this drummed into me while I lived with her—as if my mama hadn't taught me a thing." She remembered the dogma of the True Woman's role, a moral code her mother had found impractical, but society women still believed. "A True Woman is dependent on a man," she recounted. "She should be married and support her husband in all he does because, after all, he is the intelligent one. Lottie always said 'A True Woman should be pure, pious, domestic, and submissive.' Although, we are a man's moral superior, he is our intellectual superior, so we serve him."

"That's bullshit," Pearl said. "I'd like to know how I end up with a miner's paycheck when he's supposed to be so goddamn smart."

"I was constantly being scolded by Lottie for being too free in my actions and thoughts." She shook her head, "But, I had to be, to survive. I mean who's going to take care of you if you're on your own?" The drive to endure hardships, to even turn them around to her advantage had blossomed in Inez; a trait that she knew would not have developed if she had subscribed to the popular code for women. In the Territory, women didn't have the advantages that presented themselves in the East. Social events, preparatory schools, edicts from 'proper' women didn't seem important or even practical in the West. Inez craved to do right, to be the woman that others spoke highly of, to have a respected place in her community, but the situations of her life had not led her in that direction. Survival or propriety, that dilemma ruled her decisions.

"We take care of each other," Pearl said. "Well, would you look at what the cat dragged in?"

A movement down the road caught their attention; the figure of Red Dale appeared on a galloping horse. He steered the roan stallion to a hitching post near the girls. After securing the reins to the post, he tipped his hat to Pearl and Inez, "Good afternoon, ladies." He smoothed a lock of auburn hair that had slipped from under his hat just as Pearl stepped in front of him.

"What brings you to Jerome?" she asked.

He looked to Inez, then back to Pearl, "Well, as you can see, I'm headed into the mercantile, thought I'd purchase a few things."

"Us too," Inez said, but instead of going in, she took hold of his coat sleeve and directed him over to the corner away from the door. "I wanted to ask you," she began in a soft, low voice, "how Sun is doing?" No need to be coy, she thought. They both knew Sun was still with him.

He removed his hat and held it in both hands, "Well, Miss Inez, she's doing fine."

Waiting for more, she patted his shoulder as her grandmother would do to comfort someone. Then as he didn't reveal anything more, she said, "The sheriff came to see you. He told you about the man I saw at the Junction with Zhen. Does that concern you?"

"No more than anybody Zhen associates with." His blue eyes held no fear or worry, only a calm demeanor. "You and the Sheriff don't need to fret over us. I can handle things."

"But, that's just it; this isn't something for you to manage. It's a matter for the law." She wanted him to trust her, but he was determined to save Sun by himself. Was it a need to show her he could? Inez knew the pride men had for being independent and acting as if they didn't need assistance from anyone. "There ain't no shame in letting your friends lend a hand in things. This might be to a point that the law needs to step in. That's all Jim is trying to do—making sure Zhen doesn't push too far trying to get her back."

He nodded his head with his eyes cast down, "Yes ma'am, I understand that."

"Inez," Pearl pulled at her sleeve.

She looked to Pearl, then to where Pearl motioned with a demure flick of her hair and the roll of her eyes toward a lone figure across the street watching them.

The mysterious man from the Junction, tall and dark, leaned against the saddler's barn observing their actions. The gun belt rode low on his hips, while he chewed on a cigar as if waiting for someone, but Inez knew he watched Red Dale, and now her and Pearl. Red Dale had turned to see what she looked at, and Pearl too. So, now the trio all stared at the man as he stared back at them.

Should she fetch Sheriff Jim? The man hadn't done anything, but he caused a shudder in her body. "Stop staring at him," she whispered and turned back to Red Dale. "Do you have a pistol?"

"No need for one," he said. "Now, ladies, please excuse me. I have a few things to get before I go back down the mountain." He started for the door, stopped and said, "Miss Inez, you stay away from that man. Don't go asking him questions. Eventually, he'll give up and go away."

Pearl grabbed her hand, "Let's go home. We got work to do before the gentlemen arrive tonight."

The man continued to watch them as they traveled up the street, and until they turned the corner out of his sight, then Inez finally felt her heart slow and some calm return to her thoughts.

After helping Mildred prepare the supper, Inez went to her room to get ready for the evening. The warm browns and yellows of her hair pleased her. Yes, she thought, Pearl did a fine job. Along with her new hair color, a new dress was in order, one that Pearl had grown tired of, and one that Inez didn't consider too revealing. The cobalt blue silk gown hugged her figure. In the past months, she had grown into a more womanly shape, maybe it was the food Mildred fixed or the fact that she had grown up physically and mentally since being in the Territory. When the mind is forced to contend with adult predicaments, the body has a way of responding to the call, and Inez had matured. She sat in her little room wondering how her life would have been different if Josiah hadn't died. A wife and probably a mother-to-be, they would have had the house almost finished, and she would have been active in the little community, helping out at church socials, attending quilting bees, assuming the role of a frontier wife. But, that wasn't the lot in life she had. A tear trickled down her cheek then she wiped it away with a determined hand knowing that she could survive anything and that maybe she was meant for something more grand than what she had expected. Certainly, Onalee and the girls thought she had more to offer; otherwise they wouldn't have let her stay in the house without earning money by entertaining the gentlemen. They were down one girl with Lois staying over at the dress shop with her son. Inez had figured the books the day before, and the money produced by the shop paid for the rent, materials, Martha's time, and left some profit for Onalee.

Glancing back at the mirror, Inez turned to admire her reflection. Yes, she thought, I could entertain if I were so inclined. The "gay deceivers" lay on the dresser; that is what Mildred had called the spring apparatus Inez fashioned for Pearl's breasts. Pearl refused to wear them again because when her gentleman reached into her low-cut neckline, one of the springs popped out and bounced off his forehead. The recollection of the story produced a smile for Inez. Unhooking the gown, she slid one side down her shoulder and slipped the device under a breast. Then she compared the effect. It wasn't as comfortable as she had thought, but she liked the look. She unhooked the gown more so she could position both springs, not worrying about them popping out into a man's face since no man would have his hands on her.

With her new figure in place, freshly colored hair, and Pearl's dress, Inez opened the door and strode down the hallway with confidence. Mildred emerged from the bathroom, just as Inez walked by.

"Katie, bar the door!" Mildred cried out. "Inez, look at you. Dang, if you ain't slicked up tonight. Them men will ignore the ladies with you serving supper." She put a fleshy arm around Inez's waist as they walked down the hall, "What's the occasion?"

"Just thought I would do something to match my new hair color. I was worried that Pearl would turn it orange again, but she's getting the hang of it."

"After you and Onalee open the doors and greet the gentlemen," Mildred said, "you can serve the drinks in the parlor. I'll finish up supper; I don't think you should get that dress stained."

Downstairs, the girls commented on how nice Inez looked. The smell of roasted turkey, glazed carrots, and buttery potatoes drifted into the parlor. As was the usual custom during the day, the girls would open windows and doors to air out the house while they cleaned, letting the stale cigar smoke and perfume from the night before drift out. The aroma of a meal was much more tantalizing for the gentlemen than sour cigar smoke. Onalee surveyed the front parlor making sure everything was in place.

"Inez," she called. "Why don't you greet the gentlemen tonight?"

"You think I can do it alone?"

"Yes, I will be at the piano if you need me; you can introduce our guests to the ladies."

A good number of the gentlemen visited on a regular basis, so she knew several of them by name, and most by sight. Any new guests to the house were usually introduced by a regular customer, but this night, customary events did not transpire.

Maybe it was her new look, Inez thought, did she do too much change at once? The mood of the house seemed askew, as if the girls were jittery and the gentlemen distracted. Onalee played spirited snappy tunes on the piano, but the gay atmosphere didn't materialize. On a busy night, two suppers took place—early and late. For a cold windy Thursday night, the house had a fair number of visitors, but warranted only one supper. Inez greeted the men and escorted them to the parlor and retrieved their initial drinks. She introduced them to each other, if they didn't already know their fellow guests. "Hello Whitney," one man hailed another. One of Toy's regulars, Whitney, shook hands with the other man and they talked and laughed over a drink. Inez chatted with a few of the other gentlemen who frequented the house, the first time she had really spent more than a passing moment with any of the guests. Small talk about the cold weather, the upcoming holidays, the increase in mining activity, she found she had a flair for engaging the men in conversation. "What an interesting accent," one would say. "A Southern Belle," another would comment. She enjoyed the attention, but kept the dignified manner of the madam of the house. All the gentlemen treated her with great respect. The girls had made their appearance and mingled with the guests. Mildred prepared drinks as the girls delivered them with a smile to their customers. With vim and vigor, Onalee's music bounced around the parlor. The mood of the house had lightened.

As the doorbell chimed, she smoothed her dress and checked her hair to receive another gentleman into the warm company of the guests, the door opened with a gust of cold damp wind. In the porch's lamp light stood the man from the Junction. His large frame filled the entryway. Dark eyes peered out from under thick brows; his hair was combed back into a slick wave. With his hat in his hand, he nodded to Inez.

The sight of the man and knowing the story that Carl had told them at the Fashion scared Inez. Every nerve in her body seemed to prickle. A deep breath helped calm her as she concentrated on the sound of it moving through her chest. The need to retreat tugged at her, but she stood firm at the door. This man would not disrupt the house; he would not scare or hurt the girls; he could not intimidate her. The music, laughter, and conversation from the parlor fortified her confidence—this was a family. No one entered who would threaten their well-being. "May I help you?" she asked.

"Nick Rees," the man introduced himself. "John from the saloon sent me over, said this was the best house in Jerome."

Even with her nervousness, she smiled. How dumb does he think I am? She stood her ground. "John who? And which saloon?"

"Miss," Rees carefully framed his words with mock gentleness. "I'm new to these parts and I don't quite recall the man's full name or the name of the establishment."

Using the same measured tone, she replied, "Sir, this is a private house with lady boarders. You do understand that only supper guests of the ladies are invited into the parlor?"

Eyes shifted from left to right, he looked over her shoulder as if to see if there was someone else he might engage in conversation to gain entry to the house, but Inez stood in the doorway. "Where is the madam of the house?" he asked.

"I have the authority to run the affairs of this house," she hated that he was questioning her. The straight line of his tight lips showed no emotion and his eyes rarely blinked. Although the poker face conveyed his coolness, he commenced fiddling with his hat held in his hand. The rules of the house have been made clear to him, she assured herself. There's nothing left to say. She began to close the door, "Have a pleasant evening."

He blocked it with his boot casually placed across the threshold. "Now, Miss, I'm not leaving without seeing the ladies."

"Sir, kindly remove your foot from the door," she began to lose her temper. "That is, if you want to keep it attached to your leg." She pulled the heavy oak door back then heaved it on his boot, but he put both hands out and stopped it before it closed. Rees pushed her aside, nearly knocking her to the ground and barged into the parlor.

"Stop," Inez yelled.

Before he had made three steps into the house, Onalee stood before him. Almost as tall as the man, she folded her arms across her chest with legs planted firm, "What is the problem here?"

Nick Rees looked at the tall, stern-faced Navajo before him, then Whitney and several other gentlemen joined Onalee. Rees' hand fondled the holster on his hip. He squeezed his hat in his other hand. Inez could see the tension in this man who tried so hard to stage a composed appearance. It seemed to her that he was weighing his options. Onalee didn't allow the gentlemen to bring guns into the house, so none of them were armed. Onalee's own pistol lay in her office off the kitchen.

The silence threatened to explode—so many minds speculating on what the others would do.

Finding herself frozen, afraid that a sudden movement would trigger the explosion, Inez only moved her eyes to see Rees' hand hovering above the butt of his pistol. Onalee's face remained unyielding, then she looked over Rees' shoulder at Inez and her expression eased.

"Sir," Onalee said with a calm deep voice, "the lady asked you to leave. The door is behind you." The gentlemen stood firm behind Onalee. She nodded to Inez to open the door to allow an easy and dignified escape for Rees.

His hand moved away from the holster and rested with his thumb hooked over his belt buckle. His left hand slapped the hat onto his head, then he nodded to Onalee and took a step back toward Inez and the door.

Cold wind swirled in through the open door as Inez held it wide for the man to back his way out. Not once did he take his eyes from Onalee or the gentlemen. As soon as he had cleared the threshold, Inez gently shut the door and locked it.

The thick tension drained from the warm room as the gentlemen re-joined the ladies with their before-supper drinks. Conversation and laughter rebuilt almost instantly as if nothing had happened, but Inez still shook from the experience. Strong arms embraced Inez and Onalee's deep voice comforted her. "You handled him well."

"I couldn't stop him from coming in."

"No one person could have," Onalee said. "He would have pushed his way no matter who had opened the door. The gentlemen will always be here to help protect the house, even if I'm not."

"What?" Had she heard her correctly? "What do you mean?"

"Don't worry little one," soothed Onalee. "Sometimes I need to leave for a few days, but it's never for long."

"Blue Jay?" Inez asked.

A sad smile graced her lips, "Yes."

"That man," Inez broke their embrace and leaned back against the door. "He's the one Lois and me saw at the Junction with Zhen. There's talk he beat up a girl in a Mexican house, Miss Linda's house."

"I know who he is. Don't worry about him. And," she added, "Miss Linda can take care of her girls."

"What if that man comes back?"

"He won't. He's not working for Zhen while visiting the houses. That type of man believes the world is his for the taking and he will take what people allow him, but as soon as you stop him, he goes for easier prey."

Slipping her hand into Onalee's, Inez led the way back to the piano. The music began again with a bouncy tune and light glowed from Onalee's face. Wanting to remind her that Rees was looking for Sun and that both Red Dale and Sun could be in trouble gnawed at Inez but as she watched Onalee at the keyboard she let it slip away. Now, no worries should come to the house, the gentlemen visited for entertainment, food, and companionship and that became her mission for the night.

Marvelous Mildred hovered in the corner with a wine bottle, tapping her foot to the music while watching the men and ladies. An exchanged smile brought Inez to her side. The reflection in a front window reminded Inez of her beautiful dress and newly styled hair. The tension was relieved. Playful music, happy gentlemen and girls—she grabbed Mildred's hand and pulled her to the middle of the floor where they performed a lively two-step spinning and gliding around the room. Pearl yanked her gentleman up and they joined the dance. Within minutes, all the girls had the men up and dancing.

Whirling Mildred toward the piano, Inez gave a laughing Onalee a quick kiss on the cheek then steered Mildred toward the kitchen so they could finish preparing supper.

CHAPTER
TWENTY-ONE

he bolt of royal blue satin fabric rode on his shoulder like a rifle. The unmanliness of carting fabric through the streets of Jerome, Inez reckoned, was why Jared carried it that way. They climbed the steep streets back toward the dress shop where Martha rushed to finish dresses for the three daughters of a mining company official. The girls' mother had decided that the girls would wear identical dresses but in different colors. "Christmas," Martha had muttered. "Everyone has to have a new outfit for their parties."

Inez had picked the fabric for the last daughter's dress, hoping that the remaining satin could be fashioned into her own new gown. It was a color that she thought would look striking on her. Jared hoisted the bolt to his other shoulder with the precise movements of a soldier's drill.

"Do they train you to use a rifle at that school?" Inez asked.

"Yes," obviously impressed that she had noticed his handling of the bolt. He stopped and stood straight, resting the fabric roll on the top of his boot. "We're divided into squadrons of cadets, and we drill on a regular basis." He gazed into the distance with his jaw set in a regal jut. "You never know when you will be called upon to defend your country." He dropped his pose as his eyes widened with a new idea, "Why, just here in the Territory, not so many years ago, military men were called upon to tame the savages."

"You mean the people who had lived on this land for hundreds of years?" she asked, knowing that he knew very little about the area or its people.

"Oh, yeah, you have to convert them to Christian beliefs and our way of life."

She laughed, and started to take the fabric from him and just carry it herself. But, he grabbed it back and set it on his shoulder again.

"What's so funny?"

"Jared," she tried to be logical since most men responded to that line of thinking. "What would you do if Mexicans came to Virginia and started building houses and a town on your school grounds?"

"Those damn Mexicans would be shot on sight trying to squat on our land. That land is legally owned by the school. This land wasn't owned by anyone."

"Legal is defined by the government, our government. The Indians had tribal governments that said the land was shared." She squeezed her hands into tight fists. "This line of thinking makes me so mad. You're lucky to be a white boy. Indians, Negroes, Chinese, and most of all women have no rights."

"You got all the rights you need," he said.

That statement stopped her dead still. "I suppose that we have no rights so the government will protect us from making bad decisions? Just let the men take care of us?" Even in the cool breeze of the day, she felt heat radiating from her face. "That is plain stupid—"

"Hold on there," he interrupted her. "Why is it that every time we get together, we end up in an argument?"

Calming her breath, she gazed out across the Verde Valley, from the San Francisco Peaks to the north, to the red rocks to the east. Tumbling clouds like great puffs of cotton rolled across the clear blue sky on their slow trek north. Why did Jared always make her mad? Being young and well-educated, he had potential to be so much more than the ordinary man. Being Lois' son, he had a hard working and compassionate blood-line. Maybe it was their closeness in age. She realized they shared more topical conversations than she did with Pearl. She and Pearl would talk about men, hair styles, gowns, and gossip, whereas she and Jared usually ended up arguing over the role of women, the benefits of statehood, and segregation of the races. Why then, even though they argued on almost every subject, did they keep spending time together? She had to admit she liked him, but not in the way she liked Sheriff Jim. Jared represented a challenge to win a point, to test her theories, to explore her opinions. Conversations with Jim, and even Onalee, didn't have the same questioning, and she knew why: she respected them and their views. Inez wouldn't dare challenge their notions on subjects of the day, but it wasn't that she didn't respect Jared. The idea that he was her equal allowed her the freedom to call him on his statements even though he was a boy and she was a girl, it didn't matter to her because she knew that she had more opinions than this Eastern schoolboy—valid opinions because she had lived more fully than someone sheltered in a school. The experiences of losing her family, traveling to the Territory alone, loving and losing Josiah, and then finding a family again in Onalee and the ladies ignited learned lessons and strong opinions that she felt should be shared with someone with less worldly knowledge.

"Let's just agree that you don't know everything," she said to him.

He laughed. "And you do?"

"I know a lot more than you. I have lived with abundance—good and bad."

"I like your hair like that," he said.

The abrupt change in subject tickled her, and the clumsy flattery he tossed to her was even more amusing. She had pulled her hair into a loose bun covered with a crocheted net, a rather old-fashioned look, but one she liked. When she glanced at him, his wide eyes stared at her, unblinking, like a rabbit standing motionless by the side of a trail, hoping not to be seen. "You are so silly," she laughed.

"No," his voice cracked a bit then found footing in the deep tone of a young man. "I'm just charming."

"If you say so," she reckoned he knew himself better than anyone and if he defined charming by his personality then he must be, at least in his mind. Gawky, gangly, awkward would be the words she would use, but he had the blush of a handsome man developing in him, if only he had the grace of understanding women and how not to be so pushy with his ideas. "Some women," she began, "like a man who doesn't always shove his opinions on people. Women have minds too—"

"That's for sure," he interjected with a laugh.

"And they don't like to be interrupted. You don't see many girls near that school do you?"

"There's a few in town, but there is a teacher's college about thirty miles away. Lots of girls there. Sometimes we have dances with them. So, yes," he said, "I have had my share of conversations with young ladies, and they usually have a very good time. As I said, I'm charming."

"I just want to give you a little advice about the women of today. The end of the century is coming up in a few years, it's a time of change, the railroad can take us all over the country, electric lamps and indoor toilets are in the nicer houses. Women are no longer fragile, we'll have the right to vote one day, and we'll change the world for the better."

"Like those women up there," he pointed at a group of about six women marching down the street ahead of them, led by Lottie. They carried signs, some on the ends of pickets that read 'Clean Up This Town' and 'Prostitutes Must Leave' and 'Enforce the Law — No Prostitution in Jerome.'

She grabbed Jared's sleeve and pulled him toward an alley that ran to the back of the dress shop. "Those women," she tried to come up with a reasonable story, "are always carrying on about some cause."

"Looks like they want the 'ladies of the evening' to stop stealing their husbands," he laughed and craned his neck to see the group again.

"Yes," she forced a laugh, "that's it."

They slipped into the back of the shop, but Inez saw Lottie watching them.

She directed Jared to place the bolt of satin in the storage room and to find matching thread in the cabinet. She rushed to the shop window, peeked out, and saw the group heading for the door. No customers were in the shop, nor was Martha at her sewing machine. "Martha," she yelled. "There's a bunch of women coming here with protest signs. We have to keep them away from the shop."

"What?" Martha asked when she and Lois emerged from the dressing room. "Protesting dress shops?"

"Look," Inez pointed toward the window. "They're protesting prostitution and they're coming here."

Lois peered out just as the women marched to the door. "We've got Josephina Cobble in the dressing room. She's the Methodist minister's daughter."

"Lois," Inez directed, "go keep her busy and don't let her out here. Martha, what are we going to do?"

Lottie opened the door and led the women in. Sweat dripped down her round face from the exertion of walking up the steep streets of Jerome. Wiping her forehead with a handkerchief, she looked around the shop then stared at Inez. "We're here to tell you that fallen women will not be allowed to stay in Jerome. This is a God-fearing, Christian community, and sinners will repent or be driven out of town."

Inez opened her mouth to respond, but the pressure of Martha's grip on her arm stopped her.

In her simple calico dress, a pin cushion strapped to her wrist, and her grandmotherly appearance, the statement directed to Martha seemed absurd. "Are you thinking we disagree with you?" she asked.

Lottie pointed at Inez, "That girl works at a house of ill-repute."

"Little Inez?" Martha asked. "You must be mistaken. She's a seamstress here with me. Does this look like a house of ill-repute? We're a dressmaker's shop. Didn't you see the sign?"

"I saw the sign," insisted Lottie, "but I know a harlot when I see one. We," she motioned to the women behind her, "the good women of this community, have an obligation to protect our children and brothers from lecherous she-devils. This girl you say works here, well, she physically attacked me in the street." Lottie rubbed her fleshy cheek for effect.

"You called me a whore," Inez blurted out, "in front of God and half of Jerome."

The women gasped. "Lottie," one of them said, "you wouldn't

use such language, would you?"

"Of course not," she swore. "I know this girl, and I saw her with a known prostitute, that dark-haired girl that wears the striped stockings." She looked to the women, "That is a sure sign of a fallen woman."

"Pearl is my friend," Inez stepped toward Lottie.

"And," Lottie said, "they had alcohol on their breath. Drinking and consorting with a prostitute makes you a prostitute too."

"Guilt by association?" Martha asked.

"Yes." Lottie straightened her sign.

"Then, that would make the Reverend Farragate a prostitute and all the women that help at his mission," Inez stated.

"Yes," a voice said from behind them. Inez and Martha turned to see Josephina Cobble and Lois in front of the dressing room. The petite red-headed Josephina smiled with her chin held high. "That reasoning would make me a prostitute too. And my father and mother. We help these women find better lives, so I too consort with known prostitutes. You women need to find a more worthy cause for your energies. Leave the soul saving to the churches." She turned to Lois, "Thank you Lois. I will come back on Tuesday for my Advent dress." She pushed her way through the women and out the door.

"That's just fine," Lottie said with gritted teeth. "The churches aren't cleaning up this town fast enough. I know this place is more than a dressmaker's shop and I will make sure that no respectable women patronize it." Like a mother javelina, she stretched her neck to the left and right assuring her pack remained intact. The women sneaked looks at each other.

Martha smiled and skimmed the brood, "Oh hello Ida. Your dress for the church Christmas recital will be ready for a fitting next week."

The stout dark-haired Ida nodded behind Lottie. "Thank you Martha." She turned and pulled another woman with her out the door.

"Oh and there's Mrs. Jobson," Martha acknowledged. "I'll be bringing my pumpkin pie to the church supper Sunday night. I'll see you there I hope."

Mrs. Jobson strained a grin.

Jared walked up behind Inez and Martha, "What's going on here?"

Taking his hand, Martha led him up between her and Inez. "This here is Lois' son. He's visiting us from his school in Virginia." She patted him on his shoulder. "Do you ladies want us to sign a petition?"

"No," Lottie grumbled as a couple more of the women backed out of the door. Finally, after glaring at Inez, she turned and left too.

⚹ ⚹ ⚹

"They got a right to protest as long as they're peaceable," Sheriff Jim kicked his boots up on the edge of his desk and clasped his hands behind his head.

"She's just mad at me because I told her off. That old cow is the most spiteful thing in the valley." Inez paced in front of him. "You should have seen how Martha handled her."

"I heard you handled Nick Rees pretty well yourself." His stern look held for a moment before releasing into a broad grin. "You send someone to fetch me if he comes within sight of you again. I know Onalee and some of the men were there to show him the door, but this man could be dangerous. I don't want you clashing with him."

"He's after Sun and Red Dale; it's just a matter of time before he finds them. Then what? Will he hurt Red Dale? Lord only knows what a man like that would do to Sun before returning her to Zhen."

Jim dropped his feet back to the floor and leaned forward on his desk. "Sit down," he motioned to the chair across from him. "All that marching back and forth is wearing a rut in my floor."

Settled in the chair, Inez smoothed her skirt and placed her hands in her lap. She stared back at him with raised eyebrows, "Yes?"

"Don't worry about none of that," he said. "I had a talk with

Zhen. Warned him about taking the law into his own hands, that's
not how we do things here, I told him. And I told him that if Rees is
a hired gun, I'd throw both of them in jail. He's a fiery little man,
but he's also a business man. If he ends up in jail, he'll lose his
business because a man like Zhen wouldn't trust anyone else to run
it while he's serving time, so those girls would just take off."

"That's it," Inez almost jumped out of her seat. "Put him in jail
and give the girls a chance to leave."

"Now," he drawled, "I can't throw a man in jail for no good
reason."

The reasons she thought of couldn't be enforced by Jim. Zhen
ran his house as most of the houses operated, including Onalee's, as
legal businesses with lady boarders who just happened to negotiate
entertainment behind closed doors. Jim pegged Zhen right—he
wasn't the type of man to get sloppy in his business dealings. If
he took a chance, it would be all or nothing, and Inez knew Zhen
wouldn't risk his business over one missing girl.

The duties of the sheriff blurred when applied to the people
of the community, not that Jim was indecisive or favored certain
people, but he weighed the circumstances and that would sometimes
bend the laws. Not all theft was equal in his eyes. Inez knew of an
instance when a poor Mexican farmer had pocketed an extra potato,
but then there was a miner who palmed a chunk of chewing tobacco
from the same market. The miner was thrown in jail for the night
and had to pay double for the tobacco, but the farmer was warned
and sent on his way with the potato still riding in his pocket. So,
his need for a good reason to place Zhen in jail wasn't a point she
would argue. Jim was a good man, an honorable man, a person
Inez admired. She knew he was no prince from a fairy tale. At
times, he would be moody and distant to people, but living with
Stella couldn't be easy, especially when the town gossiped about
her frequent trips to Prescott. Sometimes, Inez wondered if the long
hours of the sheriff's office had wedged Jim from Stella's life. He
was lonely. She could see it in his eyes. He often stared into the
distance, maybe waiting for something—or someone.

Reaching across the desk, Inez took hold of Jim's large, strong hands. She just sat there holding them in hers, not saying anything, just enjoying the touch and feel of his hands. The under-deputies were out on patrol and the door to the jail cells was locked. Slanting beams of afternoon sun illuminated dancing sparkles of dust in the air. Jim lifted her hands to his lips and he kissed them once, then again, and again.

Her chair pushed back on the pine floor as she rose from it, and not letting go of his hands, skirted the desk to be pulled to his lap. He withdrew his hands from hers and wrapped his arms around her waist. The gray of his eyes glistened in the fading sunlight as she leaned in to place her lips to his. As if nothing else existed, she felt only the slight pressure from his mouth, the gentle rake of his mustache, and the passion surging from her own body. No other experience had been so complete since she met him; the single kiss by the river and the innocent flirting somehow led to this moment where just the act of her reaching out to touch his hands exploded into a passionate embrace and kiss that she prayed would last forever.

Forever lasted only a few seconds as Zhen and Rees opened the door and walked into the sheriff's office.

CHAPTER TWENTY-TWO

"Excuse us Sheriff," Rees said. "I can see you're keeping the town safe from unsavory elements."

Inez almost fell from Jim's lap as he jumped from the chair. Shame smacked Inez as if Lottie herself had walked in on them, or worse, that Jim's wife Stella had. The abrupt action of Jim, springing to his feet when the door opened, confirmed to Inez they had both lost themselves in the moment, a moment that although satisfying to her, now held confusion and guilt. She didn't care what Zhen and Rees thought, after all they were nothing but criminals, but what did Jim think?

Did he believe she was what Lottie had accused? Was she? Her mind considered the possibility that living and working with the ladies had incited her to become more free with herself just as Lottie said. Association with women that gave their affection so easily didn't mean she would do that too, yet here she stood, ashamed and embarrassed that she had been caught acting on an urge. Arms crossed in front of her chest, she backed into the corner of the office as Jim rounded the desk to stand in front of the men with his thumbs hooked on his gun belt.

"What can I do for you gentlemen?" he asked glancing at Rees then to Zhen.

"Sun," Zhen began, "had customer come see her all time. He not around no more. How he know she was gone?"

Rees leaned against the door frame staring at Inez then with slow deliberate movements he straightened up and walked to the window to look out at the street. "What Zhen is saying is that this man Red

Dale frequented his place, always there to see Sun. Since she's been gone, he ain't been back." He turned to face Sheriff Jim. "Ain't that peculiar? I mean, all these Chinese sows are the same."

Zhen bristled at the name Rees called his girls, but said nothing.

"So, the way we figure it, Red Dale knows where she is. He's getting his—" He stopped short and nodded to Inez. "Excuse me, Miss. He's paying his visits to her somewhere."

"Why do you reckon he didn't go to another house?" Jim asked.

"My girls keep customers," Zhen defended. "They good girls. Please men good."

"No other Chinese houses around here," Rees said. "Once a man gets 'yellow fever' he don't go back." He laughed at his joke and pulled a match stick from his vest pocket and stuck it between his teeth. "Same with all the girls, men tend to find a type and stick with it: Mexican, Chinese, Negro, Blonde, Brunette," he flashed an oily smile at Inez, "or sweet Southern Belle." His eyes moved back to Jim, "Right Sheriff?"

"Like I told you before," Jim positioned himself between Rees and Inez, "you leave this to the law."

"Law ain't doing a damn thing," Rees said.

Zhen's beady eyes jerked from Rees to Jim. "I get Sun back."

"You'll get her back when I find her and if she wants to come back," Jim said. "You can't hold that girl as a slave. She has a right to go where she wants."

"I got contract."

"You want to take that to the Judge over in Prescott?" the sheriff asked.

Zhen scratched his head. Pulling up a chair, Rees sat down and propped his boots on the desk. "You know we don't want to force this in the court, but there is an agreement made before the girls come to the Territory. It's China law that upholds the contract, not American."

"That's fine with me. I'm an American lawman. I can't enforce Chinese laws."

"We'll get her back," Rees said. "Either with your help or I'll do it my way. Zhen hired me for the job, but I told him I like to enlist the help of the local law officers to keep things smooth." The match stick twitched between his teeth as he waited for Jim's response.

The air felt thick and stagnant. Wood in the corner stove popped and hissed, and the scent of pungent smoke hung in the room. Jim reached up and rubbed his chin then walked to the corner of the desk and with a swift kick, knocked Rees' feet from the desktop. "You are in the office of the Sheriff and in the presence of a lady, get your feet down."

Rees grinned and sat up straight in the chair.

"The way I see it, no crime has been committed." Jim stared Rees in the eyes. "I come down hard when there's a crime committed in my jurisdiction, especially when I give fair warning. Sun is probably long gone from here. Red Dale has been seen at other houses."

"Yes," Inez spoke up, hoping to help. "As a matter of fact, I have had the pleasure of Red Dale's company on several occasions." She figured she wasn't lying since she had talked to him a few times since Sun's disappearance.

"Just the same," Rees said. "One girl leaving is a bad example for the others, and Mister Zhen can't have bad examples. So, I'll go about this my way." He stood up and reached for the door knob. "Oh, I note that I was warned by the Sheriff to keep things legal."

"You step out of line," Jim warned, "and you'll be answering to me."

Rees grinned and swaggered out of the office with Zhen hurrying behind him.

Left alone, Jim and Inez stood looking at the door in silence. So many things she wanted to say, to ask, but she didn't know where to start. How did he feel about their embrace and kiss? What could have happened if Rees and Zhen hadn't interrupted them? Had their actions steered their relationship forward or veered it into a ditch? She decided to voice her most immediate anxiety, the concern she had about his safety.

"Rees," she began, "will cause trouble. That's just the type of man he is. Please be careful. He wouldn't think twice in drawing his gun..." She didn't want to follow the thought.

His arms embraced her, and she let her head rest against his shoulder. "Don't fret over what he was saying. Men like that strut and crow, but there's little action." He lifted her chin and brushed a strand of hair from her face then gently kissed her forehead. "Now go on home, I got some law to uphold," he winked at her.

⚔ ⚔ ⚔

The sun rode low in the sky, casting long shadows across the valley. Frenchy, Inez, and Onalee sat in rocking chairs on the kitchen porch husking corn, breaking beans, and peeling potatoes for Mildred.

"Don't worry about this man," Onalee said referring to Rees.

Inez had explained about the exchange at the Sheriff's office and her concern about Sun and Red Dale's safety. More of her concern settled on Jim's wellbeing, but she didn't voice it to Onalee or Frenchy. "Zhen won't leave them alone. He'll hound them forever or until Rees pulls his gun and someone gets killed."

"Red Dale isn't in Cottonwood," Onalee stated as she continued to shuck corn.

"Where is he?" Inez asked.

"He's helping me."

As was Onalee's custom, she would only offer the information she thought was needed, and Inez knew that she could ask more questions but it wouldn't guarantee more answers. But she ventured anyway, "Is Sun with him? I just wondered if they were both safely away from Rees and Zhen."

She smiled, and her high cheekbones and dark eyes delivered the comfort that Inez needed. Something about Onalee calmed Inez, maybe her serenity inspired the same in others, so for now, the simple smile was all the reassurance required.

But, Frenchy apparently did not abide by the same understanding. Always a little louder and flashier than the other ladies, Frenchy didn't mind prodding for information, whether she was interested in the subject or not. The woman enjoyed conversation. She had told Inez once that she wished she could make money by just talking to people, but the parlor house was the next best thing since most of the customers really just wanted to talk and have someone listen. "So, is Red Dale out looking for Blue Jay?"

The question hung in the air as Onalee pulled the husk from the corn in a slow measured motion.

Not deterred by her unanswered question, since she had grown accustomed to Onalee's ways, Frenchy continued, "If he finds Blue Jay, what then?" The question seemed almost a musing. "Would he come here to the house and live with us? He would scare the gentleman, a Navajo Brave," she snapped a bean from her lap and placed it in the bowl next to her chair. "I once worked in a house that allowed the Indian men to visit. I tell you, some of the things those Braves taught me," she winked at Inez. "I mean they got no shame, anything goes," she rocked back in her chair. "Yes, maybe we should take a trip down to the reservation."

"The reservations," Onalee said, "are the white man's reservations. They want to teach us the Christian way and have us forget our old way. No, when Blue Jay returns, he will not live here."

Inez sensed an unsaid conclusion, so she stated it, "You and Blue Jay will leave Jerome."

Onalee nodded.

The prospect of Onalee leaving one day disturbed her. Inez set her knife down on the potato peels in her apron and she breathed. A slow breath of the cool air helped to relieve her. Situations change, she knew that. But the family that had developed in the house meant safety and love. Imagining the house without Onalee seemed impossible because the house was Onalee—her demeanor, her dignified style, her evenhandedness. Those characteristics molded the appeal of the parlor house to both the gentlemen and to the ladies. But above the business, the ladies tended to call Onalee 'Mother' in their quieter moments, and Inez had come to see Onalee as a mother and father to her. "Of course," Inez said, "you and Blue Jay deserve a happy life together." She realized her tone had not conveyed the encouragement she had intentioned.

Onalee reached over and took her hand, "That is my reason for everything here."

"I can tell you one thing," Frenchy began, "whoever you sell the place to, had better be a classy madam. Our customers expect quality and grace in the service that you provide." She gestured with a green bean at Onalee. "This is the best house I ever worked in, and it attracts the best customers. The mines are producing more every year, more men are coming to make their fortunes, and more ladies are setting up houses. But, there is plenty to go around. Last night, a gentleman gave me fifty dollars," she looked to Inez with wide eyes. "Can you believe that? Fifty dollars. And it was nothing bizarre he wanted. He said he had just sold his mining claim to the United Verde."

Molly opened the door to the porch, "Onalee, Mildred and Pearl are into it again. Mildred is chasing her around the house with a butcher knife." Her calm manner in delivering the report assured them that Mildred did not intend to catch Pearl, but just chased her to put the fear of God and Mildred into her.

"She probably called Mildred a cow again," Frenchy dropped more beans into her bowl.

With a sweep of calfskin, Onalee followed Molly into the kitchen.

"If Mildred has time to play with Pearl, then why in the world are we doing chores for her?" Frenchy set the beans on the floor. "Ain't that a sight," she pointed across the valley as the sunset lit up the red rocks to the east. "That's the color I wanted my hair, but it's fading a bit. I'll get Pearl to refresh it—if Mildred ain't killed her." A laugh banged out her ruby lips then she took a deep breath and brushed bean pods off her apron. "I feel like a queen sitting up here on the side of this mountain watching the world go by."

Thoughts of Sheriff Jim occupied Inez. Wondering about what he was doing at that very moment; his sparkling eyes watching Stella fix his dinner, or was he at the jail working? Would their attraction lead to something it shouldn't the next time they found themselves alone? She couldn't get out of her mind the nagging sense that her emotions were wrong and sinful. No, she thought, it's not the desire, but that he's a married man. "Frenchy, how do you reconcile having," she chose her words with care, "relations with men who might be married?"

"That's the least of my worries," she said. "Married, engaged, single, young, drunk, or sober, they all have a right to companionship. The married ones usually take the most care and time. Sometimes they have a little guilt, but not much. The wives tend to not enjoy the carnal arts, so the husbands wander. And," she leaned back in her chair, "That's fine by them. Few married couples stick side by side like lovers, and those that do, do it because they are religious." She absently picked up the beans again and continued to snap them in two. "Take Onalee, her and Blue Jay have been separated for years. She could work the house and make good money, but they were joined up as teenagers, in a marriage of some sort that the Navajo do for Berdaches and Braves. That's their religion and she takes it seriously. I suspect that Blue Jay is in prison somewhere. Rumor has it that he fought the white authorities that tried to make the Navajos like white men on their own reservation. So, she's trying to reunite with him, and she doesn't entertain. Now, I was in a house once that had both girls and some young boys. There's a market for everything."

"Doesn't that hurt them? Doesn't it hurt you?" Inez asked.

"You're talking emotions now. No, to keep in this profession and I hear it's been around since the beginning of time, you learn to know the difference between companionship and love. One is just physical and doing what the animals do; the other is giving your whole self. I never give that. These men don't know me. I play a part. Hell, I'm not even French."

Nodding, Inez tried to act a little surprised.

"The gentlemen pay for companionship and a little activity in private. I keep the real me safe inside. Oh, sometimes I meet a man who is sweet and becomes a regular, but I learned to keep my heart at a distance because sooner or later he doesn't show up anymore." She cocked her head at Inez like a red rooster, "You ain't thinking about joining us, are you?"

Heat flooded Inez's cheeks. "No, I just wondered how you set your mind in the job."

"Like any job I guess. No different from the miners. They have to justify spending their days in those tunnels, never seeing daylight, breathing dust and blasting out copper. The good pay comes from removing yourself from the work—just get it done, collect your pay, and then spend the money to make yourself happy."

The sound of it didn't appeal to Inez. "Have you ever been married?" she asked wondering how Frenchy became a parlor house lady.

"I'm married now. Don't know where he is. So, I figure that makes me a widow, since no man alive and in his right mind wouldn't be by my side." She raised a painted eyebrow at Inez as if waiting for her agreement.

"Of course," Inez said. "That only makes sense. Did he work in the mine?"

"That man hardly did any work. I made the money and he gambled it away."

How a husband could let his wife sell herself was unimaginable to Inez. The marriage of her parents, although not perfect, held no resemblance to the frontier marriage tales she had heard. She knew that if Josiah had lived they would have had an old-fashioned union, her raising a family and him working as a farmer, happy in their lives.

"After he took off," Frenchy continued, "I worked in Prescott for Miss Linda. Pearl said you had seen her over here checking on her girls. She ain't as bad as some say. I tend to think that when Onalee finds Blue Jay, this house will be sold to her."

Fear tightened around Inez since she knew the reason she stayed in the house without entertaining gentlemen rested with Onalee. If she left and Miss Linda became madam, then Inez would have to choose to become one of the ladies or find other employment.

A staccato pop split through the air. The sound cracked the mountain's evening song. A bang Inez didn't recognize at first until Frenchy pushed aside the bean bowl and went to the porch railing. "Gun fire," Frenchy whispered.

A hardware store and millinery backed to the parlor house and edged the street below. The slope of Jerome stacked the roofs of those buildings lower than the porch railing, but Inez could only see part of the road. The store clerk ran from the hardware store, motioning for someone to follow him. His stocky frame hurried up the street, and soon, one of the sheriff's deputies shot past him on a racing horse. The shop girl from the millinery stood between the buildings with her hand over her mouth, staring after the deputy.

"Hey Lila," Frenchy called from the porch. "What's the ruckus?"

The girl turned to look up at them. "The sheriff's been shot."

CHAPTER TWENTY-THREE

In a rush of calico, petticoats, silk, and deerskin, Inez, Frenchy, Pearl, and Onalee dashed down the alleyway to the street below and up toward a crowd of people gathered between a livery stable and a saloon. A few of the town's women cried and pointed, while men with stern faces pushed to the front. A deputy named Thaddeus kneeled by Sheriff Jim. Inez could see only Jim's right arm and empty holster at his hip. She rammed her small form between the onlookers and to the place where Jim was stretched out on the dirt.

His left hand moved up to his right shoulder and rested there. Blood flowed, turning the ground beneath his wound a rusty puddle. He was alive. She stepped by the deputy then dropped to her knees. He glanced up at her and twisted out a half-smile, "Guess I wasn't quick enough."

"Shh," she soothed and cradled his head on her lap. A tear slid off her cheek and dripped on his blue shirt turning the spot dark like a storm cloud. The blood had soaked the other side of his shirt to a deep brown that she couldn't keep from watching as it spread further. "Where's the doctor?" she pleaded to Thaddeus.

"He's coming," he said, but not as convincingly as she needed to hear.

Just as she tried to concoct a way to carry Jim to the doctor, a strong hand gripped her arm and she turned to see Onalee squat down next to her. She slipped a large hunting knife from her boot and asked the deputy and Inez to give her some room. They sat back while Onalee, in one swift motion cut the shirt from Jim's wounded shoulder. Blood billowed from the bullet hole, set free from the soaked cloth. She reached over with the knife, and before Inez knew what she had in mind, cut off a length of Inez's cotton petticoat and began to wrap it around the sheriff's wound. She tied it in place with her buckskin belt. "Pearl, Frenchy," she directed, "go get Ben at the livery to bring a wagon so we can get the sheriff to the hospital."

The new hospital had been built several streets up Cleopatra Hill, so Inez knew they couldn't have carried him that far, but that had been her immediate reaction. She was glad Onalee had the presence of mind to think clearly.

She stroked his hair and whispered, "We're getting a wagon to take you to the hospital. Relax."

"Sheriff," Thaddeus started, "who did this?"

"That can wait," Inez snapped. "We have to get him to the doctor."

Unfocused eyes wavered between Inez and Thaddeus then Jim tried to speak again, but couldn't form words.

The clopping of a horse and rickety wagon alerted Inez that Pearl and Frenchy had retrieved transportation. "Onalee," Pearl yelled, "we got one."

With careful and deliberate movements, Onalee, Thaddeus, and several of the town's men lifted Jim and carried him to the wagon bed. Frenchy had piled up several blankets to lay him on.

"Hold up there," called a tall white man being led down the side street by a little Mexican boy. The man swung a doctor's bag in his hand as the boy pulled him toward the wagon.

"Doc," Thaddeus waved him over, "we got him in the wagon."

Hoisting himself into the wagon bed, he told the deputy, "Don't go anywhere until I look him over. The ride might be too much for him." He studied the make-shift bandage, "Good job, Onalee. I know your handiwork anywhere. Looks like it's slowed down the bleeding. Sheriff? You there? Can you hear me?"

Inez climbed on a wagon wheel spoke to monitor Jim's care.

His eyes squinted and he tried to nod to the doctor.

"Is he hurt anywhere else?" the doctor asked no one in particular.

"No," answered Inez as she scrambled up into the wagon next to Jim. "That's all the bleeding we saw, but he left a lot of blood back there on the ground."

"Thaddeus," the doctor commanded, "take us to the hospital, real slow and easy." Then he looked to Inez, "Who are you?"

She considered what her relationship would be to the sheriff and why she should ride to the hospital with them, but simply said, "I'm Inez."

Onalee climbed on the back of the wagon too. "Inez and I will take care of him."

The sun had edged behind the ridge deepening shadows and dropping the temperature. The doctor kept steady pressure over the wound and directed Inez to place an extra blanket over Jim. "This damn town is growing so fast, every outlaw in the territory thinks this is the place to make his name." Jim stirred under the blanket, a wince of pain. "Thaddeus, pick up speed a bit. I don't want him out here in the cold too long."

Climbing around a sloped curve in the road, the wagon slid into a rut with a jolt. They all cringed for the sheriff, but he remained still.

A horse galloped up to the wagon with another deputy. "Thad, how's he doing?" the rider asked.

"He's not good," he said to the young deputy. "Cyrus, you find anything about who done this?"

"Nobody seen a thing."

Inez kept her eyes on Jim. Zhen and Rees, she thought. They had to be the ones. But the deputies couldn't do a thing until Jim identified the shooter.

After the deputies had no success locating Jim's wife Stella, Inez stayed by his bedside during the night. The doctor had extracted the bullet and a chip of bone from the sheriff's shoulder and he predicted a solid recovery with rest and time to heal. Jim's morphine-clouded mind had him slipping in and out of consciousness while Inez tried to find a way to notify Stella. I have to get word to her, Inez thought.

I'm sure Jim knows where she is, but he can't tell us.

When Onalee stopped by the hospital the next morning, Inez had a plan to find Stella. "You knew Stella's parents and sister in Prescott didn't you?"

"Yes, but her parents died years ago. Her sister still lives there. I'm not sure where, but I sent a message to the telegraph office. They should know where to find her." Onalee watched the sheriff sleep. "Did he rest last night?"

"Some. I think the medicine for pain dulls his mind, so he fights it trying to stay alert. I think he wants to tell us who shot him, but the medicine won't let him collect his thoughts."

"Why don't you go home and get some rest?" she told Inez. "The nurse can watch over him."

"Zowie wowie," Jared peeked through the door.

Behind him, Lois delivered a plate of ham biscuits and placed them on the dresser. "Marvelous Mildred thought somebody might get hungry," she explained.

Jared's breathing raced as he surveyed Jim lying in the bed. "This is the sheriff? And he got shot in a gun fight?" He looked to Inez as if she had lied about such things happening in Jerome. "Is he dying?"

"No," Inez nipped the word.

"The bullet was removed and he just needs to rest and heal," said Onalee. But, while she talked, Jared stared. He hadn't met Onalee before and seemed to not understand her. Her tall frame and broad shoulders would confuse most people not familiar with berdaches, Inez figured, and she recollected her own first bewildering encounter with Onalee not knowing to say ma'am or sir. Braided hair, her shapeless smock of deerskin, her coal-black eyes, Onalee presented an exotic character to those new to her. And Jared growing up in the East certainly had little contact with anyone unlike himself, that Inez knew. Lois didn't seem to realize that Onalee's appearance mystified her son, so when he introduced himself and stuck out his hand for a handshake with Onalee, Lois fumbled for the words to acquaint them properly.

"Oh, Jared," she began, "This here is... This is my friend Onalee.

She's from the Navajo Tribe."

In his confusion, he dropped his initiated handshake since that was proper only for greeting gentlemen, and he bowed to Onalee, "Pleasure to make your acquaintance." His eyes stayed on her as if trying to concoct in his mind what and who Onalee was.

"The pleasure is mine," Onalee nodded to him. "Your mother has told me many wonderful things about you. She tells everyone at the dressmaker's shop what a fine young gentleman you have become."

A blush colored his cheeks as he glanced at Inez and his mother then back to Onalee. "Are you a real Indian?"

With a deep baritone laugh, she answered, "Yes, but I live here, not on a reservation."

"The cavalry lets you leave?"

"Only if I behave myself," she smiled.

The sheriff didn't stir as Inez watched him, but she was concerned that all the people in the room produced too much commotion. "Let's go outside and allow the sheriff some quiet," she suggested.

Lois and Jared said their good-byes while reminding Inez that Jared would be traveling back to the train station the following morning. She promised to ride with them to the Junction.

"You know," Inez said to Onalee as they walked back toward the house, "since I'm going to the train depot tomorrow morning, why don't Lois and I catch the train to Prescott and find Stella. I know she would want to be told her husband's in the hospital."

"I'll check the telegraph office to see if she has been located," Onalee said. "If they can't find her, then I'm not sure if you and Lois can. She must be at her sister's house and the people there know them. Surely, she received word by now and is on her way back here."

The urge to repeat the gossip about Stella was more than Inez could suppress. "They say," she began, "Stella has a beau in Prescott she visits. If that's true, then the telegraph office won't be able to find her."

"Whoever told you that is just repeating rumors." Onalee turned the corner and headed up the street toward the United Verde's accounting offices which housed the telegraph machine and operator. "Walter will tell us if she's been located."

They found Walter, a small balding man with a broad smile, at his desk tapping on the telegraph. His mouth moved in quiet motion as he tapped the patterns on the machine as if he read the message to himself and his hands automatically converted it to Morse code. Inez and Onalee waited in silence for him to finish the current message.

The tapping ceased, and Walter looked over to them. "What may I do for you ladies?"

Onalee began, "Walter, you sent that message to Prescott for the sheriff's wife. Has she retrieved it? Did she reply?"

"Yes," Inez added, "we need to ensure it was delivered."

"No message came back." He turned back to the machine and tapped the metal bar down against the plate of steel sending his electronic cipher across the wires. He waited for a reply from Prescott. The clicking and clacking came back and he wrote what he heard, then read the message to himself. "Pete says the sister doesn't know where Stella is." He glanced up at them. "Sorry, the message is undeliverable."

Thanking him again, they left the office and strolled down the hill to the hospital, just to confirm that the sheriff rested and the nurse monitored him.

Jim slept, the blankets pulled up to his neck. Onalee uncovered his shoulder to check the bandage; it was clean. Inez touched his hand—the warmth reassured her. The doctor and nurse promised to fetch them and the deputies if he woke.

"Might as well go," Inez said as they left the hospital, "I mean we'll be at the train depot. It's just a short ride to Prescott. I would want to know if it were my husband." I wouldn't be out whoring around, she thought, if he were my husband. Maybe she had more than one message to give Stella. Was that what was driving her to find her?

✕ ✕ ✕

The next morning, the wagon loaded with Jared, a tearful Lois, and a distracted Inez climbed the hill toward Jerome Junction. The sheriff stayed on Inez's mind and what exactly she would say to Stella when they found her. Jared drove the wagon a bit faster than he should, and the jolting over the rutted road brought disapproving glares from Inez.

"Slow 'er down," she said. "You're rattling your mama."

Lois only sniffed and wiped her eyes with her handkerchief. This trip, she had forgone the calico mother outfit and bonnet for a more fashionable tailored skirt and blouse. She wore a new hat topped with orange feathers and tan wool coat that matched. She had grown more comfortable with Jared and her true personality had emerged during his visit, even if her true occupation never did.

Jared leaned over and kissed Lois on the cheek. "I had a great visit. I'll long for the time that we can get together again."

"Oh, next time will be sooner," Lois promised. "You're growing so fast. I feel like I miss out on so much."

While he had visited, Martha had let the hems out on his pants and jacket, but Inez swore it appeared he'd grown even more during his two week visit. Although still gangly and rather awkward, he would mature into a fine man, she knew that. He was just a puppy stretching into his size. "Now, you be nice to those girls at that neighboring school," she said.

"After this trip, I have to be," he said with a crooked grin.

What is he up to? she thought. But, she didn't want to ask in front of Lois. They had established a peer association, and although she and Lois were like sisters, she had to admit she and Jared had enjoyed their sparring conversations. "What do you plan to do in Santa Fe with your school friend?" she asked.

"Oh, we will stay a few days with his family then catch the train back to Virginia. School starts up again soon."

Rolling over another slight hill, Jerome Junction rose on the horizon. The morning sun warmed them and the dry air of the brilliant azure sky held no clouds. But, Lois' mood was low and blue. She gave Jared some last minute motherly advice, while Inez nodded to add her endorsement.

At the train station, Inez let Lois and Jared have time for their private good-byes, while she went to the ticket window and arranged for the trip to Prescott. A nagging feeling caused her to look over her shoulder as the ticket agent wrote up the tickets and checked his schedule chart. The lobby had been the first place she'd seen Rees, and his presence lingered in her mind. He had shot Jim, she knew it. But, how could the deputies prove that? No one had seen the shooting but Jim, and so far he couldn't get a thought put together under the pain medicines the doctor had administered.

The train heading toward Ash Fork had arrived and Jared's bags were loaded. Lois pressed some money into his hand then wiped her eyes once more.

Jared turned to Inez, "It was a pleasure to meet you." Hesitating, he leaned in to either shake her hand or hug her.

She held out her arms and grabbed him in an embrace. "Now you take care and write me and your mama."

He blushed a bit, and then with his back to his mother, he raised one eyebrow, "Say so long to Pearl for me." Out of his right coat pocket, he pulled a lacy yellow garter and held it close so that only Inez could see it.

Recognition sank in—it was Pearl's. "No," she whispered so Lois wouldn't hear.

"Yes," he grinned then turned and hugged his mother and climbed onboard the train.

CHAPTER TWENTY-FOUR

"How will we find her?" Lois asked as they rode the train toward Prescott. She seemed to be regaining her parlor house composure, now that her son was on his way back East.

Lois rouged her checks right there in the passenger car as if everybody did it. Inez could see maybe in a female car, but this was in front of men. Oh, hush, Inez told herself, you're being as bad as Lottie. And from all the things you've seen, a woman applying rouge in the presence of gentlemen is nothing to think twice about. She laughed at her own false propriety.

"What's so funny?" Lois asked. "You think Stella will be waiting at the train platform to meet us?"

"No, I caught myself thinking the way old ladies think," she pulled Josiah's coat up around her; someone forward in the car had their window open, letting in the cold.

"Fine to think that way, but you're smarter than most, and you know it." Lois put her rouge back in her purse. "Now what will we do?"

"Ask around," Inez said. "Someone is bound to have seen her in town."

"Darling Inez," Lois started. "If a married woman is courting another man in a town where her family is known, they don't go to fancy balls and the opera. They're holed up in that man's house, living the fantasy of newlyweds."

Rattling through dells of granite pillars scattered like a giant's building blocks, the train curved through the landscape. The smooth gray slabs of stone poked through the dirt at odd angles, as if some superhuman force had erected a ghostly haphazard cemetery of massive gravestones. As tall as a man, and some loomed higher than the train, the granite rocks seemed menacing and disconcerting. Inez pointed to the large boulders, but couldn't express her wonderment.

"Those are only found around here," Lois said. "Prescott is known for granite slabs sticking out of the ground. It's a bit eerie and dangerous."

"Dangerous?" Inez asked.

"Used to be," Lois sat back and straightened her hat, "bandits would hide behind them and rob travelers as they came by. Many a prospector lost his find to an ambush. Long ago, Indians used them to conceal themselves before attacking settlers. But, don't worry, those days are long gone."

"That's what I thought about gunfights in Jerome," Inez said.

"Did you see the sheriff this morning?"

"He was still sleeping when I went by the hospital. They're taking real good care of him. I had never been in a place big enough for a hospital, but I like having it near."

"Welcome to the big town," Lois laughed.

The thoughts of Jim lying in the hospital with a gunshot wound still scared her, but she knew her duty was to find his wife so she could be by his side like she should. She'll feel so bad; Inez put herself in Stella's place. Discovering her husband was hurt and her nowhere to be found.

The train arrived at the Prescott station, and Inez, impressed by the size of the town, stared out the window. "I didn't realize the place was so big."

"It will be a difficult time finding that woman," Lois said. "But, we've got three hours before there's a train heading back to the Junction."

Disembarking from the train, they stood on the platform and watched the other people go into the station or off to waiting buggies and wagons. Ornate homes with gingerbread-style trim like Inez had seen in the East mixed with the plain pine board buildings seen in Jerome and other western towns. The city seemed to be a mix of East and West, and definitely more cosmopolitan than the simple fast-built mining town of Jerome.

Lois began to walk through the depot and toward the street as Inez tagged along behind her. "We should go to the Square, that's where the courthouse is," she said, "and most shops and saloons."

A strange sensation fell over Inez as they left the station and walked up Cortez Street, as if the streets seemed out of place or disjointed. She stopped and placed her hand on her forehead.

"You alright?" Lois asked.

"Yes, ma'am. But maybe it was that jostling train, but I'm feeling a bit dizzy."

"Oh, that," Lois smiled. "You're getting your level legs. After spending so much time living on the side of a hill, you tend to get a little lop-sided. We're on flat ground now." She pointed up ahead of them. "The Courthouse Square is two blocks that way. On the west side of the Square is Whiskey Row; that's the pleasurable street." She winked at Inez.

"You mean parlor houses?"

"The girls work back behind Whiskey Row. One end is the ladies, the other end is Chinatown. Seems neither us or the Chinese can take a front row place in Prescott, but the men know where to go."

Considering the city's layout, Inez doubted they would find Stella on Whiskey Row, but that was the direction Lois headed. Some of the buildings around the Square sported lavish carvings at the roofs and doorways; in addition, buildings had been constructed of stone and brick giving them a feeling of permanence that she hadn't seen since coming to the Territory. Most of Jerome, built with fast and furious construction, and coupled with the town clinging to the side of Cleopatra Hill, engendered a sense of precariousness.

The courthouse rose from the middle of the Square's grass lawn where oak-lined walkways led to its doors from each of the four directions. Orderly, that's how Inez labeled the town, orderly in that the city was divided into neat blocks with straight streets, unlike Jerome's twisting and inclined roads always climbing or descending the hill. Not that she liked Prescott better, it was different in a way a sweet potato is different from a rutabaga. Lois interrupted Inez's musings by pulling her into a saloon on the edge of Whiskey Row.

Nicely dressed gentlemen, along with a few dungaree-clad cowboys, stood at the bar having a midday drink. The girls working the bar seemed a bit prettier and younger than the saloon girls of Jerome. They didn't have the worn, haggard appearance that Inez now associated with the descent down the hierarchy of frontier working girls. These girls were just starting out in their careers. "They could do better than this," she whispered to Lois and nodded toward the girls. "Why, in Jerome, we could train them in the social graces and have them in the finest parlor house in town."

"They're young ones. They couldn't tell us a thing about Stella. Let's ask one of the gentlemen, they seem like the crowd Stella would associate with." Lois walked up to a handsome man with slicked back graying hair and sporting an excellent bushy mustache. "Excuse me," she batted her eyes then touched his sleeve. "We are looking for a friend of ours. Her name is Stella Phillips; she's a right pretty woman with chestnut-brown hair and fair skin."

He let his eyes scan Lois then glanced at Inez in her cowboy hat, Josiah's coat, fitted skirt and boots. "She a sporting girl?" he asked.

"Stella?" Inez was shocked that they had been identified so easily, but then 'respectable' women didn't go into saloons. "No, Stella is the wife of a friend in the hospital."

"I don't know many wives. I'm more a 'single gal' man." He turned back to his drink.

Someone tugged on Inez's coat and she turned to find a thin Chinese boy, probably no more than thirteen, and small for his age. His shaggy black hair gleamed in the lamplight of the saloon and his eyes caught the low lights transforming them to sparkles. Although diminutive, evidence of his growing showed in the ill-fitting jacket and short trousers. His smooth skin showed between the hem of his pants and the tops of his socks. He tugged at her coat again. "You looking for lady from out of town?" His English was better than she had expected.

"Yes," Inez said. "She's about my height, trim build, brown hair, usually pulled into a bun," she demonstrated on her own head, "and she has large eyes, a very handsome woman. Oh," she added, "she moves like a cat; you know, real slow and deliberate."

He smiled at the description. "I can help you look... For a fee."

"That's the game," Lois snapped. "We can look on our own."

"Hold on," Inez held up her hand. Whispering to Lois, she asked, "Wouldn't another person help? He knows the town. Maybe he can find her?" She turned back to the boy. "How much?"

"I get fifty cents an hour."

"That's a lot of money," Lois said. She scrutinized his manner, "I know what you are." A smile came to her painted lips, and he smiled too. "What's your name, boy?"

"Call me John."

"Okay, John. You have a deal. Let's go outside and discuss this." She led him out the door and Inez followed.

They settled on a bench in the Courthouse yard that faced Montezuma Street. A cool breeze ruffled the feather in Lois' hat. Inez pulled her coat close around her, as she wondered about this boy. He seemed to be quite intelligent, but very poor. Frequenting saloons was not the place for a boy his age or his race unless the bartender let him work odd jobs for a cut of the proceeds. A nice face, Inez decided, I like his broad smile and dark eyes.

After explaining the situation to John, the women asked him where he thought they might find Stella.

"White women won't be found in saloons, unless they working ladies," he scratched his head and stared toward Whiskey Row. "You think she might have a man here," he repeated their notion of Stella's numerous visits to Prescott. "Could it be something more?"

The posed question confused Inez. "What? Not a man?"

Twisting his mouth and furrowing his thin brows, John rolled his eyes up in concentration. "Follow me." He sprang from the bench and headed down toward Granite Creek. In the flood plain behind Whiskey Row, a ramshackle community had grown just as

Lois had said. Anchoring one end, rows of cribs hosted the lowliest of prostitutes; waiting for their next customer, the women stood in the doorway of their little shacks beckoning and negotiating with passing men.

"Lois," Inez whispered, "you don't think Stella is—"

"No, not at all. John, where are we going?" she asked the boy.

"Chinatown, down at other end of street." He pointed to more shacks, again with men congregated around the buildings, but these men were mostly Asian. "Many white people come for restaurant, laundry, but most come for opium."

"Opium," the word glowed in Inez's memory. "Onalee said Pearl had a fondness for it. What exactly is it?" she asked Lois.

"A plant the Chinaman smokes. Makes you a bit dizzy and drunk. I tried it once, but didn't like it," she held her hand to her neck, "burned my throat. I can't tolerate smoking anything."

A mud-caked cowboy tipped his hat to Lois as they passed down the alley.

"Honey, I'm not working today," she said and nodded to him then laughed with Inez. "A randy cowhand can pick out a working girl in a crowd faster than lightning striking."

John stopped and pointed at the street of busy Chinamen and a few loitering white men and women. "Not sure," he began, "but I seen pretty cat-like woman here. Not always, just some time. She usually with handsome man, big spender, good to John."

"Opium den?" Lois asked.

"Yes," he nodded his head, thick hair flopping.

She glanced at Inez, "Sounds like the best place to start. I've known plenty of people, high society to beggar that get obsessed with that weed. It's like a lover."

"Which place do you remember seeing this woman in?" Inez asked John.

"Follow me. Mister Yao has place behind restaurant. Good food," he rubbed his stomach, "but smoke brings more people."

A grassy path squeezed between two buildings led them to a plain pine door at the back of the restaurant, no sign or markings identified it as a place of business. John rapped on the door twice, then twice more, rattling the rickety planks.

"Is this legal, opium?" Inez asked. "It just appears that we're going somewhere we ain't supposed to."

"No law against it," Lois said, "that I know of, but most people say it's a Chinaman thing and won't admit they do it since that means they are associating with the Chinese."

The door opened and an old man peered out, his long thin pigtail hung over his shoulder, his squinting eyes scrutinized them. He chattered something in Chinese to John.

John replied in a rapid retort, gesturing to Inez and Lois. Neither man nor boy smiled or showed any pleasant expression during the exchange. Inez began to worry that they wouldn't be allowed in. The chatter stopped as the old man examined them again. Then he stepped back and permitted them to enter the dark rooms.

More sensual than Inez had expected, thick red silk drapes hung from the low ceiling creating intimate chambers within the series of rooms. Somewhere, someone played a stringed instrument, not a guitar or banjo as she was accustomed to hearing, but some other instrument with plucked strings. She liked the sound it made: slow and contemplative. A sweet smoke drifted through the place, so thick she could see it waft behind Lois and John as they walked ahead of her. Glimpsing between partially opened curtains, she peered into the chambers. White men and women lounged on large pillows on the floor, smoking small pipes. Few spoke to each other; mainly they just stared and seemed to listen to the strange music. The Chinese men sat together and babbled on in their way, much more animated than the Whites while they smoked. The Chinamen shared a large polished wood contraption with hoses that they smoked from. The long wood tube spouted several hoses like arms; with each of these, a man would puff smoke from the main tube—a shared pipe. A clever idea, Inez thought, and very social to be able to smoke with friends. John escorted them to an area with piles of pillows and one of the shared pipes, a hookah or waterpipe as Lois explained, where they could see anyone entering or leaving the establishment. Trying to sit gracefully on the pillows, Inez tumbled off but caught herself before rolling into a neighboring group of hookah smokers.

"So much for blending in with the crowd," Lois teased.

"It ain't ladylike to sit on the floor," she straightened her skirt and assumed a side-saddle posture on the pillows. "Should I try this?" she asked lifting one of the hoses from the waterpipe.

"Yes," John said. "Very relaxing and make you happy."

"Maybe you shouldn't," Lois shook her head. "We have to get back to the train and opium tends to make you forget about schedules and commitments." She thanked John for the offer, but asked him to bring tea instead. "Tea brewed without opium," she added as he went to retrieve it.

They sipped their tea and watched the people come and go. John ambled around the place, checking for the woman he thought might be the cat-like Stella.

"It's getting late," Inez said. "We should get back to the station so we don't miss the train." She set her tea cup down on a tray. "I feel like we wasted the afternoon."

"Where's that John?" Lois craned her neck to find the boy. "He wouldn't leave us without collecting his money first. Well, let's go." They began to pull each other up from the pillows when John came running to them. "See," Lois said to Inez, "I told you he'd show up before we left."

"Handsome man is here with woman," he whispered. "I talk to man, take him to back room so you can tell lady about husband."

Nervousness shook Inez's hands, what would she say to Stella? What would Stella say to them—her in an opium den with a strange man?

"We can get her on the train with us," Lois was saying, "that way she's back in Jerome by nightfall."

"Where is she?" Inez asked John. He guided them around a few corridors to a private draped area with a brass hookah that a young blond man and a laughing Stella inhaled from. The sweet white smoke swirled within the silk curtains. John entered first, whispered to the young man then led him through the drapes leaving Stella.

Agreeing to not overwhelm Stella, Inez told Lois she would go in alone. A deep breath helped calm her nerves, or maybe, she considered, the opium smoke in the room relieved her nervousness a bit too. When she parted the curtains and walked to Stella, she didn't receive any reaction. Maybe Stella didn't recognize her from the dress shop. "Stella," Inez began, then deciding she should sit next to her, lowered herself to a pillow. "I'm Inez from the Jerome Dress Shop. I come to fetch you back to Jerome."

Stella only watched her lips move and nodded.

"Your husband is," Inez didn't know how to tell her, but she didn't want to upset Stella. "Your husband is in the hospital, but he's doing fine."

She waited for a reaction from Stella.

The eyes shifted to look in Inez's eyes then the head moved to catch up to them. "Jim?" she asked.

"Yes, Jim is in the hospital. He's doing fine, but we thought you should be with him. That's why I come here to get you."

"What happened?" Her voice was slow and measured, completely calm.

"Well, not that it matters now, but he was shot in the shoulder. What matters is that he's hurt and his wife should be with him." Inez felt the calming effects of the environment melting away. "And you are his wife, so get off your ass and come with us to be with him." She stood and reached for Stella's arm, jerking her to her feet, the hookah hose clanged against the brass pipe.

"Now, hold on," Stella growled. "I'm not going anywhere with you. I've heard of these tricks, you want to take me into white slavery. Where's Burt?" She twisted free of Inez's grip. Terror filled her large eyes as she looked at Inez, as if Inez were some headless monster ready to carry her into the wilderness. "Burt!" she yelled.

Rushing in to try to calm her, Lois soothed, "Stella, it's just Lois and Inez from the dress shop. We need you to come see Jim. He's in the hospital."

"Burt!"

Old Mister Yao appeared along with another Chinaman.

The sight of them panicked Stella into hysterics. "Burt! Help me!"

The young blond man and John came running through the drapes. "What happened?" the man asked Stella.

"We were trying to tell her that her husband," Inez stressed the word, "was in the hospital and that she needed to come back to Jerome with us."

Taking Stella by the shoulders, he turned her to face him. "Stella, it's alright. These people are your friends, they mean you no harm." She buckled into his arms, crying. He addressed Inez, "I'll bring her home tomorrow. Just tell Jim, she's at her sister's."

"I will not." Inez felt disgust for both Stella and Burt. "I will not lie to that man. He deserves better than that. She needs to get herself to the hospital."

"She needs time—" he began.

"Stella? What about Jim?" Inez fired back. "What kind of wife is she? Stop coddling that woman. She should be a wife, not some slobbering child."

Stella's head stayed buried in Burt's shirt.

"Let's go," Inez said to Lois. "I have to get back to take care of her husband."

CHAPTER
TWENTY-FIVE

"It don't surprise me a bit," Molly pulled curlers from her brassy hair. Lois and Inez had returned to Jerome and the parlor house just as the women prepared for the evening. Pearl set up shop again in the corner of the kitchen as Mildred cooked supper.

"Why, oh why," Mildred wailed toward Pearl's general direction, "do you girls have to fix your hair in my kitchen? There's hair of unnatural colors flying all over the place."

Ignoring her, Pearl continued finishing Molly's tresses as Toy questioned Inez and Lois about Stella. "She was having delusions?"

"Rambling on about white slavery," Inez said, still with her coat in her hands since they had only just walked in the door. "I tell you I think she was gone, out of her mind. Of course, I don't know her that well, but this wasn't normal."

"Opium," Pearl added, "that will make you do strange things. Some people see things that aren't there. I worked with a girl who smoked opium like a kitten lapping up milk. Well I can tell you one thing, she didn't last long. Always in a haze, the gentlemen stopped requesting her because she just stared off into space, didn't smile or even attempt to act like she enjoyed it—nothing but a rag doll." She stopped her work on Molly's hair, put her hands on her hips and raised a dark eyebrow, "This one time, she was flying high on opium, drifted off to some place in her mind while a gentleman was courting her up in her room, then we heard her screams. We rushed in," she stopped and narrowed her eyes, "blood was everywhere. That crazy girl had cracked the wash basin over the man's head.

Killed him dead. Split his noggin right down the middle," she traced a line across Molly's scalp.

"Stop that," Molly jerked with a shiver.

"All I'm saying is Stella has gone to another place. If she's hooked on that stuff, she may never be back."

The look in Stella's eyes haunted Inez as she thought about Pearl's story. Not a tinge of recognition came from Stella as she had tried to tell her about Jim, the woman seemed to know nothing of her husband. Would she ever come back to Jerome? To Jim?

Pearl helped Molly remove the remaining curlers. "Did you see Sheriff Jim at the hospital?" she asked.

"No, coming back into town, the nurse said we were too late to visit. The patients were having their supper and last evening check with the doctor," she sat down at the table, hugging her coat in front of her as if it gave comfort. "Although, she said he was awake and talking to the deputies." She had wanted to be by his bedside when he woke, but instead she'd gone off trying to make Stella the wife she should be. Why? She asked herself, why do I figure I can fix things between other people? He deserves better, but then I wasn't there either.

"I'm going to go take a bath," Lois announced, "so if anybody needs the toilet, go now—I don't want to be disturbed."

"We're glad to have you back," Toy said. "How'd Jared enjoy his visit?"

Immediately, Inez glared at Pearl. She still could not believe Pearl had de-flowered Jared—if a boy could be de-flowered. Pearl grinned in her sly way, but kept working with Molly's hair.

"Oh, he had a lovely time," Lois said. "I want to thank you all for helping me while he visited. I didn't want him to think bad of his mother."

"What about the dress shop?" Toy asked.

The shop continued to do well; in fact, it gained new customers each day. "We got commitments for gowns, especially for Christmas," Inez said. "After that, we can see how business goes. I wouldn't mind keeping it going. It's making money." Pride for what they had accomplished warmed her. The venture began as a front for Lois, but now stood on its own.

"Maybe we should put Pearl into a hair dressing shop," Toy laughed. "Inez has a knack for running shops."

Pointing at her with a comb, Pearl warned, "You watch yourself little Toy, or I'll fluff up your hair so big, you will fall right over from the weight of it. Anyway, I like my work here at the house." She gazed off dreamily, "So many interesting gentlemen, so kind, so patient, so concerned about my pleasure."

The women laughed, but Inez wondered if there could be a better life for her friends.

As the evening progressed and the gentlemen were served their after-dinner drinks, Inez's growing eagerness to see Sheriff Jim could not be contained. Curiosity about his condition got the best of her, so after she and Mildred straightened the kitchen and dining room, she asked Onalee if she could take a few minutes off to visit the hospital.

"Of course, but I doubt they will let you in this late. They have rules about visitors and when the patients sleep," Onalee said. She played the piano as they talked. The smell of cigars and perfume gathered in the parlor.

"It's still early," Inez reasoned.

"Only to us, the ladies of the evening. The rest of Jerome sleeps." Onalee slipped a few measures of a lullaby into the song she played then pulled it back to in high spirited melody. "Go ahead. See Jim, if you can, but don't be disappointed if they refuse your request. He might be sleeping."

She walked the few blocks to the hospital; the wind gusting around the town felt like icy fingers going through her silk gown. A wool scarf protected her ears and the curls in her hair, Josiah's coat shielded most of her dress, but she wished she had changed shoes; boots would have been warmer than her silk slippers. At the hospital, she quietly opened the door, now glad for the quiet shoes, and relieved to find no one at the desk, she crept down the hallway to Jim's room. She peeked in to see the bedside lamp still burning, but Jim lying on his back with his eyes closed. A warm glow colored his relaxed face. She saw no sign of discomfort in his easy breathing. Creeping in, she silently closed the door and edged up to the bed. She sat in the chair beside the lamp and watched him sleep. Thoughts about Stella's odd behavior and Pearl's nightmarish story engaged her until she heard his voice, low and a bit raspy.

"An angel in green silk," he smiled.

"I didn't mean to wake you. I just wanted to see how you were." She touched the blanket covering his arm.

"Fine as frog's hair," he tried to laugh, but grimaced a bit.

"You been talking to the deputies?"

"Don't remember much."

"Who did this?" she asked.

"That's the question of the day," he raised himself up and Inez repositioned the pillow for him so he could sit up and see her better. The blanket slid down to reveal his bandaged shoulder and his bare chest.

The neat clean bandage provided comfort to her distress about the seriousness of the wound, but the sight of his naked chest, black hair with a dusting of gray that covered his strong torso, bestowed a wave of passion on her. She craved to touch him so much so that her hands began to quiver.

"I told Thad and Cyrus I couldn't identify who done the shooting. That corner at the livery stable," he said slowly, "there was a ruckus. Like an argument. Sounded like a Chinaman and white man."

"Zhen and Rees," Inez whispered.

"I reckon so, but I didn't see nobody, just heard a bang that knocked me down, then felt the warm blood flowing." His eyes watched hers.

"The whole town came running," she said. "They all love you," her eyes welled with tears and overflowed down her cheeks.

"Now, don't go messing up your pretty face."

With a corner of her wool scarf, she dabbed her eyes and sniffed back more tears. "Did," she began, "did they find anything? The deputies, have they talked to Zhen?"

"They talked to him, but 'course he denied knowing anything."

He pushed himself up more and pulled the quilt up to his chest. "Please excuse my appearance. The doc don't let me dress properly for gentle ladies."

She laughed softly at his modesty. "They have to put him in jail. What if he…" She didn't want to think about it. Then, terror struck her. "Jim, no one stopped me from getting in here; in fact, the desk at the door was abandoned! What if—"

"Now, don't worry. Rees won't come here."

"Even so, one of the deputies should be at the door."

"The nurse is probably checking on someone, just away from a moment."

"A moment is all it takes." She walked to his door and peered down the hallway. The desk was now occupied by a stout woman wearing a white dress and apron. When Inez looked back, Jim's eyes had drooped. "You need your rest," she placed her hand on his. The warmth of it reassured her of his recovery. Hesitating then giving into her impulse, she bent down and lightly kissed his lips.

He smiled. "I'm glad you're here."

"But, you need sleep." As he scooted down in the bed, she arranged his pillow and pulled the quilt up to his chin. "Good night," she whispered and turned down the wick of the lamp. As she closed the door, she focused on the nurse at the desk. The woman glanced up as she approached.

"What are you doing here?" she asked stern-faced while she surveyed Inez in the emerald gown, satin shoes, and a man's coat slung over her arm.

"I came to check on the sheriff. The door was unlocked and you weren't at this desk. Why, I could have been anybody, maybe even the man who shot him."

The nurse's walnut eyes widened.

"That's right," Inez added glad that the woman grasped the seriousness. "You keep that door locked, and it wouldn't hurt to have a gun in that desk."

"Gun?" The nurse seemed shocked. "I will not have a gun in this hospital. We're healers, not murderers."

"Prevention," Inez said, "prevention is better than healing."

She opened the door to the cold night and pulled the coat over her shoulders.

While walking down the dark deserted street she realized that Jim had not mentioned Stella. She would not tell him what she and Lois found in Prescott, but knew he must worry on his wife's whereabouts.

"How could she?" Inez steamed. Stopping, she looked back at the hospital, fighting the urge to go back and stay by his bedside. The shadow of the nurse moved across the door's glass.

✕ ✕ ✕

The next day, Inez visited the sheriff's office before going back to the hospital. Deputy Thaddeus worked at the front desk as she opened the door. "Good morning, deputy." She wondered if the two young deputies could manage without Jim. "I visited the sheriff yesterday and realized there was no one guarding the hospital at night. Wouldn't it be wise to have a man stationed at the door, just in case the shooter decides to come back?"

"Nope," Thaddeus leaned back in the chair, "just got word that the sheriff will be released from the hospital about noon. Doc said he was healing so good that they didn't need to keep him any longer."

"That can't be," she sat down across from Thad. "He was shot. How can they send him home...? Alone? Stella? Do you know if Stella is back?"

"Ain't seen hide nor hair of that woman," he said and took out a pouch of tobacco and rolled a cigarette.

My fault, she thought, I scared that old cow of a nurse by saying someone might try to get to Jim, so they're throwing him out. Stella ain't home. He can't be alone. But there's no way I can get him to stay at Onalee's—just wouldn't be right to have the sheriff living at a parlor house.

"If Stella can't take care of him," Inez started, "who will? Would you and Cyrus let him stay with you?"

"There's barely enough room for the two of us in that shack," Thaddeus began to pace the floor. "You're right. Stella's not around to tend to him." He stopped and addressed Inez, "Of course, I expect he'll be right here most of the time. He ain't the type to sit at home when there's work to be done."

The thought to move in and take over Stella's place in Jim's home was more scandalous than she could imagine, but it made the most sense to her. Then she didn't think good social judgment was her strong suit. The clock on the wall read eleven-twenty, so she didn't have a good deal of time decide what to do when Jim left the hospital. "Are you going to fetch Jim home?"

"Sending Cyrus over with a wagon," Thad glanced at the clock too. "I better go remind him. Anything else I can do for you?" he asked as he headed for the back of the jail.

"No thank you," she said and left the deputies to their work. Standing by the street, she strained her wits about Jim. Clouds rolled in from the west and she could see the snow low on the San Francisco Peaks; it wouldn't be long before snow came to Jerome. Martha worked on a wool dress for Inez—the thought brought a smile to her and excitement formed in her mind. That was it, the perfect solution. She ran down the street to the parlor house, hoping Onalee would think her idea was as grand as she did.

At noon, Inez waited with Cyrus as the doctor checked Jim over before releasing him from the hospital.

He walked down the hall smiling, obviously glad to be out of bed and leaving the hospital. "Well, I got a welcoming committee," he said. With his shoulder still bandaged and immobilized by a sling, he gave Cyrus a one-armed hug, then Inez the same, although he gave her a quick kiss on the cheek too.

"Just until," Inez began, "that wife of yours shows up, we don't want you up there in your house alone. You will be staying over the dress shop. Lois moved back to the house after her son left town, so the apartment is ready for you." She waited for his reaction.

His brow worked as if he mulled over the offer. "Now, I can take care of myself."

"No one is questioning that," Inez replied.

"That's a lot of trouble," he said. "No, I can just stay at home.

I can't put you ladies out."

Etiquette seemed to dictate that he must be hog-tied to accept the offer, so Inez countered each objection with as many ropes of common-sense she could muster. Finally, Jim stood there for a second scratching his head, apparently trying to think of one more declaration of his independence, when Inez nodded to Cyrus the decision had been made and he would stay in the apartment.

"Sheriff," Cyrus helped him up in the wagon, "you take some rest time. Me and Thad got things smooth as China silk, no need to hurry back."

Jim glanced at Inez sitting next to him on the wagon seat then back to Cyrus. "So you found the man that shot me and he's locked up?"

The grin faded from Cyrus' face, "Well, not that smooth—if you want to get specific."

"But," Inez added, "the town is not sliding off the hill. People are still going about their business. You can rest a bit."

"Oh, the mayor asked about you," Cyrus steered the horse and wagon down School Street. "Said he'd talk to you when you felt better."

"I can talk to him today," Jim said.

"First, you need to get settled in. Deputy Thaddeus brought over some of your clothes," Inez explained as they helped him down from the wagon in front of the dress shop. "And I'll have your supper ready by five o'clock. So, the mayor will have to wait until tomorrow."

That evening, Inez arrived to prepare Jim's supper in the little kitchen of the apartment. The excitement of cooking for him in the cozy space and tending to his needs sent so many thoughts careening through her head that she didn't notice no lamps had been lit until she opened the door to an empty apartment.

CHAPTER
TWENTY-SIX

Inez paced the apartment, stopped at a table and lit an oil lamp, then marched to the window in search of Jim coming up the street. She considered starting the preparations of supper, but wasn't sure Jim would be there to eat. "Where did he go?" she peered out the curtains again. "He knew I was fixing his meal for him." The thought occurred that he might have decided to go to his house, but she found the box of clothes the deputies had brought still sitting on the bed in the back room. "Well, I'll just go ahead and fix supper, then leave it for him... If he shows up and has a cold meal, then that's his own fault."

Feeling a bit rejected, she fired up the stove. The perfect cozy supper wasn't going to happen. "Here you are," she said to herself, "trying to play house with the sheriff. He's got his own life and you're trying to make it what you want." She began to flour a couple of pieces of steak. The stove warmed the rooms, but she still felt chilled. With the steaks frying, she cut potatoes and onions and placed them in a separate skillet, then rolled out biscuits and placed them in the oven. While the meal cooked, she checked the window again; no sign of Jim. Busying herself at setting the little table with plates, napkins, and some candles, she didn't hear the door open.

"Something smells mighty good in here." Jim stood grinning at the door.

Her heart soared at the sight of him and her doubts fell away. Yes, she thought, it will be what I imagined.

"I had to talk to the mayor," he explained. "He offered supper with him and his family, but I said 'No thank you, I have supper waiting on me at home.'"

Home, Inez savored the word. Jim considered this place, with her cooking his supper, his home. As he shucked off his coat, Inez hung it on a peg by the door and then added his hat. "Sit down and relax. You shouldn't be traipsing around the town just out of the hospital. You're probably plumb worn out."

"The mayor had a few things to talk about," Jim settled on a divan by the window, a bit awkward on the small settee Lois had moved over from the parlor house. "Seems like," he began and tried to arrange his arm sling to a comfortable position, "people are concerned about me being out of commission."

"Rightly so," Inez said.

"But I assured him Cyrus and Thad can handle things. Our territory extends to Cottonwood and surrounding areas. That's difficult enough for three, but now down to two... And two young ones."

The steaks sizzled low and steady as Inez flipped them in the pan. "What does he want to do?"

"Send to Prescott for some help. I can patrol as needed especially here in town, but the traveling to the valley will have to go to Thaddeus and Cyrus. They're good boys, but I don't know..."

She smiled, "Deputize me. I can help."

His laughter shook his whole body.

"It wasn't that humorous."

"Sorry Inez, I think you would do a better job than the boys— on some days." His face became serious, "The mayor had another problem. Seems that woman from down the hill has complained about the ladies in Jerome. He hated to bring it up, but she said the laws weren't being enforced."

"Lottie?" she asked. "Short and stout?"

"He didn't say her name, but joked she reminded him of a javelina."

"That's Lottie. She and her troop of righteous ladies came by the shop downstairs a while back—protesting prostitutes." Inez explained how she had come to the territory and stayed with Lottie and Sam; then how Lottie took Inez as a project of training her in social propriety. "I'm sure I am a thorn in her side, living in a parlor house and fraternizing with 'soiled doves' as she would delicately phrase it."

Iron skillets clanged as Inez finished preparations for their meal and filled the plates. She helped Jim to his feet and to the table.

"Looks and smells wonderful," he complimented.

"Thank you. Now, what did the mayor want you to do about Lottie?" the issue worried Inez. Lottie could stir up a hornet's nest when she set her mind to it.

He sighed. "Well, there are some things that need done. I been overlooking them for bigger game, but the cribs need to be cleaned up and some of the saloons can't be so blatant." A smile came to his face as he tasted the steak. "Mighty good, Inez."

"Glad you like it," she said. "But, what about places like Onalee's?"

"If this Lottie is targeting the high-class places, then that makes it harder. I need to pay her a visit and listen to her concerns. That would make the mayor happy."

As they ate supper, Jim discussed his talk with the mayor and how the deputies were doing while his shoulder healed. He never mentioned Stella or her absence from his life which caused Inez to wonder if this type of separation had become common in their marriage. The lamplight flickered in his gray eyes as he talked; after he sipped his coffee, he'd dab at his mustache with his napkin; when recounting an effort to make a point with the mayor, Jim would lean in over his plate, stare her in the eyes, as he did the mayor, and explain his supporting arguments. The more he talked, the more she adored him, and she wished the evening would continue for the rest of her life.

With supper finished, she gathered the empty dishes and spooned apple cobbler onto dessert plates. They ate and laughed and talked until she realized Jim needed his rest and she needed to get back to work. While she washed the dishes, he insisted on drying and stacking them. "You go sit down," she ordered.

"No ma'am, I can do this. See" he held the dish he his right hand, restricted by the sling, and dried it with the dish towel using his left. "Not as helpless as you think."

"Just so, I'm done. Now, do you need anything before I go?"

A wicked grin flashed across his face, before he must have caught himself and only said, "Not that I can think of."

She wrapped her arms around his waist and pulled him to her, then on tiptoes kissed him gently on the lips—the taste of coffee on both their breaths. Not wanting to tire him with talk or anything else, she knew to keep their good-night quick. "Get your rest," she patted his chest and then kissed him quickly again just because she couldn't contain herself.

Mildred prepared the house supper as Inez pulled on an apron to assist. The ladies primped and primed themselves upstairs, and Onalee scribbled in her account books in her office by the kitchen.

"Glad you could make it," Mildred handed Inez a tray of biscuits to slide into the oven.

"Sorry to be late, but I fixed supper for Sheriff Jim. You know he's staying at the apartment over the dress shop?"

"Ain't that cozy?" Mildred batted her eyes. "And what does Mistress Phillips have to say about you feeding her husband?"

"Stella," she shot back, "is nowhere to be found. That woman is no good. Here her husband has a bullet pulled out of his shoulder and she's off gallivanting around." She slammed the biscuits in the oven, "Besides, Marvelous Mildred, it's our duty to take care of the men in this town, especially when the 'good women' of the community are too busy with their causes and their own desires to bother with anyone else." The thoughts of Lottie and her new campaign and Stella with her beau made her furious since these were the very women who would run the ladies out of town for being a menace to the community. She stopped mashing potatoes to get Mildred's attention. "Do you know that we're having a pine board walk installed outside the house? And, Onalee just gave the school money to help build on an extra room? Now, what business can claim that kind of charity?" Gripping the wooden spoon, she smashed the potatoes with hard intense strokes.

"That's it girl," Mildred laughed, "you crush those taters."

"Well," she stopped and looked at the remnants of the potatoes, "we're doing creamed potatoes aren't we?"

"Are now."

The bell rang at the front door, and Inez and Mildred looked at each other. "It's a might early for gentlemen." Mildred nodded toward the parlor, "You're more presentable than me, go see who it is."

She hadn't changed for the evening, but still wore her street clothes of calico, so she stopped by the entry mirror to check her hair and blouse before opening the door. Red Dale stood on the step with his hat in his hand, and behind him, a tall dark Indian in buckskin breeches and shirt peered over his shoulder as if searching for someone within the house.

"Dale," Inez said, "what a surprise and a pleasure to see you." She wondered where Sun was hidden and what the Indian was doing with him. "Come in." She stepped back to allow entrance to the house.

"Good evening, Miss Inez," Red Dale nodded and a lock of auburn hair fell across his forehead. His blue eyes scanned the parlor. "Is Onalee around?"

The Indian caught her attention because at the mention of Onalee's name, he straightened his shoulders and neck as if coming to military attention. The man was a large, handsome brave. His dark face held few rigid lines, but the hard angles of his chin and cheekbones gave him a sculptured look. His eyes seemed sensitive and caring in the way they searched the room as if he believed it was an intrusion to look around without permission. But, his eyes continued to explore the parlor as Inez and Dale talked.

"I'll fetch her," she said. "Please come in and make yourselves comfortable." The men walked to a sofa and stood. Inez realized etiquette called for men to stand until she sat or left the room. Odd, she thought, that Red Dale and this Indian brave possess the good manners that escape even the top officers in the mining company. Before she left the room, she held out her hand to the brave and said, "I'm Inez, and you are?"

For the first time, his eyes settled on her and he took her hand in his. "I am Blue Jay."

Onalee's mate—she took a step back. The man Onalee had been searching for, all across the Territory, now stood in front of her. How would Onalee react at seeing Blue Jay after all the time she'd spent searching for him? She knew that they would want privacy, time to talk and explain.

At Onalee's office door, she asked Onalee if she could receive a visitor in her private room—a large bedroom and sitting area on the main floor of the house that few people entered—it was Onalee's sanctuary.

"Of course," Onalee said as she shuffled her papers on the desk and set them aside. "Who?" she asked without looking up from the desk.

"Red Dale and another man," she didn't want say too much since she knew their meeting should be in private. "I'll bring them around."

Onalee closed the door to her office and went to her room, while Inez retrieved the men from the parlor. "I didn't tell Onalee that Blue Jay accompanied you," she whispered to Dale. "I reckoned they would want to talk alone without the girls or Mildred knowing he was here." She walked them through the back of the house away from the kitchen and to Onalee's door. She knocked softly.

Blue Jay fidgeted with the sleeve of his shirt then ran his fingers through his long hair. His eyes focused on the closed door like a dog waiting for his master to return home.

With another quiet knock, Inez opened the door, revealing Blue Jay. She and Red Dale stood back and let him enter. A gasp came from Onalee, then a few tentative words in Navajo. The expression of the words was cautious, then calm, then a slurry of words in an excited and joyous trill.

Taking Red Dale's hand, Inez led him away from the back room and back to the parlor. She hugged him and said, "Thank you for finding Blue Jay, I know she's been looking for years."

"I know. Me and Onalee have been searching and we have a deal. When I found Blue Jay, she would pay off Sun's debt to Zhen."

Her happiness faded. Although she loved seeing Sun and Red

Dale free from Zhen's hunt, she didn't think Zhen deserved to be paid for Sun. "You can't give that man money. He's taken so much from Sun to begin with," she paced across the carpet. "Keep the money and leave the valley."

"Now, Miss Inez, we know he brought in that hired gun to find her, we just got to pay his price to be free of him." He watched her pace.

"No, Rees shot Sheriff Jim. He will answer for that. You can't reward Zhen for his bullying and crimes."

"I hate to do it, but it's the only way I see," Dale headed for the door. "How is the sheriff?" he turned and asked.

"He's doing much better. Some rest and he'll be back at full strength." She closed the door behind Dale and returned to the kitchen.

Mildred slapped the ham on her work table and began to carve it into slices. "Who was at the door?"

"Red Dale," Inez tied her apron back on.

"He come calling for one of the girls? He staying for supper?" Mildred probed.

"No, he left."

"What'd he want?"

"Mildred," Inez put her hands on her hips, "he had business with Onalee. That's it. Now, I don't think Onalee will be playing the piano tonight. Do you know where the discs are for the music box? All we need is a little music to set the mood."

"They'd be in that chest by the staircase. Why won't Onalee be out tonight?"

Wanting to avoid direct questions about Onalee, Inez changed the subject again, "I got to get changed. The gentlemen will arrive anytime."

"Girl," Mildred called after her, "I got work for you, come back here."

"Sorry, I'm hostess tonight." She sped up the back staircase to her room.

As the evening progressed, the gentlemen dined and the ladies ordered drinks. Inez kept the tabs and assisted Mildred in serving. From time to time, Inez expected to see Onalee and Blue Jay emerge from the back, but they stayed put. The remembrance of Frenchy's thoughts about Onalee selling the house came back to haunt her. She'd mused that if Blue Jay was found, then Onalee would leave Jerome. The house would be sold, and then she knew her days of hosting would be gone and she'd have to entertain or leave the house.

The large mahogany music box required steel discs to play tunes; she switched the disc to one of lively music and gave the box a good crank. The music pinged across the room as the gentlemen lit cigars and the ladies ordered their after-dinner cordials. Pearl courted two young gentlemen, but as she salvaged a near-empty bottle of wine from the dinner table, she stopped to ask Inez, "Where's Onalee?"

"Had some business to attend to," Inez wouldn't look her directly in the eyes and busied herself with gathering dishes.

Pearl swigged down what was left in the wine bottle. "These two boys are hinting they want to both go upstairs at the same time." She set the empty bottle down. "This ain't no two for one, they both will pay."

"Oh," Inez began before she thought better, "give them one for free like you did little Jared."

Laughing, Pearl popped a chocolate into her mouth.

"I still can't believe you did that," Inez hissed. "He's just a boy."

"Don't you be my conscience, you are no innocent. Sheriff Jim can attest to that."

"You have had enough to drink, Pearl. I ain't done nothing like that with Jim." She loved Pearl, but knew that with a few drinks, Pearl could get right direct in what she thought. "Besides, he's hurt, I'm taking care of him."

"That reminds me," she lifted her skirt so far that Inez hurried to shield Pearl's legs from the parlor inhabitants. She pulled a small gun from her garter, "Here take my derringer." She pushed it into Inez's hand.

The steel, warmed by Pearl's thigh, felt heavy and deadly in her palm. The shape fit naturally into her grip. The lamp light glinted off the barrel.

"It's loaded, so be careful," Pearl warned. "Since you are around the sheriff and that man is still roaming the streets, you may need it."

A protest formed in her throat, but she stared at the pistol and thought about the fear she'd had at the hospital. "Thank you," she said and stepped behind the curtain separating the dining room from the parlor and slipped it into her own garter.

CHAPTER
TWENTY-SEVEN

They sat in front of the ladies like guardians of the future. Blue Jay's face showed little emotion, but Onalee beamed with unbridled happiness; a sensation Inez hadn't seen on her in the many months she'd known her. It was as if Onalee's dreams had come true, her goals fulfilled, and her prospects unlimited.

On the other side of the room, the women seemed sad and melancholy. Mildred picked at her apron, Toy and Frenchy sat straight-backed on the couch while Lois and Molly stood together, Inez guessed they had to be worried because they were the oldest. She and Pearl flanked the couch in soft upholstered chairs. The morning light streamed in the front windows as the sound of passing horses and wagons clopped along the street.

"And so," Onalee concluded, "I have to decide what to do with the house."

"We," Molly spoke first and motioned to the women, "could buy it from you and run it ourselves."

Pearl let out a sigh and shook her head. "Can you imagine us trying to do this on our own? We barely get dressed and downstairs to greet the gentlemen on our on accord. And who would manage Marvelous Mildred? That woman needs a stern hand to get anything done."

"Now wait a minute missy," Mildred said. "I ain't no child and I can do things myself. Hell, I do all the cooking and serving and—"

"You do a fine job too," Onalee interrupted. "I haven't decided anything yet, but I wanted all of you to know."

Her stomach churned as Inez thought about the possibilities and the shattering of their little family. Onalee had been the strong constant thread that bound them together; now, it seemed they would unravel without her.

"Thank you," Molly said. "You have been like a mother to all of us. Lois and me know most high-class houses wouldn't have kept us this long. Maybe Inez can use us in the dress shop."

"The dress shop?" Inez repeated. "What will happen with that?"

"You and Martha have it making money, enough to pay for itself," Onalee said. "So, I think that will stay with the two of you."

A bit of relief settled over her, but Inez knew the shop didn't have enough profit to support all the ladies, they would have to stay with the parlor house. "When will you and Blue Jay be leaving?"

"When the time comes," was all she said. Blue Jay rose and returned to the back of the house and with that, the ladies seemed to relax and started peppering Onalee with questions.

"Where are you going?'

"Can we keep the dresses?"

"Will you start another house in a different town?"

"Mother, say it isn't true."

"Please take us with you."

"How much money would we need to raise to buy the house from you?"

"Can Molly take over as Madam?"

"Why her?"

"Why not?"

"Don't listen to Pearl, she can go to another house easily."

While the commotion continued, Inez felt tears build up in her eyes. She didn't want to cry in front of Onalee, especially now that she was so happy to be reunited with Blue Jay.

"No matter what emotions burst out now," she said over the clatter, "we only want the best for you." The room quieted. "You've been mother and father to us and given opportunities that others wouldn't. Thank you."

"Yes, thank you." Lois seconded.

"We just have some shock to get over," she told all the women. "Things will work out." A deep breath helped her hold back the tears. "I know it will."

"You are my family," Onalee said. "I will make sure none of you are left on the street."

After Onalee joined Blue Jay in her quarters, the girls huddled and complained, reasoned, and justified their feelings.

✕ ✕ ✕

She found Jim in the sheriff's office working on papers while the deputies patrolled. "Seems like everything is changing," she began and then told him of Blue Jay's return and Onalee's plans to leave the town with him. "Oh, and Red Dale found him. He and Onalee had an agreement that she'd pay off Sun's debt. We can't let Zhen get that money; it just ain't right. He should go to jail."

"I don't have a thing I can charge him with." Jim eased back in the desk chair and placed his boots on the desktop. He winced a bit, but moved his shoulder to a more comfortable position. "Speaking of charges, your friend Lottie is still on the warpath about the houses. I talked to her this morning. This is her crusade, and she's not about to stop. This might be a good time for Onalee to close down."

"No," she perched on the edge of the desk, "those women have no place to go. Lois and Molly will probably end up in a saloon, or worse, the cribs."

"Don't worry about that," he said. "Those women have wits about them. They can find other work."

"What? Doing laundry for Zhen? Serving drinks? Serving food? What opportunity do women have?" she sighed and calmed her voice. "Onalee's house is a safe and happy place for those women. I won't have Lottie tossing them out on the street. What does the mayor have to say?"

Jim shook his head. "He wants to keep his job too. Elections are coming up and with more families moving into town, their votes count as much as the miners'."

"Do you have any idea how many 'family' men come to

Onalee's?"

He laughed. "Probably more than the single men, but in public they'll side with their wives."

The jail door squeaked open as Thaddeus dusted off his jacket, "That darn Mabel has been fighting again. Says that one of the girls stole her money, so she yells across the alley anytime a man stops at the other girl's crib, she yells 'watch your wallet mister, she's a thief and a lousy lay.' Excuse my language Miss Inez."

"Is it true?" Inez asked.

"Which part?" Thad smiled. "I mean the girl might have stole the money, but for Mabel's accusations about her talents, I can't testify to that."

"Don't encourage him Inez," Jim said. Then he turned to Thad, "You put her in the ladies' jail?"

"Yeah, that should cool her down for a while." He sat at his desk across the room.

Inez decided to leave the men to their work and maybe visit Lottie to see if she could talk to her. But, as she considered it that was the worst thing she could do. "You boys get to work," she said as she opened the door to leave, but on the other side of the front step, stood Miss Linda in all her feathered finery.

The woman dressed from head to toe in yellow. Topped with an elaborate canary-colored hat with ostrich feathers arching over her ruby hair, Linda swept into the room. Her fitted skirt and balloon-sleeved jacket, both in the same canary tone, lent her an air of sophistication, even though Inez considered the color would look better in the spring months than during the dead of winter.

"I'm here to get Mabel," she said to the sheriff.

He pulled his boots from the desktop and stood. "She needs to simmer down for a few hours. Thad here just got her settled."

Linda glided across the room like a graceful bird. "The longer she stays here, the less money she makes. What's her bail?"

"Until she learns her lesson about fighting with the other girls," Jim countered, "the more often she's going to find herself locked up."

For the first time since entering the office, Linda glanced over at

Inez. "You're one of Onalee's girls—Inez, right?"

"Yes ma'am. I work in the kitchen."

"I hear Onalee is selling the place."

Inez looked to Jim, "Word travels fast in this town."

She continued to watch Inez as if thinking about Onalee now instead of Mabel. "Sheriff, you're right. Let Mabel stew here for awhile." She held out her gloved hand toward Inez, "Are you on your way back to the house? I'll accompany you. I'd like to pay my respects to Onalee. We've known each other for such a long time."

With a bit of reluctance, Inez took her hand not knowing why Linda wanted to walk with her, but reckoned the camaraderie had to do with the sale of the house. She shot a look of distress toward Jim as they left the office and he winked at her as if to boost her confidence.

"Now, Inez," Linda began as they strolled down the street, "Onalee is selling her house? I did hear that, but you know how rumors fly in our little community. Why would she leave?"

"It's not my place to say. She has some personal reasons, and I'm not sure if she has decided anything yet." She didn't want to speak for Onalee, and she wasn't completely in favor of this woman wanting to take over the house.

"Running a quality house takes experience, a bit of savvy in the business world. Few women possess that skill." Linda held her head high and the ostrich feather waved in the breeze. "You have the girls to deal with and all their complex relationships between each other, the customers who must be given the utmost attention and care, the laws that have to be weighed and balanced to continue operations... Oh, Inez, it is a most complicated business. Only a woman such as myself has the abilities to make that house successful."

"The house is very successful," Inez said. "We're the best parlor house in town."

"But," Linda added, "I can make it the best in the Territory, better than any in Prescott, Bisbee, Tombstone, Tucson, or Phoenix."

Lottie came to her mind. "Let me ask you a question then. If the town had a group of wives that wanted to shut down the house, what would you do?"

She smiled, "You mean like here? I know about the campaign by a few of the women in this town. It happens often when the place starts to grow beyond a mining camp.

"Running a house requires good relations with the sheriff and town leaders," Linda continued. "Those men become part of the business. They go on payroll to some degree."

"No, you must be mistaken." Inez couldn't believe tactics like that happened, "Why, that can't be legal."

Laughter chirped out of Linda's carefully painted lips. "Dear, legal is whatever works for a town."

The sharp sound of hammering greeted them as they rounded the corner. Jedediah and some of the ladies' other customers nailed down pine boards, building the plank walkway in front of the house.

"Nice idea," Linda said.

"I thought it would help stop mud from being tracked in," Inez said, but didn't mention that the dress shop also had a walkway. She considered it really none of Linda's concern that they were running the dress shop too. As they approached the door, Inez decided to let Linda go in alone. She didn't want the fact that she accompanied her into the house to feel like her endorsement of the woman. The other women would surely think that if they entered together. "I still got some things to do. You go on in." With that, Inez turned and walked away.

The method Linda used with her businesses didn't set well with Inez. Bribes, corruption, moving women down the line as they got older, well, she thought, that's just not how you treat a family. Of course, Linda had successful enterprises, but was it worth the money? She waited behind a post and watched Linda enter the house without speaking to the men who worked on the walkway, she just stepped past them.

Dealing with Lottie did not mean putting the town officials on the payroll; that would only make her more determined to change things. Stubborn, that's what Lottie was, stubborn and inflexible. But Inez knew she had the advantage because she could be quick and agile, her history showed that.

Once inside the dress shop, she helped Martha with a few chores and added the receipts to the accounting book, but the sale of the house stayed on her mind. The problem tumbled around in her head while she came up with solutions, but then dismissed them as impractical. One idea kept rising to the top, and it took the sure steady voice of Martha to skim it from the rest.

"Why don't you take over the house?" Martha stitched lace on a petticoat. "You do a fine job here. Wouldn't it be similar?"

"Well," Inez thought out loud, "there's a bit more to it than the dress shop, but I have managed while Onalee was out of town." She sat down next to Martha. "Do you think I could?"

"You won't know 'til you try." Martha said.

"But, the money? How would I pay for the house?"

No words came from Martha; she just raised her eyebrow and tapped her forehead.

"Yes, ma'am, it is a brain teaser." She glanced toward the door wondering what Linda was doing at Onalee's. She knew she could keep the house running and making money. That was a mark she'd attained, but for her skills for handling situations like Lottie, that left doubts clouding her target.

An urgent knock on the back door startled her and Martha.

"Lord, who's banging on that door?" Martha looked to her.

Inez rushed to the storage room and unlocked the door to find Red Dale and Sun out of breath and shaking.

"Miss Inez," he said as he and Sun pushed the door shut behind them. "Rees has been hanging around the blacksmith's barn. He knows Sun was there." His blue eyes pleaded even before he said the words. "Could you, would you let her stay here for awhile? I can't let anything happen to her."

"Yes," she said before she had time to consider it. "I guess I can put a little cot here in this room. The sheriff is staying upstairs in the apartment…" Another crisis she wasn't sure she could handle, would someone like Linda know what to do? "For now, you can stay here." She moved a bolt of satin so Sun could sit on a chair.

"Thank you," Sun bowed to her.

Inez bowed back then looked to Dale. "It's not comfortable, but

I need time to think of something better."

"It's safer than my place," he said.

"Didn't you give Zhen the money?"

He rested his hand on Sun's small shoulder. "Not yet, I thought about what you said about leaving town, and I was doing some figuring, but Rees is like a damn bloodhound and I don't know what to do."

"Sun," she squatted down to be on eye level with her. "You stay. Stay in that chair. Martha is working in front, but you stay. Dale and me are going to see the sheriff." Talking with Jim gave her confidence and helped her sort out ideas.

Sun sat still in the chair, but her eyes stayed on Dale.

He repeated what Inez had said, reassuring her that she'd be safe and to stay put. "We'll get back soon," and he kissed her. A smile strengthened her face.

On their way to the sheriff's office, Red Dale scanned the alleys and streets for any trace or whiff of Rees. With each step, the gun strapped to Inez's thigh reassured her a bit.

Jim's injured shoulder limited him to office work, and as they entered, Inez could see how it wore him down. He treaded the floor from desk to cabinet to window to gun rack to table to desk. He motioned them in, "You two look like rabbits being chased by a coyote pack."

"We are," she said. They explained how they needed to move Sun for safety as Rees closed in on them.

Irritation sharpened Jim's face when they spoke of Rees. His eyes darted as he considered the situation. Finally, he said, "I'll have to lock her up."

"What?" Dale asked.

"Put her in jail." He glanced from Dale to Inez. "That's the safest place for her, and Zhen will find out," he raised his hand to stop Inez from her protest, "but that's good."

"Why?" she blurted out.

"Like we talked about before, when the law gets involved, Zhen scurries back into dark corners. With Sun in jail, he won't come before the judge to get her back. He'd have to explain why she is indebted to him."

"But that won't stop Rees," Dale said.

"It might," Inez said. "If Zhen can't get her back, then he doesn't need Rees anymore. He will send him away." She hoped that was the case, but she didn't believe it any more than Dale or Jim seemed to.

CHAPTER TWENTY-EIGHT

Jim, Inez, and Dale retrieved Sun from the dress shop and placed her in the ladies' jail, each explaining to her that she wasn't in trouble, but that the jail was a safe place from Zhen. She seemed to doubt their intentions, even with Red Dale sitting with her in the cell, she huddled in a corner.

The cell's only solid wall consisted of a rough brick that backed to a dark street lined with cribs. The rest of the cell was enclosed with iron bars that gave the ladies little privacy except for a drape that could be pulled closed when the women needed to wash themselves. Never having been in a jail cell before, Inez tested the bars for strength, the cot for comfort, and the window for its view. "Which was here first," she asked Jim, "the cribs or the ladies' jail?"

"Well, there wasn't a need for a ladies' jail before the cribs set up shop, so I figured the best place for it was down here where the girls work."

Although not a large space, the jail housed eight cells—four on each side of the aisle. Sun had been lodged in the corner closest to the stairway. Mabel, Miss Linda's girl, slept in the cell at the other end of the hallway.

"Jim," a voice called from the sheriff's office upstairs.

"Just a minute," he yelled back. "Red Dale, you stay as long as you like, just shut the cell door when you leave."

Realizing that Dale and Sun would want some private time to adjust to the new situation, Inez decided to leave too. When she and the sheriff reached the top of the stairs and walked through the men's jail, they discovered the mayor sitting at Jim's desk. A thin lanky man, he appeared to Inez to look more like a farmer than a mayor except that he was dressed in wool trousers and waistcoat. The farmer aspect of his appearance stemmed from his weathered face, lined with the deep furrows of a man who tills the fields.

"Jim, Lottie Bemis is sitting in my office."

The mention of Lottie's name stopped Inez from walking out the door.

Jim took her hand and guided her to the chair across the desk from the mayor. "Mayor, this here is Inez. She knows Mrs. Bemis."

The mayor rose to his full height, towering over the desk like a high-class scarecrow and nodded to Inez, "Glad to make your acquaintance, Miss Inez." He sank back down to his seat and addressed Jim, "She's a thorn, a thorn in the ass of this town."

He didn't apologize for his language as most men would. As she thought about it, she liked that. She'd certainly heard worse from the ladies.

"Miss Inez," he continued, "since you know her, you can testify that she's an old hound that's got us by the seat of the pants. She ain't a bit worried about the cribs; it's the high-class houses she complains about. Hell, she's a widow and I think she's mad that the men would rather go to the parlor houses than court her."

"Well, that may be part of it," Inez said, "but I could be the other." She told the mayor how she had lived with Lottie and then left after Josiah was killed. "When I came up the hill and started working for Onalee instead of skulking back to Lottie full of apologies, I think Lottie took that personally."

"She did mention Onalee's place," he said.

Jim scratched his head, leaned against the desk, and stared across the office to that blank wall he tended to use for thinking. Inez watched knowing that something would come to him.

"Inez," he asked her, "how does Onalee make money?"

"Well, she serves supper to the ladies and their gentlemen guests which the gentleman pays for."

"And how does she make money from the ladies?"

"They pay her for room and board," the statement brought a smile to her face. "That's right. Onalee runs a ladies boarding house. What does Lottie have against that? In fact, I used to pay Lottie room and board."

The mayor grinned. "That's it. Young lady, sheriff come with me, I'm pulling this old thorn out of my ass for the last time."

His office sat a block away on the second floor of a hardware store. The three of them entered to find Lottie waiting and occupying her time with a cross-stitch loop. Her round face drained of color when she saw Inez.

"Mrs. Bemis, please come into my office," the mayor said as he walked past her.

She glared at Inez and set her face into a mask of mule-headed determination. "Mayor," she said while stuffing the cross-stitch into her bag and following them into his office, "I have a group of ladies who are just as outraged as I am. We are forming a group to better this community and make it safe for children and families."

"Wonderful," he said and motioned her to a chair in front of his desk. Inez seated herself next to Lottie and Jim leaned against the window sill adjusting the sling that held his wounded shoulder in place. "Now, Mrs. Bemis, you are bringing some mighty serious charges up against the fine ladies at Onalee's house."

"Yes sir, they're whores, prostitutes, corrupting this town."

He sat silent for a while and Inez wondered if he hand changed his mind about dismissing Lottie's notion.

"Miss Inez here," the mayor nodded to her then looked back at Lottie, "I believe you know her?"

"Yes, she's fallen in with them. I tried to steer her on the right track, but I fear the death of her husband-to-be was more than her simple mind could take."

Inez jerked in the chair and opened her mouth to protest, but Jim laid his hand on her shoulder to settle her.

"What was your relationship to Inez?" the mayor asked.

"She boarded at my home and we were business associates in the laundress business. That was until she decided it wasn't exciting enough for her and she stormed out of the house and took up with harlots." Lottie kept her eyes on the mayor and never addressed Inez directly.

"Miss Inez, what do you do at Onalee's house?" he asked.

"I work in the kitchen, preparing supper for the ladies and their guests. Onalee's lady boarders will invite friends to dine with them and I work with Mildred to cook and serve the meal."

"That sounds right neighborly and like a service to the community of gentlemen who can't cook for themselves." He turned his attention back to Lottie, "What did you and Miss Inez do at your home?"

"You can't compare my home to that place." Her face flushed.

He waited for her to answer.

"Like I said, we did laundry for people."

"Another fine service for the community," he nodded. "Now the way I see it, Onalee's operation is like yours, now why would I take exception to her and not to you? Why would the ladies you have corralled have a problem with this boarding house and supper kitchen?"

"They do more than that," she twitched in her chair causing the wood to creak.

"Can you give me a first-hand account?"

"No."

"I can," Inez said. "I'm working there and I worked for Lottie, boarding at both places. It isn't the same. Lottie had a servant and master business, where Onalee has a family—those women board there because they're like sisters. They have fun; the gentlemen treat the place like their home too. I never have heard a cross word, unlike I did at Lottie's."

"Cross words?" Lottie fumed. "This isn't about me," she straightened herself in the chair and wiped a trickle of perspiration from her temple.

The flat odor of sweat and face powder drifted from Lottie, and Inez knew the nervous tension caused by the questions had begun to wear Lottie down.

The mayor stretched his tall frame up from his chair. "I don't like wasting my time on accusations that can't be backed-up." He lit his pipe and puffed the smoke in three quick huffs: "Rumors... Gossip... Hearsay... Mrs. Bemis, I can only conclude that Onalee has a boarding house, like you." He looked to Jim, "Sheriff, do you know of any laws Onalee has broken?"

"Not a one. In fact, she's a pillar of the society. She just gave money to help the school add another room to handle more children."

"That's a fine example of citizenship," the mayor smiled. "Now, Mrs. Bemis, I'd suggest you follow Onalee's example and take that group of women you riled up and put their enthusiasm to use—the school needs new books."

Lottie continued to sit looking from the sheriff to the mayor.

"Good day, Mrs. Bemis," the mayor walked to the office door and held it open for Lottie.

She pushed herself out of the chair and lumbered out of the office without another word.

Containing her joy until she and the sheriff had left the mayor's office, Inez squealed and hugged Jim on the street. "Can you believe he told her to follow Onalee's example?"

"Yeah, the man can talk circles when he wants to. I was ready to give Onalee and the ladies an award for their civic service."

The afternoon sun warmed the hillside as they walked, and Inez felt as contented as she had in many months. Lottie seemed to be out of her life.

A couple of galloping horses approached with Thaddeus and Cyrus riding side by side, excitement in their eyes. "Sheriff, there's a disturbance at Zhen's place!" Thad yelled.

Jim perked up and his right hand started for his holster before the sling pulled it back.

"We got it," Cyrus called as they dashed by.

He watched them disappear around a corner, "Maybe I should get down there."

She didn't want him to go especially without the use of his right arm, but then a more important concern came to her. "Who's watching the jail?"

"We only have one drunk in the cell," Jim still watched the corner where the deputies had gone, "and Mabel downstairs in the ladies' jail."

"What about Sun?"

He turned to her, eyes twitching, connecting the disturbance at Zhen's with Sun left unguarded at the jail. "Let's go."

He ran toward the jail with Inez following close behind. They rushed to the door and into the empty sheriff's office. Behind the desk, Jim searched a drawer then stared at the hallway to the jail. "The keys are gone. Maybe," he said to Inez as if trying to convince her, "Thad took them with him."

Inez started for the jail, but he stopped her.

"No, you stay here. I'm going to check on the prisoners."

"No," she said in a soft voice. "I'll go with you, but I think we should be quiet about it."

He seemed to think about it for a second then slipped the sling off his arm. When he reached to grasp his gun from the holster, a shudder made him stop then he tried again and slid the pistol from its leather sheath.

The walk down the corridor of the men's jail seemed slow and noisy as floorboards creaked with each step. The drunk snored low and even. The ladies' jail, scored into the hill below the men's, lay only a staircase below. Their footsteps would easily be heard.

At the top of the steps, Inez held up her hand to stop Jim. "Sun," she yelled down the stairs, "it's Inez. Are you hungry? I got some supper for you."

No answer came—not from Sun or from Mabel. She whispered to Jim, "Let me go first. If someone is down there, they don't care about me. Or if they took Sun, then I can find that out."

"No," he said and pulled her behind him as he stepped down the stairs. They couldn't see the area surrounding the bottom step, and the shadow of Cleopatra Hill kept any afternoon sun from streaming in the small high basement windows.

As Jim's boots reached the step visible from the lower floor, someone grabbed and jerked his feet causing him to tumble down the last six stairs to the hard stone floor.

Inez rushed to his side.

Blood flowed again from his wound where he had landed on his right shoulder, but he scuttled away from the staircase until he sat back against the bars of a cell, his left hand holding his shoulder and his right hand empty. He searched the floor for his gun, without looking up to see who had tripped him.

Inez hunched by Jim's side stared into the wild eyes of Rees.

A crooked smirk darkened his face. His right thumb hooked over his low slung gun belt, his revolver still resting in its holster. He watched Jim then turned to see what Jim had spotted—the sheriff's gun had slid into an empty cell. "So, Sheriff, you want to make this difficult. I can play that game."

To the left of Rees, Sun struggled with handcuffs binding her hands behind her back, her cell door open and the keys snagged in the lock.

"Should I lock you two up or just kill you?" He raised an eyebrow, "Now, the girl might be worth taking with me. I kill you, leave this Chinese sow with Zhen, and take the girl here on a little honeymoon."

His words dragged icy fingers down her spine. She pulled in closer to Jim, and something poked the outside of her thigh. Pearl came to mind, pulling up her gown and handing Inez the derringer. It was tucked in her garter since she had made a habit of wearing it as Pearl had. She pushed her leg against Jim again hoping he would feel the steel of the pistol.

His face turned toward her, his eyes flashed down at her skirt. She blinked back to him.

Then trying to find a way to get the gun to Jim, she leaned in front of him, blocking him from Rees and kissed his lips with passion.

Rees snickered and said, "You go right ahead Sheriff, get your last taste of her."

While they kissed, Jim's left hand ran under her skirt and up her leg to the garter then slipped out the pistol. Concealed under the folds of her skirt, he held the gun as she pulled away from him.

A slimy smile crossed Rees' face. "Now, it's my turn," he said and reached for Inez. As he grabbed for her arm, the shot popped.

Inez smelled the scorch of her cotton petticoat and skirt.

The iron bars rattled as Rees stumbled back and hit the cell behind him, but before he could recover from the shock of the little derringer, Jim sprang up and tackled him.

Dust flew as they struggled for Rees' revolver, both men grabbing at the holster.

"Get the damn gun," Mabel yelled and pointed to Jim's pistol lying inside the bars of the cell opposite hers.

Reaching as far in as she could, Inez flicked the barrel with her fingertips and it spun around a bit closer to her. She grabbed it and turned toward the men.

The blur of their bodies struggling made Inez unsure as where to aim. She couldn't get a good shot at Rees without Jim getting in the line of fire.

"Shoot him," Mabel yelled again.

Rees looked up and saw Inez aiming the gun, just an instant of hesitation, but enough for Jim to snatch the revolver from the holster.

The sheriff scooted back from Rees with the pistol aimed at his chest.

The derringer lay forgotten by Rees' boot, but he glanced at it, then to Jim, then to Inez. "Well, well, I got two guns aimed at me." He glanced at the little gun again.

"Don't think about it," warned Jim.

"Do I have a choice?" He lunged at Jim while grabbing the derringer.

Shot after shot fired until smoke billowed through the jail.

The empty click of Inez's spent gun kept going as she continued squeezing the trigger, aiming at the bloody body of Rees. She dropped the gun when she came out of her haze and saw Jim staring at her.

"I think he's dead," Jim pushed himself up from the floor. "You alright?"

Her hands trembled and then her shoulders began to heave from the stress. His hand reached out and helped her to her feet. "I'm shaky, but fine. Did he shoot you?"

"I'm good, just tore up that wound again."

"Did I?" she began while staring at Rees' body and the dark

brown puddles soaking into the stone floor. The prospect of taking a life terrified her. But he would have killed Jim, she told herself. Her hands shook and the gun fell to the floor with a thunderous clang. Hot stinging tears filled her eyes as Rees' body jerked one last time. "Did I?"

The sheriff pulled her to his chest with his good arm, "No, no, I took care of it. You didn't hurt anyone."

✗ ✗ ✗

"Linda has offered to buy the house," Onalee sat in the small parlor of her quarters in the back of the first floor. Blue Jay fidgeted in the corner, carving something with his knife. Inez knew he longed to be out of town and back in the mountains.

She wanted to ask Onalee not to sell it to Linda, to let things keep going as they were, to allow them to stay together, but that wasn't fair to Onalee. She had worked to make the house successful and now was her time to benefit from that. "She may be a good woman to work for," was all Inez could manage.

"I wanted to talk to you privately because you are doing the job of Madam of the house."

She waited for Onalee to continue. But, she only watched Inez.

"Would it be possible," Inez filled the silence with what had been simmering in her mind for days, "that we could continue as we are? I mean, I can run the house and the dress shop." She studied her apron. "But, I don't have money to buy the house from you."

"What would I do with money?"

The question surprised Inez. "What do you mean?"

"We're going back to the tribal lands, to the wilderness of our ancestors. Money is a product of the white man."

"But, it isn't right that you don't get something from this place, after all you did."

Her calm face held a slight smile, "If you and the ladies are happy, that will be my payment."

The thoughts collided and didn't make sense to Inez. She

couldn't just take over the house, could she? Onalee would just walk away from it? Without taking anything? It wasn't fair in Inez's mind, she couldn't do that.

"You believe in me enough to trust the businesses to me?"

"You are the only one I trust to continue the job." Onalee leaned forward, "Linda's experience would benefit the profits, but I know her single vision might disregard the well-being of the women here. I am not interested in profit, which will follow when you do your best in all the things that are connected to you. You have shown me you are wise and brave. All of Jerome knows of your bravery in the face of that man who tried to kill the sheriff." She chuckled, "No one will attempt anything against this house with your new reputation."

Excitement stirred in her. The possibility of running the house enlivened her thoughts about the future, but she couldn't shake the feeling that Onalee deserved money. "I will set money aside each month for you and Blue Jay."

"No need," she said.

"But I want to, I have to. This is your business."

"No, it is now your business." She stood and straightened her doeskin smock. Blue Jay nodded to Inez as if adding his agreement. Onalee said, "Come with me, we have papers to sign to satisfy the law."

❊ ❊ ❊

The gentlemen had left for the evening and the ladies had retired to their rooms. Inez locked the front door and collected a couple of abandoned wine glasses as she surveyed the parlor, then the dining room on her way to the kitchen. The warmth of the house embraced her. The ladies, 'her girls' as she had begun to refer to them, clattered upstairs as their evening drifted into night. Mildred had left some soapy water in the sink, so Inez pushed up her silk sleeves and washed the remaining glasses.

"Not what I expected to see," Jim said as he walked through the back door and swung his arm to loosen up his shoulder. "I don't know if it's a good idea to have the Madam of the most popular parlor house in Jerome washing glasses."

"It has to be done," she said.

He walked up behind her, slid his arms over hers, and skimmed his hands into the water. "I'll help you then." His fingers intertwined with hers and the glass slipped to the bottom of the sink.

His lips kissed her neck.

She leaned her head back and turned slightly toward him.

Their mouths met.

Pulling back, Jim said, "Let Mildred finish that in the morning."

⚹ ⚹ ⚹

The sun cut through the lace curtains of her private quarters in the back of the house. Jim had already been up and made coffee, carrying it back from the kitchen wearing only his Levi's. He set the cups down on the bedside table then climbed back under the quilt with her.

"Good morning," she said and sipped the coffee. The sunlight filled the room. The warmth and the presence of Jim left her content—comfortable as hot coffee.

She wondered what Josiah would think of her? Her, Inez, transported to the Territory as a mail-order bride, now the Madam of a parlor house, and in bed with the sheriff. Then she felt his laugh—a warm hearty chuckle from the past, a past that seemed to her long ago, but had only been a year. The hurt of losing him had faded, but his memory made her strong. His optimism for the future never wavered. Yes, she had learned from him, and she'd discovered her strength from Onalee and the ladies. "I'm setting aside a bank account for Onalee and Blue Jay, but we still haven't heard from them."

"I doubt you will," Jim said. "Knowing the Navajo ways, she won't need it or ever claim it."

"That's fine. It's there just in case."

He nestled down in the bed beside her, neglecting his own coffee. "I heard what you and the ladies did for the mine widows' fund. You're doing great things, Inez."

"In a way, I'm a mine widow. I don't want other women to go through the despair I did." She felt a little uncomfortable talking about the money she'd donated. Onalee had taught her to take care of her ladies and the house, but with resources above that to contribute to the community, since they were all connected. "It's the Navajo way," she added.

She wondered about Jim and Stella. For the past six months, the sheriff's wife had not contacted him. Although a relief to Inez, she knew it weighed on Jim's mind. No one in Prescott had seen Stella or Burt, and Inez felt certain they had left the Territory together. Jim lived in the house alone, not yet ridding himself of her clothes or other belongings. Not that he thought she would return, but as he would often say, it just didn't seem right to give them away. She ventured the subject, "Any word from Prescott or Stella's sister?"

"She claims Stella will be back one day," a bit of sadness clouded his eyes. "I doubt it."

"Marriage is a strange thing," Inez said. "Red Dale and Sun can't marry because she's Chinese. Onalee and Blue Jay can't marry because, honestly, they're both physically men. And I don't think it matters one smidgen to them. They live their lives together happier than other couples I see."

He wrapped his arms around her, "And us?"

"You're still married to Stella," she said partly in jest.

"That doesn't mean that I love you any less. Do you want to get married?"

The thought had occurred to her, but now as he suggested it, she remembered how happy Sun had been with Dale as they loaded a wagon and headed to Phoenix, and the smile on Onalee's face as she and Blue Jay rode off to the north. "That is a white man's institution," she said. "As long as we're together, that's what matters."

He kissed her, and she set her coffee back on the bedside table as they snuggled down into the feather bed.

RESOURCES

To learn more about Jerome, Arizona; ladies of the West; "Two-Spirit" Native Americans ("Berdaches"); and territorial life in the Southwest; investigate the following resources:

Butler, Anne M. *Daughters of Joy, Sisters of Misery: Prostitutes in the American West 1865-90* (Urbana and Chicago, Illinois: University of Illinois Press, 1987)

Butruille, Susan G. *Women's Voices from the Western Frontie*r (Boise, Idaho: Tamarack Books, 1995)

Jacobs, Sue-Ellen, Wesley Thomas, and Sabine Lang, eds. *Two-Spirit People* (Urbana and Chicago, Illinois: University of Illinois Press, 1997)

Mulvey, Kate and Melissa Richards. *Decades of Beauty: the Changing Image of Women 1890s – 1990s* (New York City, New York: Octopus Publishing Group, 1998)

Seagraves, Anne. *Soiled Doves: Prostitution in the Early West* (Hayden, Idaho: Wesanne Publications, 1994)

Williams, Walter L. *The Spirit and the Flesh: Sexual Diversity in American Indian Culture* (Boston, Massachusetts: Beacon Press, 1986)

Young, Herbert V. *Ghosts of Cleopatra Hill* (Jerome, Arizona: Jerome Historical Society, 1964)

Young, Herbert V. *They Came to Jerome* (Jerome, Arizona: Jerome Historical Society, 1972)

Printed in the United States
200978BV00027B/7-15/A